D0961062

"One of the most gifted writers
working today."
—*NEW YORK TIMES BOOK REVIEW*

Jeanette Winterson's *Christmas Days* gives the reader a portal into the spirit of the season, where time slows down and magic starts to happen. From trees with mysterious powers to a tinsel baby that talks, philosophical fairies to flying dogs, a haunted house and a disappearing train, Winterson's innovative stories encompass the childlike and spooky wonder of Christmas. Perfect for reading by the fire with loved ones, or while travelling home for the holidays. Enjoy the season of peace and goodwill, mystery, and a little bit of magic courtesy of one of our most fearless and accomplished writers.

Born in Manchester, England, **JEANETTE WINTERSON** is the author of over twenty books, including the national bestseller *Why Be Happy When You Could Be Normal?*, *Oranges Are Not the Only Fruit*, *Sexing the Cherry*, and *The Passion*. She has won many prizes including the Whitbread Award for Best First Novel, the John Llewellyn Rhys Prize, the E. M. Forster Award, and the Stonewall Award.

GROVE PRESS
an imprint of Grove Atlantic
Distributed by Publishers Group West
COVER ILLUSTRATIONS © KATIE SCOTT
groveatlantic.com   PRINTED IN THE USA

CHRISTMAS
DAYS

Also by Jeanette Winterson

CHRISTMAS
DAYS

12 Stories and 12 Feasts
for 12 Days

JEANETTE
WINTERSON

Grove Press
New York

Published simultaneously in Canada
Printed in the United States of America

First published by Jonathan Cape in 2016

First Grove Atlantic hardcover edition: December 2016

Library of Congress Cataloguing-in-Publication data available for this title.

ISBN 978-0-8021-2583-5
eISBN 978-0-8021-8974-5

Grove Press
an imprint of Grove Atlantic
154 West 14th Street
New York, NY 10011

Distributed by Publishers Group West

groveatlantic.com

16 17 18 19   10 9 8 7 6 5 4 3 2 1

To the loved ones in my life who really can cook.
My wife Susie Orbach and my friends
Beeban Kidron and Nigella Lawson.
You can't beat a Jewish Christmas.

CONTENTS

CHRISTMAS-TIDE

ise men trekking across the desert following a star. Shepherds in the fields with flocks by night. An angel, fast as thought and bright as hope, turning eternity into time.

Hurry! A baby will be born.

Believers and unbelievers know this story.

Who doesn't know this story?

An inn. A stable. A donkey. Mary. Joseph. Gold. Frankincense. Myrrh.

And at the heart of the story, the mother and child.

Until the Protestant Reformation in Europe in the 16th century, the Madonna and Child was the Christian image everybody would see every day; stained glass, statue, oil painting, carving, and the homely shrines people made for themselves.

Imagine it: most people can't read or write, but their minds are vivid with stories and images; images are more than the illustration to the story – they are the story.

When you and I go into an ancient church in Italy or France or Spain, we cannot read the myriad scenes in the vaulted ceilings, or the frescos, or the hung paintings, but our ancestors could. We stand with our guidebooks looking for clues; they threw back their heads and saw the mystery of the world.

I love the written word – I'm writing it now, reading it now – but in societies that are not literate but are culturally alive the image and the spoken/sung word are everything. It's a different kind of liveliness of mind.

After the Reformation, Mary, who had been treated like the fourth member of Godhead, was demoted. The Reformation wasn't good for women; we soon hit the Europe-wide witch burnings, and of course the Pilgrim Fathers who landed at Plymouth Rock in 1620 were Puritans of the most uncompromising sort – cue the Salem witch trials in the 1690s.

In New England the Puritans banned the celebration of Christmas in 1659 and that law wasn't repealed until 1681. In England, under Cromwell, Christmas had already been banned since 1647, and remained so until 1660.

Why? Too pagan in its origins, as we'll see later, too party-time, too pleasurable (why be happy when you could be miserable?) and too dangerous to let Mary back out of the kitchen and into the starring role.

What ordinary people missed most about the break with Catholicism was the cult of Mary.

In Catholic countries in Europe then and now, and in Latin America now, the cult of Mary, the mystery of the Virgin birth, the union of mother and child is still powerful and persuasive. Every time a woman gives birth she is the fleeting tableau of the holiest of happenings. Daily life and devotional life are held together in this image.

And it's an image with its roots deeper than Christianity.

If we look back into Greek and Roman history we can see that gods and marvellous mortals are usually born of one divine and one human parent. Hercules's father was Zeus. Zeus also fathered Helen of Troy. She was trouble, but beautiful women with a touch of the god are always trouble.

Romulus and Remus, founders of the city of Rome, claimed that Mars was their father.

Jesus was born in the Roman Empire. The New Testament was written in Greek. The Gospel writers wanted to fix their Messiah in the roll call of superheros with a divine dad.

But why did Mary have to be a virgin?

Jesus was a Jew. Jewish lineage is through the mother, not the father, so the emphasis in Judaism on the purity and sexual abstinence of women is a predictable way of trying to control who's who.

If Mary is a virgin then the divine parentage of Jesus isn't in doubt.

All that makes sense, but there's something else too. Sitting further behind this story is the potency of the Great Goddess herself.

Goddess-worship in the ancient world was uninterested in chastity as a virtue. Even Vestal Virgins were allowed to marry once they left the service of the goddess. Temple prostitution was normal, and the goddess was a symbol of fecundity and procreation – crucially, she never belonged to any man.

So the Mary myth brilliantly manages two magnetically opposed forces: the new religion of Christianity offers a tale of god-into-man divine birth. Mary is special and singled out – like in the hero stories. Her pregnancy is no ordinary domestic arrangement; she has been visited by a god.

At the same time, her purity and submission allow the new religion to break away from the riotous pagan sex cults and fertility rites that the Jews hated.

Right from the start, Christianity had the knack of fusing together core elements from other religions and cults – ejecting any problematic elements, and then telling the story in a new way. That has been part of its global success story.

And the most spectacular of its success stories is Christmas.

The birth of Jesus is only written about in the gospels of Matthew and Luke, and their versions are different. Mark and John don't discuss the birth story at all. There is no mention of December 25th anywhere in the Bible.

So how did it happen?

The Roman festival of Saturnalia is part of the story. This was a typical midwinter festival celebrating the turning of the sun (the shortest day of the year is December 21st, the winter solstice). The pagan Emperor Aurelian declared December 25th Natalis Solis Invicti – the birth of the invincible sun. The festival included gift-giving, party-going, wearing silly hats, getting drunk, lighting candles and roaring fires as sun symbols and decorating public places with evergreens. This festival was swiftly followed by Kalends – where we get our word calendar. They liked to party in the old days.

In Celtic Britain the winter festival of Samhain began on what is our Halloween – All Hallows' Eve – a festival of the dead, and, as in Germanic and Scandinavian countries, the Celts celebrated the December solstice with bonfires and merriment. This period of Yule or *Jól* is where we get our words Yuletide and jolly. Evergreens, the holly and ivy, emblems of ongoing life, were used both as decorations and as sacred installations.

In the Germanic tribes, white-bearded Odin roamed around during Yuletide and had to be appeased with little gifts left out at night.

The Church took the sensible view that if you can't beat 'em, join 'em, and incorporated all the elements people were reluctant to give up – the singing, the celebrating, the evergreens, the gift-giving and, of course, the time of year – into Christmas.

December 25th is a great day for Christ's birth because it means that Mary was impregnated by God on March 25th – Lady Day (the Feast of the Annunciation) in the church calendar – and this allowed the Church to celebrate the spring equinox of March 21st without life getting too pagan about it. It also allowed Christ's conception and crucifixion (Easter) a neat symmetry.

Santa Claus himself is one of the many mixed messages of Christmas.

Nicholas was a Turkish bishop of Smyrna born around 250 years after the death of Christ. He was rich and gave gifts of money to people in need. The best story about him is that one night, trying to throw a bag of gold through a window, he found the window closed and had to shin up onto the roof and drop the sack down the chimney.

Who knows? But as usual a cult grew up around him, notably of sailors, who naturally enough went sailing, and as the cult spread northwards this Turkish bearded gift-giver merged with the bearded god Odin, who had the advantage of travelling on a flying horse – with eight legs.

St Nicholas was Sinta Klaus to the Dutch, and it was the Dutch who brought Sinta Klaus to America.

New Amsterdam, now New York City, was a Dutch settlement. By 1809, in spite of the best efforts of the descendants of all that New England Puritan stock, Santa is riding a wagon over the treetops in Washington Irving's *A History of New York*.

In 1822 another American, Clement Moore, nailed the definitive Santa in his poem 'A Visit from St Nicholas'. Everybody knows those opening lines: ''Twas the night before Christmas, when all through the house/Not a creature was stirring, not even a mouse.'

This is the moment when St Nick gets his reindeer.

But he was still wearing green – his colour as a pre-Christian fertility god.

Enter Coca-Cola.

In 1931 the Coca-Cola Company commissioned a Swedish artist, Haddon Sundblom, to give Santa a makeover. Red it had to be, and from then on, thanks to the advertising might of Coke, Santa's robes are red.

The Christmas tree is an ancient symbol of the power of life to survive and thrive through the dead of winter. What did our ancestors think, trudging through the dark, bare forests, when they came across an evergreen?

Famously Queen Victoria and Prince Albert managed the first modern celebrity photoshoot when they posed in front of their Christmas tree at Windsor Castle in 1848.

Actually it was a drawing in the *Illustrated London News*, but after that everyone had to have a Christmas tree.

Prince Albert was German, and the earliest record of winter trees being brought indoors for the midwinter festival is in the Black Forest in Bavaria.

Martin Luther, the man responsible for the Protestant Reformation, was a German, and the story goes that he decorated his own Christmas tree with candles to mirror the million stars in God's sky.

Trees themselves are sacred objects. Think of the apple tree in the Garden of Eden, the World Ash Tree, Yggdrasil, worshipped in Norse and Germanic mythology, the Druid Oak. James Cameron's *Avatar* features a goddess tree, and in the Tolkien sagas the Ents, the talking, walking trees, are brutally cut down by Saruman and the Orcs, enemies of the sacred forest.

Christ, like other sacrificial gods, dies on a tree.

So the tree is symbolic across centuries and cultures, and the evergreen tree a symbol of life's persistence.

The Massachusetts Puritans hated all those pagan connections, but they couldn't stop the moment in 1851 when two sled-loads of trees were hauled from the Catskills to New York City, to become the first retail Christmas trees sold in the United States.

The 19th century is the century when Christmas becomes the Christmas we celebrate now: the Christmas tree, Christmas cards, season of goodwill, gift-giving, robins, feasting, charity to the poor, snow, supernatural agency of some kind – whether ghosts, visions or a mysterious star.

It's in the 19th century that all the great Christmas carols we love to sing were composed.

It's the 19th century that invents the Christmas card. Henry Cole worked for the London Post Office and realised that the Penny Post (1840) was a great way of sending simple greetings cards, so in 1843 he got his friend to draw some, and before you could say plum pudding the Christmas-card craze was off.

It was more than thirty years before the Christmas card caught on in America. Blame the Puritans. I do.

Cards, carols and, the most Victorian of all, the Christmas Ghost Story.

Telling stories round the fire is as old as language. And, as fires are lit at night and/or in wintertime, the winter festivals were natural story-telling opportunities.

But the ghost story as a phenomenon is a 19th century phenomenon. One theory is that the spectres and apparitions claimed in so many sightings were a result of low-level carbon-monoxide poisoning from gas lamps (it does cause fuzzy, drowsy hallucinations). Add in the thick fogs and plenty of gin, and it starts to make sense.

But there's a psychological side to this too. The 19th century was haunted by itself. Its new industrialisation seemed to have unleashed the very powers of hell. Visitors to Manchester called it the Inferno. The English writer Mrs Gaskell wrote of her visit to a cotton mill, 'I have seen hell and it's white…'

And the new poor, the factory slaves, the basement-dwellers, the toilers in iron, heat, filth and degradation, appeared like spectres, thin, yellow, ragged, semi-human, half-dead.

That this is also the century of organised charity and philanthropy is not a coincidence. And that it is the century of Christmas at its most inspired as well as its most sentimental should not surprise us. Christmas becomes a magic circle, the season of goodwill where those who have benefited most from the mechanised desolation of their fellows can both make amends and soothe their own souls.

That is why Charles Dickens's *A Christmas Carol* begins with Scrooge's refusal to give money to help the poor: 'Are there no work-houses?'

Scrooge, the polar opposite (pun – sorry) of Santa Claus, can't give and won't give, and finds himself visited by three spirits, plus the ghost of his dead partner, Jacob Marley.

This is a story of hard hearts and second chances. Of the mis-rule of Christmas, where ordinary laws are turned upside down, of clock-time being out-chimed by significant time (a lifetime happens in a night). And of goose, pudding, fires, candles, fearsome hot cock-tails (Smoking Bishop), snow so thick the city sleeps and 'A Merry Christmas to us all…God Bless us every one!'

This is a story so powerful it can survive the Muppets.

In America, Christmas wasn't declared a federal holiday until 1870 (after the American Civil War as a way of reuniting north and south in a shared tradition).

Yet in spite of the Puritans' best efforts, and in spite of the fact that Christmas is most certainly not a Jewish celebration, Americans and

American Jews have contributed as much to the folklore of Christmas as any star, shepherd, Santa or angel.

It's a Wonderful Life, Miracle on 34th Street, Meet Me in St Louis, The Polar Express, How the Grinch Stole Christmas, Trading Places, Scrooged, Home Alone 2, White Christmas – the movie list is only getting longer…

And when you're singing along to 'White Christmas', 'Rudolph, the Red-Nosed Reindeer', 'Santa Baby', 'Winter Wonderland', 'Let it Snow, Let it Snow, Let it Snow', or humming about roasting those chestnuts by an open fire, raise a glass to those Jewish songwriters who saw a good opportunity for a tune and gave us the classics we love.

Christmas was banned by the Puritans in the UK and the USA because it is such a gaudy ragbag of a festival with something borrowed from everywhere – pagans, Romans, Norsemen, Celts, Turks – and because its celebratory free spirit, its gift-giving, topsy-turvy misrule, made it anti-authority and anti-work. It was a holiday – holy day – of the best kind, where devotion has joy in it.

Life should be joyful.

I know Christmas has become a cynical retail hijack but it is up to us all, individually and collectively, to object to that. Christmas is celebrated across the world by people of all religions and none. It is a joining together, a putting aside of differences. In pagan and Roman times it was a celebration of the power of light and the co-operation of nature in human life.

Money wasn't the point.

In fact, the Christmas story starts with a demand for money:

And it came to pass in those days, that there went out a decree from Caesar Augustus, that all the world should be taxed. (Luke 2:1)

And ends with a gift – *'unto us a child is born.'*

The gift of new life is followed by the gifts of the magi – the gold, frankincense and myrrh.

In the best-loved of all Christmas carols the poet Christina Rossetti poses the question of what we can give that is not about money or power or success or talent:

> *What can I give Him, poor as I am?*
> *If I were a shepherd, I would bring a lamb;*
> *If I were a Wise Man, I would do my part;*
> *Yet what can I give him: give my heart.*

We give ourselves. We give ourselves to others. We give ourselves to ourselves. We give.

Whatever we make of Christmas, it should be ours, not something we buy off the shelf.

For me, feasting with friends is a lovely part of Christmas-tide, so I've included some recipes here that have personal stories attached to them. I am hopeless with quantities and cook by eye, texture and taste. If pastry is too dry, add water or egg. If it's too wet, add flour – that kind of thing.

There was a big fight with my editor over whether the recipes should be in metric or imperial – 'Even Nigella has gone metric,' she argued.

I asked Nigella and she said, 'Have both.'

And where I say things like 'cabbage', the query came back: 'What size cabbage?'

There are so many things to do every day – and wondering what size cabbage isn't one of them.

These recipes are a little disorderly, the kind of thing we'd make together, and I'd say, 'Damn, I forgot the mushrooms,' and then we'd just do without them. So don't worry too much. Cooking has become a lot like cycling. By which I mean people used to pop out on their bikes – now everyone has to wear Lycra and goggles and beat their own speed and distance record. Cooking at home is not an Olympic sport. Cooking is an everyday ordinary miracle.

I like cooking but I prefer writing.

Stories are where I live – they are physical three-dimensional places to me. When I was a kid and locked in the coal hole for various crimes, I had a choice: count coal – a limited activity. Tell myself a story – an unlimited world of the imagination.

I write for the delight of it. Sitting down at a keyboard to play. Christmas has a special delight – as though the season is cheering you on. It's a time for tales, presided over by the Lord of Misrule, who must be the guardian spirit of creativity, as he is of the ancient twelve days of Christmas-tide.

And strangely, in a house that was generally unhappy, Christmas was a happy time for me when I was growing up. We don't lose these associations; the past comes with us, and with luck we reinvent it, which is what I am suggesting we do with Christmas. And everything is a story.

Stories round the fire at Christmas, or told with frosty breath on a wintry walk, have a magic and a mystery that is part of the season.

Writing is an epiphany of its own, in the sense of something un-expected being revealed. Christmas, which seems so familiar, maybe even worn out, is a celebration of the unexpected.

Here are the stories I have written so far. Twelve of them for the twelve days of the season. Here are ghost stories, magical interven-tions, ordinary encounters that turn out to be not ordinary at all, small miracles, and salutes to the coming of the light.

And joy.

SPIRIT OF CHRISTMAS

I t was the night before Christmas and all over the house nothing was stirring because even the mouse was exhausted.

There were presents everywhere: square ones with bows, long ones with ribbons. Fat ones in Santa paper. Thin ones tantalising as a diamond bracelet, or disappointing as a chopstick?

Food supplies had been stockpiled like a war-warning; puddings the size of bombs were exploding off the shelves. Bullets of dates were stacked in cardboard rounds. A line of grouse, like toy warplanes, hung outside the back door. Chestnuts were ready to heat and fire. The free-range organic turkey – nothing that a good vet couldn't revive – was crouched next to hangar-loads of tinfoil.

'Good thing the Twelfth Night pork is still eating windfall apples in an orchard in Kent,' you said, trying to squeeze round the kitchen table.

I was staggering under the weight of the Christmas cake – it was the kind of thing medieval masons used to choose as the cornerstone of a cathedral. You took it from me and went to pack it in the car. Everything had to go in the car, because we were going to the country tonight. The more you loaded, the more likely it seemed that the turkey would be doing the driving. There was no room for you, and I was sharing my seat with a wicker reindeer.

'Hackles,' you said.

Oh, God, we had forgotten the cat.

'Hackles doesn't celebrate Christmas,' I said.

'Tie this tinsel round his basket and get in.'

'Are we going to have our Christmas row now or shall we wait until we're on the road and you've forgotten the wine?'

'The wine is underneath the box of crackers.'

'That's not the wine, that's the turkey. He's so fresh I had to tape him in to stop him trying to claw his way out like something from Poe.'

'Don't be disgusting. That turkey had a happy life.'

'You've had a pretty good life but I'm not thinking of eating you.'

I ran and bit your neck. I love your neck. You pushed me away – in play – but do I imagine that you push me away not in play these days?

You smiled a small smile and went to repack the car.

Soon after midnight. Cat, tinsel, tree with flashing lights, reindeer, presents, food, my arm out of the window because there was nowhere else to put it – you and me set off to a country cottage we had rented to celebrate Christmas.

We drove through the seasonal drunks waving streamers and singing about Rudolph in red-nosed solidarity. You said it would be quicker to go right through the middle of town so late at night, and as you were slowly pulling away from the traffic lights down the main street I thought I saw something moving.

'Stop!' I said. 'Can you reverse?'

The street was completely empty now, and you took us backwards, the engine whining under the weight of the effort, until we were outside BUYBUYBABY, the world's biggest department store, finally and reluctantly closed from midnight Christmas Eve for an entire twenty-four hours (online shopping always available).

I got out of the car. The front window of BUYBUYBABY had been arranged as a Nativity scene, complete with Mary and Joseph in ski-wear and a number of farm animals keeping warm under tartan dog coats. There was no gold, frankincense or myrrh – these three kings had bought their presents from BBB. Jesus was getting an Xbox, a bike and an apartment-friendly drum kit.

His mother, Mary, had been given a steam iron.

Flitting about in front of the Nativity, her nose pressed inside the window, was a tiny child.

'What are you doing in there?' I said.

'Trapped,' said the child.

I went back to the car and tapped on your window.

'There's a child left behind in the shop – we've got to get her out.'

You came and had a look. The child waved. You looked doubtful. 'She probably belongs to the security guard,' you said.

'She says she's trapped! Call the police.'

The child smiled and shook her head as you took out your phone. There was something about her smile – I felt uncertain.

'Who are you?' I said.

'I am the Spirit of Christmas.'

I heard her clearly. She spoke clearly.

'I can't get a signal,' you said. 'Try yours.'

I tried mine. It was dead. We looked up and down the strangely deserted street. I was starting to panic. I pulled and pushed at the doors to the store. Locked. No cleaners. No janitors. This was Christmas Eve.

The voice came again. 'I am the Spirit of Christmas.'

'Oh, come on,' you said. 'It's a publicity stunt.'

But I wasn't listening to you, I was fixed on the face in the window, which seemed to change every second, as though light was playing on it, shrouding, then revealing, the expression. The eyes were not the eyes of a child.

'She is our responsibility,' I said, quietly, not really to you.

'She is not,' you said. 'Come on, I'll call the police as we drive.'

'Let me out!' said the child as you turned back towards the car.

'We'll send someone, I promise. We're going to find a phone— '

The child interrupted. 'You must let me out. Will you leave some of your gifts, some of your food, in the doorway, just there?'

You turned back. 'This is crazy.'

But the child was hypnotising me.

'Yes,' I said and, half-dazed, I went to the car and flipped up the back and started dragging wrapped shapes and bags of food towards the doorway of the department store. Every time I put something down, you picked it up again and put it back in the car.

'You've gone mad,' you said. 'This is a Christmas stunt – we're being filmed, I know it. It's reality TV.'

'No, this isn't reality TV, this is real,' I said, and my voice sounded far away. 'This isn't what we know, it's what we don't know – but it's true. I'm telling you, it's true.'

'All right,' you said, 'if this is what it takes to get us back on the road – here's the bags. OK? Here and here.' You slammed them down in the doorway, your face flushed with tiredness and exasperation. I know that face.

And you stood back, hands in fists, not even thinking about the child.

Suddenly all the lights went out in the window of the store. And then the child was standing in between us on the street.

Your face changed. You put your hand on the smooth glass, as clear and closed as a dream.

'Are we dreaming?' you said to me. 'How did she do that?'

'I'm coming with you,' said the child. 'Where are you going?'

And so, past one o'clock in the morning, we set off again, my arm inside the car now, the child on the back seat next to Hackles, who had climbed out of his basket and was purring. I looked in the wing mirror as we left and saw our bags of food and gifts being taken away, one by one, by dark figures.

'They are the ones who live in the doorways,' said the child, as though reading my thoughts. 'They have nothing.'

'We are going to be arrested,' you said. 'Theft of in-store display. Dumping on a public highway. Abduction. Merry Christmas to you too, Officer.'

'We've done the right thing,' I said.

'What exactly have we done,' you said, 'except lose half of what we need and collect a lost child?'

'It happens every year,' said the child. 'In different ways, in different places. If I am not set free by Christmas morning, the world grows heavier. The world is heavier than you know.'

We drove along in silence for a while. The sky was black, pinned with stars. I imagined myself, high above this road, looking back on Planet Earth, blue in the blackness, white-patched, polar-capped. This was life and home.

When I was a child, my father gave me a glass snow-scene of the earth shook with stars. I used to lie in bed and turn it over and over, falling asleep with the stars behind my eyes, feeling warm and light and safe.

The world is weightless, hanging in space, unsupported, a gravitational mystery, sun-warmed, gas-cooled. Our gift.

I used to fight off sleep for as long as I could, squinting out of one closing eye at my silent, turning world.

I grew up. My father died. The snow-scene was in his house, in my old bedroom. When we were clearing I dropped it, and the little globe fell out of its heavy, star-shot liquid. That was when I cried. I don't know why.

I must have reached across the car seat then and taken your hand as we cruised along on the night road.

'What's the matter?' you said, gently.

'I was thinking about my father.'

'Strange. I was thinking about my mother.'

'Thinking what?'

You squeezed my hand. I saw your ring finger glinting under the low green dashboard lights. I remember that ring and when I gave it to you. I see it every day but today I see it.

You said, 'I wish I'd done more for her, said more to her, but it's too late now.'

'You never got on.'

'Why is that? Why do so many parents and children never get on?'

'Is that why you don't want us to have children?'

'No! No. Work... We always said we'd think about it... but... yes, perhaps... Why would I want my child to hate me? Isn't there enough hatred in the world?'

You never talked like this. Glancing at your profile, in the eerie green light, I could see the tension in your jaw. I love your face. I was about to say so, but you said, 'Ignore me. It's this time of year. A family time, I guess.'

'Yes. What a mess we make of it.'

'Of what? Of our families, or of Christmas?'

'Both. Neither. No wonder everyone goes shopping. Displacement activity.' You smiled, trying to lighten the mood.

I said, 'I thought you liked the presents under the tree?'

'I do, but how many do we need?'

I was about to remind you that you had yelled in my face less than an hour ago, when a voice from the back seat said, 'If only the world could rid itself of just some of its contents.'

We both glanced round. I realised that the green light in the car wasn't the instrument panel; it was her. She was glowing.

'Do you think she's radioactive as well?' you said.

'As well as what?'

'As well as…well, as well, as I don't know, as well as…'

'Suppose she's who she says she is?'

'She hasn't said who she is.'

'Yes, she has, she's…'

'I am the Spirit of Christmas,' said the child.

I said, 'And suppose something extraordinary is happening to us tonight.'

'An unknown child on a wild-goose chase?'

'At least it's seasonal.'

'What?'

'The wild goose.'

This time you squeezed my hand and I saw the muscle in your jaw lower just a little.

I want to tell you about love, and how much I love you, and that I love you like the sun rising, every day, and that loving you has made my life better and happier. I know this will embarrass you, so I don't say anything at all.

You switched on the radio. 'Hark! The Herald Angels Sing.'

You sang along. '"Peace on earth and mercy mild…"'

I saw you watching the child in the rear-view mirror.

'If this goes according to plan,' you said, 'we should be seeing Santa and a team of reindeer about now. What do you think about that, Spirit of Christmas?'

The voice from the back seat said, 'Turn right here, please!'

You do. You hesitate, but you do it, because she's that sort of child.

You took the dark bend, accelerated forward and stalled the car.

Just touching down over the roof of a handsome Georgian house, holly wreath on the blue front door, was a sledge pulled by six antlered reindeer.

Father Christmas smiled at us and waved. The child waved back and climbed out of the car. Locks didn't seem to make any difference to her. Hackles jumped out and followed her.

Santa clapped his hands. The house was in darkness but a sash window on the first floor was pushed up by some unseen inside hand; three bulging sacks thudded to the ground. Santa Claus shouldered them easily and loaded them onto his sledge.

'He's robbing the place!' you said, opening the car door and getting out. 'Hey, you!'

The figure in red came forward convivially, stamping his boots and rubbing his hands.

'We can only offer this service once a year,' he told you.

'What bloody service?'

Santa Claus took the opportunity to fill his pipe. He blew star-shaped smoke rings, blue into the white air.

'In the old days we used to leave presents, because people didn't have much. Now everyone has so much, they write to us to come and take it away. You've no idea how much better it feels to wake up on Christmas morning to find it all gone.'

Santa rummaged in one of the bags. 'Look, hair curlers, a year's supply of bath salts, more socks than anyone can have feet, baked garlic in olive oil, an Eiffel Tower embroidery kit, two china pigs.'

'And now what?' you said, half-furious, half-fazed. 'Car-boot sale for New Year?'

'Well, come and see if you like,' said Santa. 'Follow me.'

He pocketed his pipe and went towards his sledge. The Spirit of Christmas went with him, and Hackles.

'Hey, that's our cat!' you shouted at the bottom of the sledge, because by now it was in the air.

The Spirit of Christmas was looking very pleased with herself.

We jumped in the car and followed the sledge as best we could, though it took the direct route across the fields.

'It's some kind of jet-pack hovercraft,' you said. 'How did we get into this?'

Now we were off the little road and bouncing up a track that was killing the car's suspension. You had both hands on the wheel.

The sledge came to land. A few minutes later we caught up.

We were outside a dark and wind-broken cottage. The roof tiles were slipping and the gutter was hung with icicles, like the electric ones people buy as decorations, except that these icicles weren't electric and they weren't decorations. The fence stakes round the house were tied together with bits of wire and the gate was propped shut with a stone. An old dog slept in the open doorway of a disused caravan.

As the dog raised his head to bark, Santa Claus threw a glittering bone through the air. The old dog caught it contentedly.

While the reindeer ate moss from their nosebags, Santa and the Spirit of Christmas went to the house and opened the front door.

'Is this a trap? Like *Don't Look Now*? Are we going to be killed?' You were scared. I wasn't scared but that was because I believed in this.

Santa came out of the cottage, stooping slightly under the weight of a moth-eaten bag. He was holding a mince pie and a glass of whisky.

'Not many people leave anything these days,' he said, downing the whisky in one, 'but I know this house and they know me. Pain and Want must vanish tonight. Once a year is all the power I am given.'

'What power?' you said. 'Where's the child? What have you done with my cat?'

Santa gestured back at the cottage, its windows lit up now with the strange green that accompanied the child. We could see quite clearly, even at a distance, that the table had a clean cloth on it and the child was arranging a ham, a pie, cheese, while our cat, Hackles, purred about with his tail in the air.

Santa smiled, and tipped the sack onto the sledge. What fell out was musty and old and broken. He picked up the pieces of a plate, a torn jacket, a doll without a head. Now the sack was empty.

Without speaking, he offered the empty sack to you and pointed towards the car. He wants you to fill it, I thought. Do it, please; do it.

But I didn't dare to say this out loud. This was for you. About you.

You hesitated, and then you opened all the doors of the car and started pushing presents and food into the sack. It was only a small sack, but no matter how much you put into it, you couldn't fill it. I could see you looking at what was left.

'Give him everything,' I said.

You leaned over and started taking things from the back seat. The car was almost empty now, except for the wicker reindeer, and that seemed too ridiculous to give to anybody.

You handed the heavy sack to the red figure, who was watching you intently.

'You haven't given me everything,' he said.

'If you mean the wicker reindeer…'

The Spirit of Christmas had come out of the house now, Hackles in her arms. He was glowing green too. I had never seen a green cat.

The child said to you, 'Give him what you fear.'

The moment was still, utterly still. I looked away like I did when I asked you to marry me, not knowing what you would say.

'Yes,' you said. 'Yes.'

There was a terrific thud and the bag fell to the ground in a great weight. Santa nodded, and with some difficulty picked up the sack and threw it onto the sledge.

'It's time to go now,' said the Spirit of Christmas.

We got in the car and drove back along the track.

The frost had brightened the ground and hardened the stars. Beyond the dry-stone walls, the sheep were in huddles in the fields. A pair of hunting horses ran along the side of the fence, their breath steaming like dragons'.

After a while you stopped and got out. I followed you. I put my arms round you. I could hear your heart beating.

'What shall we do now that we've given it all away?' you said.

'Haven't we got anything left?'

'A bag of food behind the front seat, and this…' You felt in your pocket and took out a foil-wrapped chocolate snowman.

We both laughed. It was so silly. You broke a piece off to give to the child in the back of the car, but she was sleeping.

'I don't understand any of this,' you said. 'Do you?'

'No. Is there any more chocolate?'

We shared the last pieces and I said to you, 'Do you remember when we first met and we had no money at all – we were paying off student loans and I was working two jobs, and we ate sausages and stuffing on Christmas Day, but no turkey because we couldn't afford one? You knitted me a jumper.'

'And one sleeve was longer than the other.'

'And I made you a stool out of that ash tree the council had cut down. They left half the trunk on the street. Do you remember?'

'God, yes, and it was freezing because you were in that horrible houseboat, and you wouldn't come home with me because you hated my mother.'

'I didn't hate your mother! You hated your mother.'

'Yes...' you said slowly. 'What a waste of life hatred is.'

You turned me to face you. You were quiet and serious.

'Do you still love me?'

'Yes, I do.'

'I love you, but I don't say it enough, do I?'

'I know you feel it. But sometimes...I...'

'Yes?'

'I feel like you don't want me. I don't want to force you but I miss your body. Our kisses and closeness, and yes, the rest too.'

You were quiet. Then you said, 'When he, Santa Claus, or whatever he is, asked me to give him what I fear, I realised that if everything were still in the car and you were gone, then what? What if our house, my work, my life, everything I have was all where it should be, and you were gone? And I thought – that's what I fear. I fear it so much I can't even think about it, but it's there all the time, like a war that's coming.'

'What is?'

'That bit by bit I am pushing you away.'

'Do you want to push me away?'

You kissed me – like we used to kiss each other – and I could feel my tears, and then I realised they were yours.

We got back in the car and drove slowly on through the last miles towards the village, the uneven roofs visible under the vanishing moon. Soon it would be day.

A hooded figure was walking by the side of the road. You pulled alongside and stopped the car, opening the window. 'Would you like a ride?' you said.

The figure turned to us; it was a woman carrying a baby. The woman pushed back her hood; her face was beautiful and strong. Unlined and clear. She smiled, and the baby smiled. It was a baby, but its eyes weren't the eyes of a baby.

Instinctively I looked round at the back seat. The cat was curled up in his basket, but the child was gone.

Above us in the sky was a drop-pointed star, and a light strengthening in the east.

'It's nearly day,' I said.

You had pulled over now. You put your elbow on the steering wheel and your head on your hand. 'I don't know what's going on. Do you?'

'She's gone. The Spirit of Christmas.'

'Have we dreamed it all? Are we at home, asleep, waiting to wake up?'

'Come on,' I said. 'If we're asleep, let's sleepwalk down to the cottage. We haven't got much to carry any more.'

The woman and child were ahead of us now, walking, walking, walking.

We got out. You took my hand.

We had noticed everything once – the water collecting on the berried ivy, the mistletoe in the dark-armed oak, the barn where the owl sat under the tiles, the smoke like a message curling up from forest-burnt fires, the ancientness of time and us part of it.

Why had we learned to hurry through every day when every day was all we had?

The woman was still walking, carrying the future, holding the miracle, the miracle that births the world again and gives us a second chance.

Why are the real things, the important things, so easily mislaid underneath the things that hardly matter at all?

'I'll light the fire,' I said.

'Later,' you said. 'I'd like to sleepwalk back to bed with you.'

You were shy. You're so tough but I remember this shyness. Yes. And yes. Asleep or awake. Yes and yes.

Outside from across the fog-ploughed fields I heard the bells ringing in Christmas Day.

Mrs Winterson's
Mince Pies

rs Winterson never gave up her War Cupboard. From 1939 to 1945, she had done her bit for victory by pickling eggs and onions, bottling fruit, drying or salting beans and trading black-market tins of bully beef. She liked things you could store, and while waiting for either nuclear war in the 1950s and 1960s, or the Apocalypse Anytime Soon, she carried on pressing beef and making things with dried fruit.

The two essential items in our lean-to kitchen both came with handles: the mangle, for wringing out the clothes on wash-day, and the Spong mincer. This was the largest Spong mincer money could buy and it lived clamped on the edge of our Formica table. One of its many uses was making mincemeat for mince pies. Mrs Winterson made her mincemeat in the autumn because we had plenty of windfall apples.

It is confusing for those whose Christmas tradition does not include mince pies to work out why the mince is not meat, but fruit.

The answer is that mince pies go back to the reign of Elizabeth I (1558–1603), and in those days the miniature mince pies were indeed made with minced meat, fruit and candied peel.

Why?

Fruit and spices were used to disguise the inevitably 'off' flavour of meat without refrigeration. This is probably why fruit was so popular in English cooking right up until the late 1960s. We are not America and fridges were expensive back then. We didn't get one until I went to secondary school in the 1970s. My dad won it in a raffle. It was a tiny under-the-counter fridge and mostly left empty. We had no idea what to do with it. The milkman delivered every day, veg came off the allotment or from the market twice a week, we had our own hens for eggs, and because we were poor we bought a joint of meat once a week – no more. The remains went through the Spong, to reappear in pies and meat pastes. If our food wasn't being eaten it was being cooked, and if it wasn't being cooked it was fresh. Who needed a fridge?

But if you want to make your own no-meat mincemeat, with or without a Spong – here's the recipe. Yes, you can use an electric blender, but a mechanical device with a handle delivers a more satisfying coarseness. If you don't want to make your own, buy some good stuff (read the ingredients – not too much sugar, no bloody palm oil et cetera), then, before you use it, tip the contents of your jars into a bowl, add more brandy and stir. Commercial mincemeat is always too dry.

FOR THE MINCEMEAT YOU NEED

1 lb (450 g) cooking apples, cored and peeled – and then grated
1 lb (450 g) nicely chopped suet (yes, suet...go figure)
1 lb (450 g) each of sultanas, currants, raisins and demerara
sugar. You can add candied peel if you like it. I hate it.
6 oz (170 g) almonds, blanched and pounded up with
a pestle and mortar
Grated rind and juice of 2 lemons (unwaxed, organic;
you are eating this stuff after all)
Teaspoon grated nutmeg
Teaspoon cinnamon
Teaspoon salt
Quarter pint of brandy – or rum if you prefer

Stuff the dried fruit through the Spong. Chuck the fruit and everything else into a big bowl. Blend it all together. Add more brandy or rum if you don't like the consistency. Not too runny but not slab-like either. Pack into jars and put in the back of a cool cupboard for at least a month.

I do mine on Bonfire Night – November 5th. You could easily choose Halloween as an equally messy celebratory night of pointlessness, so why not do something useful while you're trick or treating or making bonfires and getting drunk?

Then you're ready to roll (the pastry) come December.

FOR THE MINCE PIES YOU NEED

Your mincemeat – home-made or shop-bought
1 lb (450 g) plain flour – I use organic; Mrs W used Homepride.
Teaspoon baking powder
½ lb (225 g) unsalted butter – I use organic. She used lard.
Tablespoon of sieved sugar or castor sugar
Plain cold water (have this at the ready or you'll cover
the tap in pastry mix)
An egg thoroughly beaten up in a cup for later

You'll also need a baking tray with individual shallow pie slots; grease these with the butter from the wrapper – or the lard from the wrapper if you want to be back in the 1960s.

METHOD

Wear an apron. This recipe is messy. Mrs W called her apron a pinny
– short for pinafore – because our 1960s were also the 1860s.

Put on some Christmas carols, Bing Crosby, Judy Garland or
Handel's 'Messiah' (it was written for Easter but soon became the
mince-pie Christmas staple).

Chuck everything except the water and the egg into a big bowl
and knead it with both hands. When Mrs W was teaching me this
when I was about seven she gave me the bowl and told me to knead
the mixture, but I couldn't work out how to get both knees into
the bowl.

When your mixture looks like breadcrumbs put in enough cold
water to turn the stuff into dough.

Now sprinkle some flour on the counter or rolling board, turn
out the mixture, roll it with your rolling pin – good for your triceps
– bang it around a bit and think of your enemies, if you are like Mrs
Winterson, until you like the texture; you should be able to throw it
at someone (your enemy) and do damage. Put this Christmas missile

back in the bowl, cover it with a robin tea towel (optional robin) and stick it in the fridge for an hour, or just put it on the windowsill if the weather is cold or snowy or seasonal. But not raining.

Mrs W never had to do this part because we had no central heating, just a coal fire, and our house was always freezing. Modern homes are too warm for good pastry. They used to say cold hands make good pastry. If you want the full 1960s experience, lard et cetera, turn off your heating the night before and wear two jumpers under your pinny.

Get out the mincemeat – your own or shop-bought. Turn into a bowl and see if you want to add any more brandy or rum. Is the mixture too dry? This matters.

Now – and this is my bit not hers – pour yourself a glass of wine and go and write some Christmas cards or wrap a few gifts; something seasonal and fun. Don't do the ironing.

Heat up the oven to 200°C or gas mark 6. You will know your own oven so do it some time during the hour the pastry is firming up. I have an Aga so I am useless at oven-work – and Mrs W had a gas oven of terrifying heat. It behaved like a castrated blast furnace roaring for its balls. Squat. Square. Short legs. Cast iron. Turn on the gas tap. Hiss. Throw in the match. Stand back. Boom. Roar. Rip of blue flame steadying to a line of unleashed orange. Inside of oven like a squash court of self-bouncing fire. Now cook.

Hopefully you have a tamer domesticated version of this feral fire-box.

So back to the fridge.

After an hour or so, get out your pastry, cut the lump in half and roll out one half onto your floured counter. Not too thick. Use a cup or a cutter to make pleasing circles of pastry and press these firmly into your greased baking trays.

Now fill each one generously, but not idiotically, with the mince-meat.

Now you have a choice.

Traditionally you roll out the other half of the pastry and make lids for the pies, sealing the joint with a bit of beaten egg and brushing egg over the top of the lid. Spear a hole in the lid with a skewer to let the steam out.

OR – make more pies and just drape an 'X' of pastry in two strips over the mincemeat for those who want less pastry. Not me.

These will cook faster, so don't burn them.

Bake for 20 minutes with lids, 15 minutes without lids. In an Aga this is not exact. In Mrs Winterson's furnace it was 20 minutes or eat them black.

Store in an old tin you have no use for but can't bear to throw out.

TIP: make twice the amount of pastry. It will keep in tinfoil in the fridge for five days. And then you can make some more mince pies quick and easy.

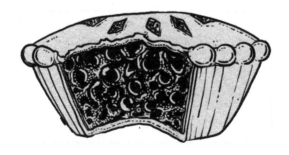

THE SNOWMAMA

t is snowing. In the English language we do not know anything about the 'it' that is snowing. It might be God. Maybe not.
Anyway. It. Is. Snowing.

What kind of snow?

There are many kinds of snow. Did you k-snow that?

There's mountain snow. And polar snow. And ski-snow, and deep snow, and snow in flutters like tiny moths, and snow in flurries like moths in a hurry, and snow in flakes like someone (it?) is grating the sky.

And snow sharp as insect bites and snow as soft as lather and wet snow that doesn't stick and dry snow that does, and wraps the world like an installation to the point in the night where you wake up and the sound is gone, to the point in the night where you turn deeper into the bed, to the point in the night where there's snow in your sleep and your sleep is as deep as snow.

*

Then
Open the curtainS Now!
Wow!

Snow on snow on snow on snow on snow.

Deep enough for the dog to disappear, ears reappearing like wings. Cars are mounds. Sounds are children excitedly.

Let's build a snowman!

Nicky and Jerry started rolling the snowball bigger and bigger and rounder and rounder. Soon they had a body bigger than either of them.

Do you think she's too fat? said Nicky.

How do you know she's a she?

Well, I don't until we put the clothes on her.

But you keep calling her her.

Because she's fat.

How do you make a thin snowman?

They tried. They rolled a pole of snow and stood it up and when they put the head on the pole it fell down.

Nicky wasn't impressed. She pulled a face. She said –

We can make her a bit more pyramidy – give her a neck or something. A fat neck is not a good look.

Jerry didn't want to make a pyramid snowman.

She said, Snow people are all fat – it's like what they have to be to keep them warm.

Nicky thought this was stupid – If they warm up they melt.

Warm on the inside, stupid! Come on, Nicky, help me roll her head.

*

Nicky's mum came out with two mugs of hot chocolate.

Hey! He's great!

He's a she. Have we got any clothes for her?

Sure! Go and see what's in the charity box.

Nicky ran inside, leaving her chocolate to steam.

Nicky's mum was attractive. She was slim with hair coloured three kinds of blonde. She smiled at Jerry. She had good teeth.

How's your mum, Jerry; is she OK?

Jerry nodded. Her mum had to work hard and she had to work nights at a hotel. Sometimes she drank too much and passed out. Jerry's dad had left them last year, just before Christmas, and he hadn't come back.

Nicky's mum shifted her weight, which wasn't a lot, from foot to foot.

Why don't you sleep over tonight? Nicky would love that.

I'll ask, said Jerry.

You can call, said Nicky's mum, but Jerry couldn't call because her mum's phone had been cut off. But she didn't want to say that; instead she said, I'll run over later and ask.

Nicky came back out with an armful of clothes. They tried a sweater, a hoodie, a dress with buttons, but nothing fitted.

This is like *Cinderella*, said Jerry.

You mean she's the ugly sister? said Nicky.

She's the princess in disguise. Here – try this.

The bobble hat fitted.

She can go to the ball!

In a bobble hat?

Yeah.

Well, she can't, because she's got no legs. How about eyes? She needs eyes. But not buttons.

No, not buttons – give me your bracelet – those green stones – they can be her eyes. Come on!

What are you doing? That's my bracelet!

But Jerry wasn't listening – she broke the bracelet and fixed the SnowWoman with great green, staring eyes.

She looks real now! said Nicky.

She needs a snose, said Jerry, or maybe a snowt.

Jerry forgot about Nicky. She made the SnowWoman a nose out of a pine cone and a mouth that was a big red smile. It was really the dog's throw-hoop cut in half but it looked like a big red smile.

By now Nicky was playing a game on her iPad. The afternoons were short and the day was cold. Soon it would be dark. Nicky's mum called out from the kitchen door – Jerry! Go and see your mother now if you're coming back later!

Jerry ran off, promising the SnowWoman she would come right back. But when Jerry got home, her mother wasn't there. The house was dark. Sometimes the electricity got cut off, but when that happened Jerry couldn't get in with the entry phone – she had to climb over the wall at the back and find the key behind the dustbins. That was what she did – but the key wasn't there, and the house was as dark at the back as it was at the front.

You lookin' for your ma? asked Mr Store, who ran the store that was called Store's Stores.

Jerry nodded. She didn't say anything. Mr Store said, Your ma's not here – went out, didn't come back; what's new?

Mr Store was horrible. He had a horrible face and a horrible stare and a horrible pair of brown overalls that he always wore. Sometimes Jerry's mum asked him for milk or bread and to pay the next day. He always said no. Now he stuffed his horrible hands in the brown pockets of his horrible overalls and went inside.

Jerry decided to wait a while and squeezed herself onto the front step, where she was out of the cold a little.

She thought about the SnowWoman – she was at least eight feet tall, bigger than anyone. When Jerry grew up she hoped she'd be eight feet tall. Then she'd show them.

She'd show them who she was.

Night fell. Why do we say that? Like night didn't mean to be here but tripped up crossing the moon. The moon was bright. Everyone was coming home now, the day done, the night cold. The windows along the street lit up one by one. Jerry stood up to warm her limbs and walked up and down the street looking in through the windows where she could. People sitting down to eat. People watching TV. People moving from room to room, saying something – she couldn't hear what, their mouths opening and shutting like goldfish.

There was a bird in a cage and an Alsatian lying across the front door, willing it to open.

All the houses had lights on now, except hers.

Maybe her mother thought she was staying at Nicky's. Maybe she should go back there now.

Jerry set off on the half-hour walk back to Nicky's house. It seemed later than it was – the quiet streets, no one driving. A black cat paced the length of a white wall.

There was Nicky's house now – and the lights were on. Jerry broke into a run to reach the gate, but as she reached it all the lights went out, just like that, and the house was as dark as hers.

What time was it? The station wagon was on the drive. Jerry rubbed snow from the window and peeped in at the clock. 11.30? It couldn't be 11.30 at night.

*

Jerry was suddenly scared and tired and not knowing. Not knowing the time, not knowing what to do. Maybe she could sleep in the shed. Jerry turned from the dark house to the garden, strangely light and white and semi-shining because of the snow.

The SnowMama was looking at her with two bright green jewel eyes.

I wish you were alive, said Jerry.

A live what? said the SnowMama. A live cat? A live circus?

Did you just speak? said Jerry doubtfully.

I did, said the SnowMama.

Your mouth didn't move...

That's the way you fixed it, said the SnowMama. But you can hear me, can't you?

Yes, said Jerry. I can hear you. Are you really alive?

Watch this! said the SnowMama, and skipped a bit sideways. Not bad for no legs. That's the way you fixed it too.

I'm sorry, said Jerry, I didn't know how to do legs.

Don't beat yourself up about things you can't change. You did your best. Anyway, I can glide. Come on! Let's go for a glide!

The SnowMama set off surprisingly fast for an object without legs, wheels or an engine. Jerry ran to catch up.

I'd say hold my hand, said the SnowMama, except that you didn't fix me any hands...

Wait! said Jerry. Would you like two medium-sized garden forks?

That would be gracious, said the SnowMama.

So Jerry fetched the garden forks (medium-sized) from the shed and shoved them firmly into the sides of the SnowMama. The SnowMama wriggled her shoulders a bit to get the fit right, then, concentrating hard, she was able to flex the tines of the forks.

Hey! Hey! Hey!

How d'ya do that? asked Jerry.

It's a mystery, said the SnowMama. Do you know how you do things? Does anyone? I just did it. So let's go.

Where are we going?

To find the others!

Jerry and the SnowMama left the garden and set off down the road. The SnowMama was much faster than Jerry, who kept falling down.

Fish in the sea, that's me, said the SnowMama. I'm in my element. Climb aboard! Just jump up and rest your feet in my tines.

Soon the two of them were speeding down the street. Jerry held her feet in the cupped tines like they were stirrups and she held on to either end of the SnowMama's scarf like they were reins. On they went, past the school and the post office, or they were nearly past the post office when a little voice called out, WAIT FOR ME.

The SnowMama slid in a skid to a halt.

She said, WHO GOES THERE?

On the top of the mail box some kids had perched a Little Snow-Man with a paper hat on his head. THIS IS SO BORING, said the Little SnowMan – TAKE ME WITH YOU!

Why are you speaking in Capital Letters? said the SnowMama. Don't you know it's Bad Manners to speak in Capital Letters?

I have no family, said the Little SnowMan, and I never went to school. Forgive me.

Well, come on, said the SnowMama, just hold on to my front, as the back is occupied, and let's see what we can see.

PLEASED TO MEET YOU, MISS! yelled the Little SnowMan to Jerry, then he remembered that was not Polite, and whispered as quietly as he could – PLEASED TO MEET YOU, MISS!

*

On they went, past the garage and the factory and through the still, silent night under the rock-diamond sky.

They came to the city park.

All day long the children had built SnowMen and now all the children had gone home and the SnowMen were still there.

They looked eerie in their brilliant white coats lit up by the brilliant white moon.

Then Jerry saw that some of the SnowMen were moving slowly towards the lake – where two of them were fishing.

A child must have built these fishing SnowMen, each with a rod and line made from a peeled stick and a length of twine.

As Jerry, the SnowMama and the Little SnowMan came near the lake one of the SnowFishers turned and raised his pork-pie hat in salute.

Welcome! This lake is full of SnowFish! The SnowGirls are lighting a fire and we hope you will join us for a barbecue. Perfect weather!

Right then his line bent and quivered and for a minute he steered something invisible and strong back and forth under the water, then with a deft flick of the line a SnowFish flew above the surface of the lake. It was more than a foot long and its scales were made of snowflakes.

You only get them at this time of year, explained the SnowFisher. Too early and they are frozen solid, too late and they melt like they were never there.

I've never seen a SnowFish, said Jerry.

That's to be expected, said the SnowFisher. Most of us can only see the world we know.

OH BOY OH BOY OH BOY OH BOY OH BOY! yelled the Little SnowMan. He was so excited he stood upside down on his head and it came out backwards: HO YOB HO YOB HO YOB HO YOB.

HO YOB!

Can he pipe down? said the SnowFisher. He'll scare away the Snow-Fish.

The SnowMama grabbed the Little SnowMan by his feet and took him over to where a group of SnowSisters were piling together a wigwam of white frosted branches. They all wore earrings made out of red berries.

Y'all staying for the barbecue? said one, taller than the rest. She's human, right?

Yes, said the SnowMama; her name's Jerry.

What about ME? shouted the Little SnowMan. Don't forget ME!

Can I leave him with you? said the SnowMama. He needs some discipline. He can fetch branches for the fire.

Sure! Come on, you little Sno' Snothin', get to work. We'll teach him a thing or two.

I'm an orphan! yelled the Little SnowMan. I got Special Needs.

You surely shall have Special Needs when the sun shows up and melts you down, said a SnowSister. Now come on! Move it!

Let's you and me take a tour, said the SnowMama to Jerry. This is all new to you, I can see.

Isn't it new to you? asked Jerry. I mean, I only made you this morning.

That's part of the mystery of history, said the SnowMama. I was not. I am. I will not be. I will be.

That was too deep for Jerry and so was the snow. As she ran after the gliding SnowMama she fell into a deep drift up to her chin.

*

SNOLLIE! Lend me a line, will you? The SnowMama was signalling to one of the SnowFishers. He came over, dropped his line and pulled Jerry out like she were a carp under the ice.

Thanks, Snollie, said the SnowMama. This is a good year for us, isn't it?

It certainly is, Mama, said Snollie. If the weather holds we should be here a week before we have to move on.

Move on? said Jerry.

Like I said, the mystery of our history. Let me tell you how we happen.

The SnowMama sat down next to a snowy figure on a snowy bench and invited Jerry to sit between them. She folded her tine hands across her white lap and began...

Every year the snow falls and children build snowmen. They give us mittens and hats and ties and scarves and beautiful eyes, like the ones you gave me made out of green glass.

Grown-ups think that SnowPeople are just snow, but children sknow better than that. They whisper to us and tell us their secrets. They sit down on the ground and pull up their knees and lean their backs against us when they are sad. They love us, and so we come alive.

Look around the park. You see how many SnowPeople there are? Every year we meet again, because once we come alive, we live forever. You see us melt, and we do, but that's us moving on, to the next place where it snows. And when the children roll the snow, there we are again.

Jerry thought about this... But if you melt...

The SnowMama held up her hand in pause...

You can't melt our Snowls. Every SnowPerson has a Snowl, and the Snowl goes on through time and space and frost and ice and you'll find us with the polar bears and the elks and the reindeer. You'll find us waiting in white clouds to begin again. When the snow falls, we're not far behind.

Jerry looked at the SnowPerson sitting motionless on the bench beside her. What about this one? Why isn't he saying anything?

The SnowMama shook her head. He will never say anything. He's not a SnowMan, he's just snow. A grown-up made him, didn't believe in him, and didn't love him. So he didn't live.

Jerry said, My friend Nicky didn't love you. She thought you were too fat.

I am just right, said the SnowMama, and you loved me, and so I was waiting for you in the garden.

What if I hadn't come back? said Jerry.

I knew you would, said the SnowMama. Love always comes back.

A SnowCat prowled past wearing a jewelled collar. Ain't that the truth? said the SnowCat. High five for Lucky Love. And he held up his paw.

They've lit the fire! said Jerry. I can see it! But the flames aren't orange or red; they're white!

Cold fire, said the SnowMama. That's no ordinary fire. Come on! Let's go and join in.

The fire was burning high, every flare and shoot of flame like a burst of snowflakes flying upwards, but strangely the white frosted branches didn't seem to be consumed. The cold fire burned through them in shimmering transparent blasts.

The SnowPeople were standing or sitting around the campfire colding their hands and feet.

Come and get colder! said the SnowMama.

I'm too cold already, said Jerry, who was shivering.

Well, look who's here, said one of the SnowSisters. MAKE WAY, MAKE WAY!

It was the Little SnowMan, carrying one end of a pole hung with SnowFish from the lake. The fish looked like they were made of crystal with pearly eyes.

Snollie was carrying the other end of the pole; he was trying to direct the Little SnowMan... Now we suspend the pole over the fire, like...

But the Little SnowMan was so excited that he walked right into the fire and right out the other side.

WOW, said Jerry, he just got bigger!

The Little SnowMan had indeed got bigger – a lot bigger.

That's what happens in cold fire, explained the SnowMama. In regular fire, things burn up so they get smaller, and then they disappear. Cold fire makes everything it touches bigger – look at the fish!

The fish were cooking, sizzling inside their snowflake scales – but now they were all twice the size.

Grab yourselves a fish, folks, said the SnowFisher.

Eat up while they're cold.

Can I have three? yelled the BIG (aka Little) SNOWMAN.

That stupid SnowBody got slush for brains – we'll get him back to size... Hey, dude, swallow this!

One of the SnowSisters threw what looked like a pine cone at the rapidly growing, now enormous SnowMan.

THANKS! THANKS! THANKS! said the BLS, his snowy head already in the branches of the trees.

Will he be OK? asked Jerry.

Sure he will, replied the SnowMama. Worst comes to worst, he'll melt.

Will you melt? said Jerry.

Yes, I will.

I don't want you to melt.

You know what I'm thinkin'? said the SnowMama. I'm thinkin' we should get you home – don't want you like Kay in *The Snow Queen* – with blue hands and feet and ice in your heart.

But she was bad, said Jerry, the Snow Queen.

Yes, she was bad, but even being good has unintended consequences. You're only human, after all.

So the SnowMama picked up Jerry and they left the SnowPeople singing winter songs round the campfire: 'Let it Snow, Let it Snow, Let it Snow', 'Winter Wonderland', 'Snobody Loves You Like I Love You', 'Ain't Snow Stoppin' Us Now'.

At the edge of the city park, the sound of singing died away and all Jerry could hear was the wind blowing in the trees and the glide of the SnowMama across the tracks. She was singing quietly to herself in a low, beautiful voice.

What's that song? said Jerry.

Shakespeare – 'Fear no more the heat o' the sun.' It's a song of mourning. We sing it when we melt.

Do you know about Shakespeare?

It's a mystery, said the SnowMama.

Soon they were on Jerry's street and outside Jerry's home. The lights were still out.

Here, said the SnowMama, let me do the door. I'll freeze open the lock.

Inside the house was cold and empty. There were dishes piled in the sink and on the counter. The floor was dirty. There was a Christmas tree in the corner of the room but it had no decorations.

It will be Christmas in a few days, said the SnowMama.

My dad left last Christmas, said Jerry. I think my mum's upset.

No one ever came to Jerry's house now. Not to play or to visit. She was used to seeing it like this. The mess and the dirt and the sadness. Now she saw it through the SnowMama's eyes.

Let's clean the place up together, said the SnowMama. You start with the dishes. I'll wash the floor.

The SnowMama's mopping method was unique. She melted a little bit of her snowskirts and spun the water round the room, shooing it straight out of the door when it was too dirty. Soon the dishes were done too, and dried, and the floor was gleaming.

All right! said the SnowMama. Now collect all the dirty clothes and the sheets and things from the bed, and we'll go to the launderette.

It's closed! said Jerry. And we don't have any money.

Trust me, I'm a snowman.

At the launderette the SnowMama sprang the lock and in they went. Operating the machines was easy. The SnowMama prised the metal front from the token dispenser with her steel fingers.

Plenty here, she said, carefully refitting the door.

While the laundry went round and round, Jerry felt herself getting warm and sleepy. She dreamed she was in a snowstorm of washing powder and that the sky was made of sheets.

A drunk walking by, second bottle of vodka in his pocket, saw or said he saw a snowman doing the washing –

I'm tellin' ya she was eight feet tall and white and built like a cube and she had these scary green eyes, and pitchforks for hands, and there was a little girl with her fast asleep on a couple of chairs.

Ya sure it wasn't Santa Claus in there with her? Ha ha ha ha ha...

When Jerry woke up all the laundry was washed and dried and folded, so she and the SnowMama made their way home.

You see to the beds, said the SnowMama; I'll be back very soon.

Jerry made up nice new beds for herself and her mother. For the first time in ages the beds looked like nice places to be, snug and warm and clean and inviting. She started to yawn. The clock said nearly 4am.

Just then the SnowMama returned pushing a shopping cart piled with groceries: fruit, coffee, cakes, vegetables, bacon, eggs, milk, butter, bread, a turkey and a plum pudding. The SnowMama's red dog-hoop mouth was a bigger, wider grin than ever.

I broke into Store's Stores!

But that's stealing!

Yes, it is.

But that's wrong!

So is a child with nothing to eat. Here...

And the SnowMama boiled some hot milk and made Jerry a big piece of cheese on toast. Jerry sat up in bed eating and drinking and nearly asleep.

I have to go now, said the SnowMama. You can see me in Nicky's garden tomorrow.

I don't want you to go, said Jerry.

I need to be out in the cold. Big goodnight – I'd give you a kiss but I can't bend down.

Jerry jumped up on the bed and kissed the SnowMama. She felt a little bit of snow melt in her mouth.

The next day Jerry woke up hearing the front door open. She jumped out of bed. Her mother had come home. She looked tired and defeated. She didn't notice the beautiful, clean kitchen or the sparkly windows or the warm, happy feeling of the house. Jerry put some bread in the toaster. It's nearly Christmas, she said.

I know, said her mother. I'll get you a present, I promise. We'll decorate the tree together. I just need to get some sleep... I... She stood up, went into the bedroom, came back out again. Did you clean everything? I've never seen it look like this.

I washed it all. And there's food. Look!

Jerry's mother looked in the fridge and in the cupboards. Where did you get the money for all this food?

The SnowMama did it.

Jerry didn't say anything about the SnowMama stealing the food from Store's Stores.

Is she, like, a charity? For Christmas?

Yes, said Jerry.

Jerry's mother looked nearly like her old self before Jerry's dad had left. I can't believe someone has helped us – been kind to us. Did she leave a number?

Jerry shook her head.

Her mother looked again at everything in their little house. This is like a miracle. It is a miracle, Jerry!

Go out and play and when you come back I'll have made dinner. Like I always did.

Jerry ran round to Nicky's house. She couldn't wait to tell her friend everything that had happened during the night. She told her about the SnowFish, and the Big Little SnowMan, and how she had ridden on the SnowMama's back. She didn't tell her about the launderette or the stealing. But Nicky didn't believe her. She went up to the Snow-Mama and pulled her nose off. See? If she was alive she'd yell at me!

Jerry grabbed the pine cone and pushed Nicky flat down into the snow. Nicky started to cry and her mother came out. That's enough, you two! Jerry, we're going Christmas shopping this afternoon – do you want to come?

I don't want her to come! shouted Nicky.

Jerry pretended to go home but in fact she hid behind the shed. As soon as the car had pulled away she ran up to the SnowMama. They've gone! You can move now!

But nothing happened. The SnowMama was still as a statue. Jerry waited and waited, colder and colder. Feeling sad and silly, she walked home through the park. The SnowMen were all there, fishing or standing in groups. She saw the SnowCat under the tree and ran up to him: Hello, Lucky Love! But the cat said nothing.

So Jerry set off home, wondering if the house would really be clean, if the food would really be in the fridge, if her mother would really be making dinner.

As she came down the street past Store's Stores Mr Store was standing grumpily on his step in his horrible brown overalls. He waved at Jerry to listen to him.

I was robbed last night! Thieves broke in and stole food. One of them was dressed as a snowman! I have it on CCTV. Can you believe it?

Jerry couldn't help smiling. Mr Store frowned so low that his horrible eyebrows were on top of his horrible moustache. It's no laughing matter, young lady.

Jerry opened the door to her house. Her home was as clean and bright as she had left it. Delicious smells filled the kitchen. Jerry's mother was listening to carols on the radio. She had made a lasagne. They ate it together and her mother was full of plans. I'll get a different job – no more nights. We'll keep this place nice. Just somebody helping us has made all the difference. Do you know that?

That night Jerry's mother had to go back to her job but it didn't seem so sad and hard as before. Jerry had a plan to sneak out and go to the park, but she found that her mother had double-locked the door. She was thinking, maybe, she could climb out of the bedroom window so that no one could see her, when she heard a tap-tap-tapping at the kitchen window.

It was the SnowMama.

Jerry opened the window.

It's so warm in there now I can't come in, said the SnowMama. I brought you these to decorate the tree.

She had a sackful of pine cones like her nose but these were all shining white and frosted.

Why didn't you talk to me when I was at Nicky's? asked Jerry. I waited and waited and you were just snow.

It's a mystery, said the SnowMama. Why don't you decorate the tree? I'll watch through the window.

Soon the tree was splendid with its cones and the house looked festive and fun.

Did you know, said the SnowMama, that there are more than a million snowflakes in just one litre of snow?

And is every snowflake different? said Jerry.

A snowflake is formed as it swirls and falls through the air, and that swirling and falling is never the same, always different, said the SnowMama. How is your mother today?

She was happy today, said Jerry, and she made a lasagne. I did the washing-up.

You have to look after each other, said the SnowMama – if not, you'll both be sad and cold, even in the summer.

Parents are supposed to look after their children, said Jerry.

Life is as it is, said the SnowMama.

Jerry looked out of the window at the frosty stars. She said to the SnowMama, Can you come and live with us? If we could keep you really cold – like get you your own freezer or something?

The SnowMama's green eyes flashed in the light.

Then everyone would know what we know – and that can't happen because everyone has to k-snow it for themselves.

What? said Jerry.

That love is a mystery and that love is the mystery that makes things happen.

Jerry slept the whole dark night of softness and quiet and a million, million stars.

When she heard her mother come in the next morning Jerry jumped out of bed and ran into the kitchen and kissed her mother, who was admiring the tree.

Where did you find these decorations?

The SnowMama brought them, said Jerry.

I wish I could thank her myself. Are you sure she didn't leave a card?

Jerry decided she would go and ask the SnowMama to meet her mother. While her mother got ready to sleep after her night shift, Jerry got dressed and ran through the park towards Nicky's.

When she got to the gates of the drive, she stopped.

There was a different car parked next to Nicky's family car. The car was parked right where the SnowMama had been.

Jerry ran in and behind the car. On the ground was the bobble hat and two old forks. Jerry dropped on her hands and knees and dug frantically in the snow. She found the SnowMama's emerald eyes. She started to cry.

Nicky came out, just wearing a jumper and leggings.

What's the matter, Jerry?

But Jerry couldn't speak, so Nicky said, The snowman got knocked down when my friends came. They just backed up in the car...sorry.

But Jerry kept on crying and Nicky didn't know what to do. She wasn't real, Jerry – we can build her again if you want. Do you want to?

But the weather was changing. Already there was rain and the snow was softening and the roofs shed great slabs of snow. Jerry ran back through the park and saw that the SnowPeople had started to move on.

Some had lost their heads. The SnowCat was just a heap with one ear, and the frozen lake was changing colour as the warmer water sat on its surface. The SnowFisher had dropped his rod and line.

Jerry went home. When her mother woke up Jerry tried to explain about the SnowMama, but her mother didn't understand. But she did understand that Jerry was upset and she held her close and promised her that their lives would be different from now on. There would be food, and warmth, and clean clothes and time.

I won't be drinking. I won't be depressed. I won't leave you alone, she said to Jerry and, though these things are easier to say than to do, Jerry's mother kept her promise and there was never another cold and hungry Christmas.

And Christmas Day came, because it always does, whether you want it to or not, and it always goes, whether you want it to or not, because life is as it is. And Jerry opened the presents under the tree, and among them, best of all, was a microscope and a book that told you everything about snowflakes.

It had all started in Vermont in 1885 when a boy called Snowflake Bentley began photographing snowflakes through his microscope. He was the first person ever to do this and when he died he had photographed 5,381 snowflakes, and every photo was different.

And Jerry went back and stood where the SnowMama had stood. But the place was empty.

Over the years that followed, Jerry built the SnowMama every winter, usually in the park by the lake, but the SnowMama never came alive again.

Jerry grew up. In time she had children of her own and they loved the story of the SnowMama, even though they had never seen her.

It was Christmas Eve.

Jerry's kids were in bed.

The stockings were hung on the ends of the beds and the cat was asleep under the Christmas tree.

Jerry went to turn off the lights. The snow was falling softly. For some reason she opened the drawer to her desk and got out the old microscope that her mother had given her so many years ago. Then she pulled on her boots and went outside.

Her kids had built three SnowPeople all in a row. Jerry pressed the microscope against the nearest cold white form and studied the snowflakes magnified in the glass. How could life be so multiple, unexpected, ordinary and a miracle?

Like love, she said out loud.

And a voice she knew replied – Love always comes back.

There was the SnowMama. Standing in the garden.

It's you! said Jerry.

Always, said the SnowMama.

But all these years – where have you been?

It's a mystery…

I'll tell the kids – they know all about you!

Not tonight, said the SnowMama. Maybe one day, who knows? I guess I just wanted to see you again; I always hoped I would.

And something like a snowy tear fell from the SnowMama's eye.

Wait! said Jerry. Wait…

She ran inside and went back to her desk drawer.

She had kept the green glass eyes wrapped up with the microscope.

These are yours, she said. Shall I put them in?

Then she kissed the SnowMama and felt a little bit of ice melting in her mouth.

It worked out, said Jerry.

I know, said the SnowMama. Sometimes a little bit of help is all we need.

Don't go! said Jerry as the SnowMama began to spin away.

I'll keep an eye on you, said the SnowMama. Ha ha. And who knows what the future brings?

And away she went, gliding as silent as the stars until she was as faint and far as a star.

A million, million stars and lucky love.

❄

Ruth Rendell's
Red Cabbage

I met Ruth Rendell in 1986 when she was fifty-six and I was twenty-seven. We were friends until her death in 2015, when she was eighty-five and I was fifty-six. I met her when she was at the age I am now – and that changes the way I think about our friendship, and her remarkable kindness to me.

I had published just one book back then – *Oranges Are Not The Only Fruit*. She was a celebrated international success. The Queen of Crime.

We met because she needed someone to house-sit while she went on a book tour of Australia for six weeks. I was writing my second novel, *The Passion*.

With her characteristic thoughtfulness for young writers, Ruth said that she too was writing her second novel – as Barbara Vine, the pen-name she had recently assumed for thrillers of terrifying psychological insight.

Ruth and I really liked each other. In some ways it was as simple as that. Over the years we started our own tradition of spending Christmas Day or Boxing Day together. Her son lives in America, and after her husband, Don, died, our Christmas times became more important to us both.

The routine was always the same. She told me when to arrive so that we could go for a long walk around London. She planned the route – there was always something she wanted to see. Her later work is full of London. She loved walking in London and Christmas Day is quiet.

After the walk, we'd eat. Ruth cooked. She was a nimble cook, no fuss. She wasn't all that interested in food, but she liked making Christmas dinner.

What did we have? Pheasant, roast potatoes, carrots, a green vegetable of some sort, usually whatever I had grown in the garden that had survived slugs and pigeons. So we might eat sprouts if we were lucky, kale if we weren't. Lots of gravy and, and this is the point of the story, Ruth Rendell's pickled red cabbage.

Ruth made the pickled cabbage in early autumn. She always rang me to tell me the day. 'Oh, Jeanette, it's Ruth; I'm pickling the cabbage and then I'll walk down to the House.'

She meant the House of Lords, where she was a Labour Peer.

It's not generally known that Ruth was a big Country and Western fan, so the cabbage-pickling was accompanied by Tammy Wynette or k. d. lang.

I was never present at the process of pickling. Ruth was her own alchemist and, whatever she did, she did it better than me. I have her recipe but not her knack. Pickling was something that Ruth's generation of women understood. Ruth was born in 1930. As a teenager in the Second World War she was pickling for victory. And her own mother was Swedish, so, if you think about it, Ruth's pickling skills go back to the turn of the century, and were learned from a tradition whose winter food-supply depended on salting and fermenting.

And of course when Ruth was growing up in London, first there was the Depression, then came the war, then rationing – and nobody had a fridge.

When her husband was alive she pickled him gherkins. He loved a gherkin. She told me she had pickled rabbits during the war.

'What did they taste like?'

'How should I know? It looked disgusting. I wasn't going to eat it, Jeanette!' And then that laugh. Ruth had a wonderful laugh, directed at the comedy of life, its absurdity.

*

It's fair to say she was a connoisseur of the pickle. She loved a pickled herring. I adore pickled cucumber and I always order it when I eat at the Wolseley Restaurant on Piccadilly in London.

Ruth liked me to take her there. Generally in life Ruth found herself paying the bill; she was both wealthy and generous, so it was good for her to be taken out, and our rule was that she never paid at the Wolseley. I always got there first so that I could order champagne without having a fight...

I find that champagne and pickled cucumber is an excellent combination. Ruth, though, never thought much of the Wolseley cucumber.

'Mine's much better, you know...'

And it was.

Ruth owned a set of ancient pickling jars with rubber seals and screw-top lids. When filled to the brim these were left to sit in the back of the larder like a question no one can answer yet.

Opening the jar was a moment of anticipation and anxiety. Fermentation is fraught. You might make something exquisite – or something that stinks.

It never went wrong – but until you open the jar you really don't know.

The colour of pickled red cabbage is exquisite, and the perfect red for a Christmas feast. Ruth served hers in a pale green bowl. The sharpness of the taste is a great counterpoint to the richness of Christmas dinner.

Apart from the vegetables, all I had to do was bring the wine. Ruth's wine knowledge was zero and left to herself a drink would be a supermarket bottle of wine-lake Chardonnay. But she loved champagne, so that's what I brought her. Veuve Clicquot.

After our meal it was TV time. Ruth was in charge of what we watched, but it had to be something scheduled in real time – no DVDs, no catch-up TV.

Ruth put her feet up on the sofa with her beloved cat, Archie. I'd lie on the other sofa, and we'd complain about the telly. It was important to be able to complain about the telly.

About ten o'clock, Ruth would zap the zapper and say, 'I can't stand any more of this rubbish, can you.' (It was not a question.) Then she followed it with a second non-question: 'Shall we have the Christmas pudding.'

The pudding – always made by a friend of hers in the House of Lords – was the size of a cannon ball and just as heavy. It was a lethal weapon disguised as dessert. Ruth let it boil for hours wrapped in a rag in a double pan – the old-fashioned way. As her kitchen ventilation wasn't that great, we spent the later part of the evening in a Hitchcock steam that smelled of washing. Even the cat coughed.

When the pudding was thought to be ready – and Ruth, the most precise of persons, never used a timer – she set about making custard. While this was happening she'd sing a bit – usually Country and Western, or sometimes Handel; she was a big Handel fan. Sometimes it was 'Jolene' medley'd with hits from the *Messiah*.

The custard was proper home-made with milk and eggs. The effort had to be encouraged by opening a further bottle of champagne – but only a half.

Then the pudding was tipped onto its dish, covered in brandy by me, and set alight by Ruth. Ruth always said she was too full to eat any, and then munched her way through exactly one half.

The next day she'd send me home with the rest of the jar of red cabbage.

The last Christmas I spent with her was 2014. Ruth Rendell had a stroke on January 7th 2015 and never recovered.

I miss our Christmases together. And the red cabbage.

Here's her recipe.

YOU NEED

Organic red cabbage – not too old or tough. Use a big one or two small ones.

Pickling vinegar. More on this below.

100 g sugar. Not all recipes use sugar but Ruth's does.

150 g good-quality coarse sea salt. The salt depends on how much cabbage you are making. The point of the salt is to draw the water from the cabbage leaves.

About the pickling vinegar: you can buy this from the shops but Ruth made her own and kept some to hand in the cupboard in case she wanted to make a Cheat's Red Cabbage (instant pickled effect). The pickling vinegar lasts ages if you keep it in a good airtight bottle and decant it into smaller bottles as the volume goes down. Here's how you make it:

Put 2 pints (just over a litre) of malt vinegar in a big pan along with 6 fresh bay leaves, a couple of teaspoons of peppercorns, some caraway or coriander seeds if you have them, mustard seeds as well, or instead (I said this was a personal recipe!), a few cloves. Whatever. For Ruth it really was a whatever, because she knew what would work.

Bring to the boil. Let it cool down somewhere that won't stink out the place with vinegar. I cover mine and put it outside overnight.

Leave all your spices in the vinegar mixture until the next day then sieve the vinegar clear. Some people start the process by putting all the spice-junk in a spice bag and throw the bag away afterwards but Ruth thought that was a faff. 'What's wrong with a sieve.' (Another not-a-question.)

METHOD

Get rid of any old outer leaves. You are eating this stuff later.

Fine-chop the red cabbage into forkful-sized shreds. Put these into a big bowl and work the salt through the cabbage. Cover and keep in the fridge overnight.

The next day bring your pickling vinegar to the boil again, let it cool off and add the sugar, stirring well. If you put in the sugar when the mixture is too hot you will get a kind of vinegar syrup like something from a disastrous chemistry lesson. Not good.

Rinse the salt off your cabbage and dry it well.

Line up your airtight jars, which have been sterilised, if used previously, and which are perfectly dry and clean. We all have to die but not of cabbage poisoning.

Fill each jar a third full of your pickling liquid, then pack the jars tight with cabbage. And I mean TIGHT! Then fill the jars to the very brim with the pickling vinegar. No air pockets!

Seal the jars, wipe any spills and store your pristine pickled cabbage in a dark, brooding place till needed.

The problem with the recipe is that Ruth was a virtuoso pickler, so if she wanted to add some red wine to her pickling mixture, or use cider vinegar, she did that. Similarly, she sometimes chopped some windfall apples in with the red cabbage. Or a little bit of onion. (I know, I KNOW.)

She just couldn't get it wrong. Unlike me.

Remember old Sam Beckett? 'Try Again. Fail again. Fail better.'

Happy Christmas, Ruth.

DARK CHRISTMAS

e had borrowed the house from a friend none of us
seemed to know.

Highfallen House stood on an eminence overlooking the sea. It was a square Victorian gentleman's
residence. The large bay windows looked down through the pines towards the shore. Six stone steps led the visitor up to the double front
door, where a Gothic bell-pull released a loud, mournful clang deep
into the distances of the house.

Laurel lined the drive. The stable block was disused. The walled
garden had been locked up in 1914 when the gardeners went to war.
Only one had returned. I had been warned that the high brick wall
enclosing the garden was unsafe. As I passed it slowly in the car I saw
a faded notice falling off the paint-peeled door: DO NOT ENTER.

I was the first to arrive. My friends were following by train and I
was to collect them the next day and then we would settle down to
Christmas.

I had driven from Bristol and I was tired. There was a Christmas
tree roped on the top of my 4x4 and a trunk-load of provisions. We
were not near any town. But the housekeeper had left stacked wood

to build a fire and I had brought a shepherd's pie and a bottle of Rioja for my first night.

The kitchen was cheerful enough once I had got the fire going and the radio playing while I unpacked our festive supplies. I checked my phone – no signal. Still, I knew the time of the train tomorrow and it was a relief to feel that the world had gone away. I put my food in the oven to heat up, poured a glass of wine and went upstairs to find myself a bedroom.

The first landing had three bedrooms leading off it. Each had a moth-eaten rug, a metal bedstead and a mahogany chest of drawers. At the far end of the landing was a second set of stairs up to the attic floor.

I am not romantic about maids' rooms or nurseries but there was something about that second set of stairs that made me hesitate. The landing was bright in the sudden way of late sun on a winter's afternoon. Yet the light ended abruptly at the foot of the stairs as though it couldn't go any further. I didn't want to be near that set of stairs so I chose the room at the front of the house.

As I went back downstairs to bring up my bag the house bell started to ring, its jerky, metallic hammers sounding somewhere in the guts of the house. I was surprised but not alarmed. I expected the housekeeper. I opened the front door. There was no one there. I went down the steps and looked round. I admit I was frightened. The night was clear and soundless. There was no car in the distance. No footsteps walking away. Determined to conquer my fear, I walked up and down outside for a few minutes. Then, turning back to the house, I saw it: the bell wire ran along the side of the house under a sheltering gutter. Perhaps thirty or forty bats were dangling upside down on the vibrating wire. The same number swooped and swerved in a dark mass. Obviously their movement on the wire had set off the bell. I like bats. Clever bats. Good. Now supper.

I ate. I drank. I wondered why love is so hard and life is so short. I went to bed. The room was warmer now and I was ready to sleep. The sound of the sea ebbed into the flow of my dreams.

I woke from a dead sleep in dead darkness to hear…what? What can I hear? It sounded like a ball bearing or a marble rolling on the bare floor above my head. It rolled hard on hard then hit the wall. Then it rolled again in the other direction. This might not have mattered except that the other direction was uphill. Things can come loose and roll downwards but they cannot come loose and roll upwards. Unless someone…

That thought was so unwelcome that I dismissed it along with the law of gravity. Whatever was rolling over my head must be a natural dislodging. The house was draughty and unused. The attics were under the eaves where any kind of weather might get in. Weather or an animal. Remember the bats. I pulled the covers up to my eyebrows and pretended not to listen.

There it was again: hard on hard on hit on pause on roll.

I waited for sleep, waiting for daylight.

We are lucky, even the worst of us, because daylight comes.

It was a brooding day, that 21st of December. The shortest day of the year. Coffee, coat on, car keys. *Shouldn't I just check the attic?*

The second set of stairs was narrow – a servant's staircase. It led to a lath and plaster corridor barely shoulder-width. I started coughing. Breathing was difficult. Damp had dropped the plaster in thick, crumbling heaps on the floorboards. As below, there were three doors. Two were closed. The door to the room above my room was ajar. I made myself go forward.

The room was under the eaves, as I had guessed. The floor was rough. There was no bed, only a washstand and a clothes rail.

What surprised me was the Nativity scene in the corner.

Standing about two feet tall, it was more like a doll's house than a Christmas decoration. Inside the open-fronted stable stood the animals, the shepherds, the crib, Joseph. Above the roof, on a bit of wire, was a battered star.

It was old, handmade in a workmanlike but not craftsmanlike sort of way, the painted wood now rubbed and faded like pigments of time.

I thought I would carry it downstairs and put it by our Christmas tree. It must have been made for the children when there were children here. I stuffed my pockets with the figures and animals and left quickly, leaving the door open. I had to set off for the station. Stephen and Susie could help me with the rest later.

As soon as I was out of the house my lungs felt clear again. It must be the plaster dust.

The drive to the station was along the coast road. Lonely and unyielding, the road turned in a series of blind bends and tight corners. I met no one and I saw no one. Gulls circled over the sea.

The station itself was a simple shelter on a long single track. There were no information boards. I checked my phone. No signal.

At last the train appeared distantly down the track. I was excited. Memories of visiting my father as a child when he was stationed at his RAF base give me a rush of pleasure whenever I travel by train or come to meet one.

The train slowed and halted. The guard stood down for a moment. I watched the doors – it wasn't a big train, this branch-line train – but none of the doors opened. I waved at the guard, who came over.

'I am meeting my friends.'

He shook his head. 'Train's empty. Next stop is the end of the line.'

I was confused. Had they got off at the earlier stop? I described them. The guard shook his head again. 'I notice strangers. They would have boarded at Carlisle, asked me where to get off – always do.'

'Is there another train before tomorrow?'

'One a day and that's your lot and more than anybody needs in a place like this. Where are you staying?'

'Highfallen House. Do you know it?'

'Oh, aye. We all know it.' He looked as if he was about to say something else. Instead he blew his whistle. The empty train pulled away, leaving me staring down the long track, watching the red light like a warning.

I needed to get a signal on my phone.

I drove on past the station, following the steep hill, hoping some height would connect me to the rest of the world. At the top of the hill I stopped the car and got out, pulling up the collar of my coat. The first snow hit my face with insect insistence. Sharp and spiteful like little bites.

I looked out across the whitening bay. That must be Highfallen House. But what's that? Two figures walking on the beach. Is it Stephen and Susie? Had they driven here after all? Then, as I strained my eyes against the deceit of distance, I realised that the second figure was much smaller than the first. They were walking purposefully towards the house.

When I arrived back it was nearly dark.

I put on the lights, blew the fire into a blaze. There was no sign of the mysterious couple I had seen from the hill. Perhaps it had been the housekeeper and her daughter come to make sure that everything was all right. I had a telephone number for Mrs Wormwood but without a signal I could not call her.

The snow was thickening in windy swirls. Relax. Have a whisky.

I leaned on the warm kitchen range with my whisky in my hand. The wooden figures I had brought down from the attic were lying on the kitchen table. I should go up and get the stable.

I don't want to.

I bounded up the first set of stairs, using energy to force out unease. At my bedroom I put on the light. That felt better. The second set of stairs stood in shadow at the end of the long landing. I felt that constriction in my lungs again. Why am I holding on to the handrail like an old man?

I could see that the only light to the attic was at the top of the stairs. I found the round brown Bakelite switch. I flicked down the nipple. A single bulb lit up reluctantly. The room was straight ahead. The door was closed. Hadn't I left it open?

I turned the handle and stood in the doorway, the room dimly lit by the light from the stairs. Washstand. Nativity. Clothes rail. On the clothes rail was a child's dress. I hadn't noticed that before. I suppose I had been in a hurry. Pushing aside my misgivings, I went in purposefully and bent down to pick up the wooden Nativity. It was heavy and I had just got it secure in my arms when the light on the landing went out.

'Hello? Who's there?'

There's someone breathing like they can barely breathe. Not faint. Struggling for breath. I mustn't turn round because whoever or whatever it is is behind me.

I stood still for a minute, steadying my nerve. Then I shuffled forward towards the edge of light coming up from downstairs. At the doorway I heard a step behind me, lost my balance and put out a hand to steady myself. My hand gripped something wet. The clothes rail. It must be the dress.

My heart was over-beating. *Don't panic.* Bakelite. Bad wiring. Strange house. Darkness. Aloneness.

But you're not alone, are you?

Back in the kitchen with whisky, Radio 4 and pasta boiling, I examined the dress. It was for a small child and it was hand-knitted.

The wool was smelly and sopping. I washed it out and left it hanging over the sink to drip. I guessed there must be a hole in the roof and the dress had been soaking up the rain for a long time.

I ate my supper, tried to read, told myself it had been nothing, nothing at all. It was only 8pm. I didn't want to go to bed, though the snow outside was like a quilt.

I decided to arrange the Nativity. Donkey, sheep, camels, wise men, shepherds, star, Joseph. The crib was there, but it was empty. There was no Christ Child. And there was no Mary. Had I dropped them in the dark room? I hadn't heard anything fall and these wooden figures were six inches tall.

Joseph was wearing a woollen tunic but his wooden legs had painted puttees. I pulled off the tunic. Underneath, wooden Joseph wore a painted uniform. First World War.

When I turned him round I saw there was a gash in his back like a stab wound.

My phone beeped.

I dropped Joseph, grabbed the phone. It was a text message from Susie: 'TRYING 2 CALL U. LEAVE 2MORO.'

I pressed CALL. Nothing. I tried to send a text. Nothing. But what did it matter? Suddenly I felt relief and calm. They had been delayed, that was all. Tomorrow they would be here.

I sat down again with the Nativity. Perhaps the missing figures were inside. I put in my hand. My fingers closed round a metal object. It was a small iron key with a hoop top. Maybe it was the key to the attic door.

Outside, snow had fallen, snow on snow. The sky had cleared. The moon sped above the sea.

I had gone to bed and I was deep asleep when I heard it clearly. Above me. Footsteps. Pacing. Down the room. Hesitate. Turn. Return.

I lay in bed, eyes staring blindly at the blind ceiling. Why do we open our eyes when we can't see anything? And what was there to see? *I don't believe in ghosts.*

I wanted to put on the light but what if the light didn't come on? Why would it be worse to be in darkness I had not chosen than darkness I was choosing? But it would be worse. I sat up in bed and pulled back the curtain a little. The moon had been so bright tonight, surely there would be light?

There was light. Outside the house, hand in hand, stood the still and silent figures of a mother and child.

I did not sleep till daylight and when I slept and woke again it was almost midday and already the light was lowering.

Hurrying to get coffee, I saw that the dress was gone. I had left it dripping over the sink and it was gone. *Get out of the house.*

I set off for the station. There was an air-frost that had coated the trees in glittering white. It was beautiful and deathly. The world held in ice.

On the road there were no car tracks. No noise but the roar and drop of the sea.

I moved slowly and saw no one. In the white unmoving landscape I wondered if there was anyone else left alive?

At the station I waited. I waited some time past the time until the train whistled on the track. The train stopped. The guard got down and saw me. He shook his head. 'There's no one,' he said. 'No one at all.'

I thought I would cry. I took out my mute phone. I flashed up the message: 'TRYING 2 CALL U. LEAVE 2MORO.'

The guard looked at it. 'Happen it's you who should be leaving,' he said. 'There's no more trains past Carlisle now till the 27th. Tomorrow was the last and that's been cancelled. Weather.'

I wrote down a number and gave it to the guard. 'Will you phone my friends and tell them I am on my way home?'

On the slow journey back to Highfallen House I filled my mind with my departure. It would be slow and dangerous to travel at night but I could not consider another night alone. Or not alone.

All I had to do was manage forty miles to Inchbarn. There was a pub and a guest house and remote but normal life.

The text message kept playing in my head. Had it really meant that I should leave? And why? Because Susie and Stephen couldn't come? Weather? Illness? It's all a guessing game. The fact is I have to go.

The house seemed subdued when I returned. I had left the lights on and I went straight upstairs to pack my bag. At once I saw that the light to the attic was on. I paused. Breathed. Of course it's on. I never switched it off. That proves it's a wiring fault. I must tell the housekeeper.

My bag packed, I threw all the food into a box and put everything back in the car. I had the whisky in the front, a blanket I stole from the bed, and I made a hot-water bottle just in case.

It was only five o'clock. At worst I'd be in Inchbarn by 9pm.

I got in the car and turned the key. The radio came on for a second, died, and as the ignition clicked and clicked I knew that the battery was completely flat. Two hours ago at the station the car had started first time. Even if I had left the lights on... But I hadn't left the lights on. A cold panic hit me. I took a swig of the whisky. I couldn't sleep in the car all night. I would die.

I don't want to die.

Back in the house, I wondered what I was going to do all night. I must not fall asleep. I had noticed some old books and volumes when I had explored downstairs yesterday – assorted dusty adventure stories and tales of Empire. As I sorted through them I came across a faded velvet photograph album. In the cold, deserted sitting room I began to discover the past.

Highfallen House 1910. The women in long skirts with miraculous waists. The men in shooting tweeds. The stable boys in waistcoats, the gardening boys wearing flat caps. The maids in starched aprons. And here they are again in their Sunday Best: a wedding photograph. Joseph and Mary Lock. 1912. He was a gardener. She was a maid. In the back of the album, loose and unsorted, were further photographs and newspaper cuttings. 1914. The men in uniform. There was Joseph.

I took the album back into the kitchen and put it next to my wooden soldier. I had on my coat and scarf. I propped myself up in two chairs by the wood-fired range and dozed and waited and waited and dozed.

It was perhaps two o'clock when I heard a child crying. Not a child who has scraped his knee, or lost a toy, but an abandoned child. A child whose own voice is his last hold on life. A child who cries and knows that no one will come.

The sound was not above me – it was above the above me. I knew where it was coming from.

I put my hands over my ears and my head between my knees. I could not shut the sound out; a locked-up child, a hungry child, a child who is cold and wet and frightened.

Twice I got up and went to the door. Twice I sat down again.

The crying stopped. Silence. A dreadful silence.

I raised my head. Footsteps were coming down the stairs. Not one foot in front of the other but one foot dragging slightly, then the other joining it, steadying, stepping again.

At the bottom of the stairs the footsteps paused. Then they did what I knew they would do; what all the terror in my body knew they would do. The footsteps came towards the kitchen door. Whatever was out there was standing twelve feet away on the other side of the door. I stood behind the table and picked up a knife.

The door swung open with violent force that rammed the brass doorknob into the plaster of the wall. Wind and snow blew into the kitchen, whirling up the photographs and cuttings on the table. I saw that the front door itself was wide open, the entrance hall like a wind tunnel.

Holding the knife, I went into the hall to shut the door. The pendant metal lantern that hung from the ceiling was swinging wildly on its long chain. A sudden gust lurched it forward like a child's swing pushed too high. It fell back at force against the large semicircular fanlight over the front door. The fanlight shattered and fell round my shoulders in shards of solid rain. Flicker. Buzz. Darkness. The house lights were out. No wind now. No cries. Silence again.

Glass-hit in the snow-lit hall, I walked out of the front door and into the night. At the drive I turned left and I saw them: the mother and child.

The child was wearing the woollen dress. She had no shoes. She held up her arms piteously to her mother, who stood like stone.

I ran forward. I grabbed the child in my arms.

There was no child. I had fallen face down in the snow.

Help me. That's not my voice.

I'm on my feet again. The mother is ahead of me. I follow her. She's going towards the walled garden. She seems to pass through the door, leaving me on the other side.

DO NOT ENTER

I tried the rusty hoop handle. It broke off, taking a piece of door with it. I kicked the door open. It fell off its hinges. The ruined and abandoned garden lay before me. A walled garden of one acre used to feed twenty people. But that was a long time ago.

There were footprints in the snow. I followed them. They led me to the bothy, its roof patched with corrugated iron. There was no door but the inside seemed dry and sound. There was a tear-off calendar still on the wall: December 22nd 1916.

I put my hand in my pocket and I realised that the key from the Nativity was there. At the same time I heard a chair scrape on the floor in the room beyond. I had no fear any more. As the body first shivers and then numbs with cold, my feelings were frozen. I was moving through shadows as one who dreams.

In the room beyond there was a low fire lit in the tiny tin fireplace. On either side of the fire sat the mother and child. The child was absorbed in playing with a marble. Her bare feet were blue but she did not seem to feel the cold any more than I did.

Are we dead, then?

The woman with the shawl over her head stared at me or through me with deep, expressionless eyes. I recognised her. It was Mary Lock. Her gaze went to a tall cupboard. I knew that my key fitted this cupboard and that I must open it.

There are seconds that hold a lifetime. Who you were. What you will become. Turn the key.

A dusty uniform fell out, crumpling like a puppet. The uniform was not quite empty of its occupant. The back of the faded wool jacket had a long slash where the lungs would have been.

I looked at the knife in my hand.

'Open the door! Are you in there? Open the door!'

I woke to blinding white. Where am I? Something's rocking. It's the car. I am in my car. A heavy glove was brushing off the snow. I sat up, found my keys, pressed the UNLOCK button. It was morning.

Outside was the guard from the train and a woman who announced herself as Mrs Wormwood. 'Fine mess you've made here,' she said.

We went into the kitchen. I was shivering so much that Mrs Wormwood relented and began to make coffee. 'Alfie fetched me,' she said, 'after he spoke to your friends.'

'There's a body,' I said. 'In the walled garden.'

'Is that where it is?' said Mrs Wormwood.

At Christmas in 1914 Joseph Lock had gone to war. Before he left for Flanders he had made a Nativity scene for his little girl. When he came back in 1916 he had been gassed. They heard him, climbing the stairs, gasping for breath through froth-corrupted lungs.

His mind had gone, they said. At night in the attic where he slept with his wife and child, he leaned vacantly against the wall, rolling the child's marbles up and down, down and up, pacing, pacing, pacing. One night, just before Christmas, he strangled his wife and daughter. He left them for dead in the bed and went out. But his wife was not dead. She followed him. In the morning they found her sitting by the Nativity, her dress dark with blood, his fingermarks livid at her throat. She was singing a lullaby and pushing the point of the knife into the back of the wooden figure. Joseph was never found.

'Are you going to call the police?' I said.

'What for?' said Mrs Wormwood. 'Let the dead bury the dead.'

Alfie went out to see to my car. It started first time, the exhaust blue in the white air. I left them clearing up and was about to set off when I remembered I had left my radio in the kitchen. I went back inside. The kitchen was empty. I could hear the two of them up in the attic. I picked up the radio. The Nativity was on the table as I had left it.

But it wasn't as I had left it.

Joseph was there and the animals and the shepherds and the worn-out star. And in the centre was the crib. Next to the crib were the wooden figures of a mother and child.

Kathy Acker's
New York
Custard

n the early 1990s Kathy Acker moved from London back to the USA. Harold Robbins had tried to sue her for cutting and pasting a passage from one of his books, *The Pirate*, into her edgy re-release, *Young Lust*.

Robbins, the mass-market soft-porn airport-novel novelist wasn't interested in Acker's life-long raid on power structures, or her deep-cut-and-paste method of ripping up existing texts – great or insignificant – to create new texts that disrupted the reader's relationship with what they were reading.

Reading Harold Robbins takes no mental effort at all so Kathy was surprised that the man who had sold more than 75 million copies of his sex and schlock formula should put so much mental effort into suing a literary bandit.

But Robbins had a high opinion of himself as a writer. Kathy's appropriation of his work had made it comically clear that out of the context of the page-turning sex-yarn – where language has no purpose except as a lubricant to slide the reader from one sex act to another – Robbins's prose was awful. That was the problem. Kathy Acker had exposed Harold Robbins – to himself.

Robbins insisted she apologise – which was really the kind of suck-my-dick attitude that Kathy hated.

Kathy, being Kathy, wrote an apology more incendiary than the crime-bomb she had detonated.

Then, in characteristic Acker-fashion, the battle-brave bandit suddenly felt vulnerable, criticised, misunderstood. She packed her things and went back to Manhattan.

But Manhattan wasn't quite right either – nowhere was ever quite right for Kathy, and not long afterwards she came to stay near me in a flat I found for her to rent. And soon it was Christmas-time.

The flat was the last gasp of English eccentricity before every single place in London was gobbled up for greed and gain. It was a vaulted, echoing basement with a stone floor in an empty, grand Georgian house. I thought Kathy would like the long windows that opened onto an overgrown walled garden. The owner had died. The heirs were waiting for probate, and yes, Kathy could stay in the flat for almost nothing, and I would be down the street.

But there were drawbacks. When I was telling this story to my wife, Susie Orbach, who is both Jewish and American, lived for a long time in Manhattan and is the same age as Kathy, she said to me, 'Wait a minute, you put a Jew raised in Sutton Place in an apartment without a fridge?'

I failed to understand. I said, 'She didn't need a fridge; there was no heating.'

This was not the right reply. Susie put her head in her hands and said, 'Sutton Place is one of the most exclusive addresses in Manhattan – it's like Belgravia.'

'But Kathy was an outlaw!'

'She was also a princess!'

True. And it explains why, that Christmas, Kathy wore her Russian fur hat indoors. I couldn't understand it at the time but I do now.

She never said anything about it, of course, because what is often forgotten about Kathy Acker, sexual runaway and post-punk icon, is that she had perfect manners.

It was Christmas. I said, 'Kathy, we need to make custard.'

The history of custard goes back to the Romans, who realised that milk and eggs make a good binder for almost anything, savoury or sweet. As the Romans went everywhere, custard went everywhere too. By the Middle Ages, crustards were filled pies, like our quiches or flans – a crusty pie using egg and milk to hold the rest of the ingredients together.

The French are fans of custard but they don't have a word for it – it's *crème anglaise* to them, but whether it's filling for an éclair or a quiche, rest assured, it's custard.

The runny, pouring custard so popular at Christmas became a big hit in the 19th century – along with Christmas itself in all its glory. For this we have to blame or praise a Birmingham chemist called Alfred Bird, whose wife was allergic to eggs. Poor Mrs Bird liked custard but couldn't eat it, so in 1837 Alfred knocked up a powdered version that used cornflour instead of eggs. Mr Bird added sugar and yellow food-colouring to his cornflour and soon Bird's custard powder was to be found in cheerful tins all over England and the Empire.

The craze for a tin of powdered stuff to be diluted with milk crossed the Atlantic when the Horlick brothers emigrated from England and in 1873 set up a plant in Chicago to produce their world-famous drink.

For some reason, from the late 19th century onwards, perfectly well-nourished men and women began to fear an entirely invented problem called 'night starvation'. Drinks like Horlicks would solve this problem.

Kathy Acker liked Horlicks and I used to make it for her. Kathy, drinking Horlicks and laughing about the impossibility of custard (she could not cook – she could not even stir), and obsessive about everything, found out for me that Dylan Thomas had invented a fantasy product called Night Custard.

In the 1930s while Dylan was dossing on the sofa of a well-paid friend in advertising, who happened to have a contract with Horlicks, Dylan thought he might make his fortune with Night Custard, and speculated that it might also be used as hair crème or a vaginal lubricant.

This rather put me off custard for a while. But Christmas is Christmas and Christmas is custard.

In fact Acker, with her bluestocking fascinations and zero culinary skills, had now blended together forever custard and New York City.

After all, Bob Zimmerman had changed his name to Bob Dylan because of his hero Dylan Thomas (maybe 'Tambourine Man' owes everything to Night Custard).

And Dylan Thomas died in New York in the Chelsea Hotel.

Whenever I make custard I think without thinking, image without imaging, a New York City now as lost as Atlantis; of Beat hotels and drunk poets and diamond voices as various as Andy Warhol and Patti Smith, Bob Dylan, Dylan Thomas and Kathy Acker...who died not many years after this time, in 1997, furiously fighting cancer and upholding Dylan Thomas's poem:

Do not go gentle into that good night...
Rage, rage against the dying of the light.

Our grand gestures and our small acts are not so far apart. We remember our friends for the insignificant and silly things we did together, and for the greatness that they were too.

Here's the custard.

YOU NEED

Pint (570 ml) of milk

Dash of cream

4 egg yolks

1 oz (30 g) castor sugar or sieved demerara

2 teaspoons of cornflour (optional)

METHOD

Whisk the egg yolks nice and fluffy in a bowl. You can use the whites
to make meringues or an egg-white omelette.

While whisking add the sugar.

Heat up the milk and cream but don't boil it.

Pour the milk mixture into the bowl with the egg mixture and
whisk, whisk, whisk!

Return everything to the pan and return the pan to the heat. Do not boil!

Yes, you can add brandy or rum. Some people like to add vanilla – in which case that goes in with the milk and cream.

And, like Mr Bird, you can add cornflour as a thickener – just a couple of teaspoons in with the egg mixture, NOT the milk mixture, and whisk, whisk, whisk.

The whisking business goes best with a balloon whisk. I use a copper whisk and a copper bowl and a copper warming pan, but that's just for looks.

The key is to keep stirring once the custard is back in the pan and heating up. If you're using some kind of a poet or dreamy type to do your stirring for you, you might end up with scrambled egg.

Pouring-custard like this should be served at once. And eaten.

CHRISTMAS IN NEW YORK

he week before Christmas me and the guys at work like to go out for a cocktail and a few plates. There's a place we know on 12th Street called Wallflower, where the ceiling's made of tin and the banquettes are made of orange stuff. It serves French food and American cocktails.

The night we went out we got talking about Christmas past – our childhoods mostly, when, according to memory, our affidavit against history, Christmas wasn't commercialised, so although no one went shopping there were always presents under the tree. Kids went sledging and came home to play board games in front of the fire. Everyone had an old dog and a grandma who played piano. We all wore hand-knitted sweaters.

Everybody built a snowman with a carrot for his nose and a scarf around his neck and sang 'Winter Wonderland'.

And on Christmas Eve you did your damn best to stay awake and see the fella in red in his sleigh – and you never did see him, but he came anyway, and drank the whisky on the kitchen counter.

'Santa was an alcoholic.'

'Yeah, but he spends the rest of the year in rehab.'

'You want another bourbon? Martini? Twinkle?'

'Come on, guys! This one's on me.'

I got up to go to the restroom. I sat down again. Seeing double.

'Sam? Are you OK?'

It was Lucille, squeezing in next to me in her little grey dress with the white collar. She works in the drawing office. I work in design. I tell her I'm fine.

'You didn't say anything when we were all talking about Christmas – don't you like Christmas?'

The fact is: I don't like Christmas. I don't know what it's for these days – except for running up bills you can't pay and fighting with your relatives. I live alone so I have an easy time of it. I live alone. That's good.

'I'm going home for Christmas,' said Lucille; 'what about you?'

'I'm staying home,' I replied.

'On your own?' said Lucille.

'Yeah. I need some me-time. Y'know?'

Lucille nodded like she was shaking her head. Then she said, 'So tell me a story about your Christmas past. Just one.'

'Choose any of them you like, they were all the same. We didn't celebrate Christmas.'

'Is your family Jewish?'

'No. Just unpleasant.'

I didn't say any more right then because the others had started singing their version of 'Fairytale of New York', which was even worse than The Pogues'.

I mean, what is this bonhomie? Is it because we're in a bogus French bar that we have to have bogus French feelings, and kiss each other like it's true?

It's not true, but here they are, my colleagues, clinking glasses and feeding each other prawns.

Lucille leaned forward and joined in and I guessed that was the end of the Yuletide interrogation. I took a deep breath, made it to the restroom one more time, and decided to cut away right there and walk home.

I took my coat from the rail and looked back at the group. Enjoy yourselves.

Outside on the sidewalk there were people laughing, arm in arm, holding their faces up to the falling snow.

What's the big deal? Snow's just rain that's been left out in the cold.

'I love it when it snows,' said Lucille, suddenly standing next to me in her Russian fur hat and Doctor Zhivago greatcoat. Lucille's OK but strange. She brings flowers to the office. She said, 'Do you want to walk for a while?'

So we set off through the white light and the gentle screen of quiet snow. The streets were noisy but didn't seem so. The snow quieted the city and lowered the pulse rate of the place. And the late air smelled clean.

'This broken world,' I said.

'What?' she said.

'Hart Crane.'

'Oh…'

So we walked; past the bars and the eateries, and the small shops open late, and the guy selling bags under a tarpaulin, and the bundle of rags sitting up in the doorway with a sign that said MERRY CHRISTMAS FOLKS. The vent next to him shot out steam and the chemical crack of dry-cleaning. Lucille gave him five dollars.

'So what was your Christmas past?'

'Nothing – *nada*, I told you. No decorations, no tree, no gifts, no family meal. My father drove trucks across to Canada – he always chose the shift over Christmas – paid triple, he said, though what it paid triple for, what he spent it on, I don't know.'

'Are you saying you've never had a Christmas gift?'

'No! I'm a grown man. I've had girlfriends. I have friends. They've given me gifts, of course! But Christmas itself means nothing to me.'

There was a small dog on a leash jumping and snapping at the snow like he could catch it.

'Christmas does mean something to you,' said Lucille. 'Christmas means sadness.'

Oh, no, I said to myself, she's New Age or she sees a shrink five times a week. Gimme a break.

We reached the corner by the deli – its plastic frontage protecting a row of Christmas trees in pots. I smelled cold pine and detergent.

'This is where I turn off,' I said.

'Your beard's white,' she said. 'Seasonal.'

I brushed the snow from my chin, pushed my hands into my coat pockets and set off down the block. About halfway I turned round. I don't know why. Lucille had gone. Of course she had gone. Girls don't stand on street corners in the snow.

I went up the stairs to my apartment – it's a one-bedroom in a building with a doorman who is dead but kept for show, and because it's cheaper than getting someone who's alive, I guess. He sits in his booth with the TV on. I've lived here two years. I've seen the back of his head but I've never seen him move.

I unlocked my door – three locks in a rectangular blank plate of unforgiving steel – and turned on the light. My apartment is like my clothes – I don't care but you have to wear something. I took this place furnished. I have never brought in anything of my own.

Right in front of me in the middle of the room like it belonged there. A Christmas tree.

I ran back downstairs and thumped on the booth where the doorman is supposed to be alive and well and willing to help the residents of the building.

No response. I swear he turned up the sound on the TV.

Then I'll have to call the police...

I'd like to report an incident.

What kinda incident?

There's a Christmas tree in my apartment.

Fella, you been drinking tonight?

No. Yes. But not a lot. I mean, somebody has broken into my apartment and left a Christmas tree.

Any material damage? Anything missing?

No.

Buddy, call your pals, say thank you, and say goodnight. Happy holidays, and goodnight.

The line went dead. I phoned downstairs to the dead doorman. He didn't pick up.

The following day was my last day at work. I got up early, which was easy as I hadn't slept much. The Christmas tree was still there. I had to walk around it to reach the door. As I looked back, as I was closing the door, I was sure the tree was smiling.

At the office I said to Lucille, 'Do you think trees can smile?' She smiled in return, an open, kind smile I had never noticed before.

'That's not like you, Sam. That's almost romantic.'

'I'm a little distracted,' I said.

It was a day of winter sun that sparkled the city into diamonds and pearls. Electric-blue sky lit like a neon. The windows of the big department stores like magic mirrors into another world.

I started to walk towards the Rockefeller Center, I don't know why. The crowds are crazy, and everyone has six bags and no one can get a cab.

Every year the city brings in a seventy-foot Christmas tree and strings it with five miles of lights and tops it with a giant Swarovski crystal star.

I went forward, I don't know why. Standing under the tree. The scale of it makes a grown man feel like a tiny child again.

Sam! Sam! You come on in now.
I want to see the tree, Mom. They're bringing the tree from the forest!
You heard what I said. Get inside now or no supper.
Into the dark house. Into bed. And nothing.

'Sam?' It was Lucille. 'What are you doing here?'

'Me, oh, I had an errand midtown.'

Lucille was still smiling – is she always smiling, and if so, why? She said, 'I love coming to look at the tree. It makes me happy.'

'It does? How does a tree make you happy?'

'Because it's free, and nothing's free in New York, and it's beautiful, and look how relaxed people are – with their children – and that old lady over there like she's dreaming something good.'

'She's probably going to be all alone at Christmas,' I said.

'Are you?' asked Lucille.

'No, no. Of course not. Listen – have a good one, Lucille; I have to…'

'I was just heading into Bouchon for a hot chocolate. Want one?'

And so we sat – and Lucille was still smiling, and I was still not, and she was chatting about the holidays and suddenly I said, 'Last night, in my apartment, there was a Christmas tree. It just appeared.'

'Are you sure?'

'I called the police.'

'You called the police because there's a Christmas tree in your apartment?'

A guy in a plaid fleece squeezed by carrying two gingerbread mochas. He leaned down and said to Lucille, audible for my benefit, 'Get yourself a better date, sweetheart.'

Lucille laughed, but I didn't see what was so funny. I called at his back, 'She's not my date!'

The guy in plaid turned round. 'So you're stupid. I get it. Happy holidays.'

'Somebody broke into my apartment! Asshole!'

But the guy in plaid had gone, and I was on my feet, embarrassed and alone. I wasn't alone. Lucille was still there.

'Did you like it?' she said.

'The chocolate's great, yeah...thanks.'

'The tree. Did you like the tree?'

I was walking back home, alone, thinking about what she had said. Do I like it that for the first time in my whole life of thirty-two years I have a Christmas tree in my home?

I rounded the corner. The Afghans who run the deli were standing outside. I said, 'Did you deliver a tree to my apartment last night?'

They shook their heads and offered me some chestnuts from the hot pan. Am I going home for the holidays? No? They would like to go home. One of them took out his wallet and showed me a crumpled printed picture of the house where his parents lived – a single-storey building made of concrete set against a steep mountain topped with snow. He didn't say anything – held the picture, like it was a light or a mirror, or an answer to a question. Then a woman came in wanting oranges.

I went inside and bought some cooked chicken with rice and cashews and apricots, and headed round the corner towards my building. My apartment is on the fourth floor with the living-room window onto the street.

There's a light in my window, coming from inside, somewhere. Like a low lamp. I don't own a low lamp. I'm a centre-light man.

I rushed into the building.

The Dead Doorman was in his booth watching TV. I stood outside waving my hands to attract his attention but all I heard was the TV set turned up louder. He's gonna explode the set.

There's no elevator in my building, so I climbed up the stairs two at a time, spilling some of the juice out of the chicken container. I opened the door – all three locks are tumbled. No sign of a forced entry. Inside, I reached for the light switch but there's no need.

The Christmas tree is lit up.

Outside on the stairs I can hear someone breathing heavily. I hang back in the doorway, tense, expecting something to happen. Instead Mrs Noblovsky from the fifth floor comes heaving by, carrying or being carried by a flotilla of gaudy bags. I can barely see her. 'Let me help you,' I say, because I have to say that.

Mrs Noblovsky pauses, panting, outside my apartment. She sees the serenely glowing Christmas tree through the door, and sighs. 'So nice, Sam; mine own iz plaztik.'

'Would you like this one? You can have it if you want it. I can carry it upstairs for you.'

'Such a good boy. A kind boy. No vank you. I am goink to my daughter tomorrov in Feel-a-del-fia. You must ve havink Christmaz here to hav that fine tree.'

And then she's on her way up the next flight of stairs, me behind carrying the bags, hearing about Christmas in Soviet Russia and her grandmother's special vodka that made anyone who drank it clairvoyant.

'When I voz three, Grandmama says to me, "Agata, you vill live in Amerika." And here I am.'

There's no arguing with that. She opens the apartment and I dump her bags in the hall. Her place is bigger than mine. I've never seen inside before.

Everything is brown – chocolate carpets, caramel furniture, velvet curtains the colour of coffee. There's a mahogany standard lamp with a seaweed-brown fringed shade and an ancient TV in a veneer cabinet on legs. The distinct low rumble from the fridge makes the apartment sound like it's digesting. It's like she's living inside a big brown bear.

Mrs Noblovsky fetches me a bottle from a cupboard. 'Vodka,' she says, pressing it into my hand. 'Clairvoyant. My babushka's recipe. My brother in Brooklyn makes it from potatoes.'

'Are potatoes clairvoyant?'

'There iz a secret ingredient. Family secret. Take it. You are a good boy.'

I protest, hesitate, hesitate, protest. Then I suddenly think of something. 'Mrs Noblovsky, the doorman – downstairs – is he alive, do you think?'

'I think zo,' she says, 'vhy?'

'I've lived here two years now and he's never spoken to me.'

'He spoke to me about twenty years ago. I had a gaz leak. Vhy you want him to speak to you? You hav a gaz leak?'

'He's the doorman.'

She shrugged and turned on the TV. I thanked her for the vodka and went downstairs.

Back in my apartment there's the tree. The glowing tree. Whoever did this had good taste in fairy lights but that is not the point. I ate the chicken and rice and cashews and left the apricots. I could have turned off the tree lights. Instead I sat staring at them. By the time I'd had four of Mrs Noblovsky's clairvoyant vodkas I almost liked the tree. I could see myself buying something similar next Christmas.

I fell asleep on the couch.

'I bought this for you, Mom. It's a Christmas present.'
'We don't celebrate Christmas, Sam.'
'Why not?'
'We never have and we never will.'
'I saved my pocket money.'
My mother unwrapped the present. It was a butter dish made of aluminum. In the shape of a clam shell. 'It's silver, I think,' I said.
'Thank you, Sam.'
'Do you like it?'

Cold light of day. The garbage truck woke me. I went to the window. Still dark on the block. More snow in the night like a secret we keep. The truck pulled away and the dirty tyre tracks were soon filled with white feathers from the snow goose in the sky.

Snow goose? What's the matter with me?

Get up and go out, get what you need. It's Christmas Eve.

I went down to Russ and Daughters. Bought lox and cream cheese and pastrami. They were handing out free cookies. I took some. Round the corner is their eat-place and I thought maybe some roe on toast and a cocktail would be the right thing at 9am on Christmas Eve.

I swung in, sat at the counter and picked up the menu that serves as a mat.

'Hello,' said Lucille.

She was drinking coffee at a table. 'Care to join me?'

Why not? I thought. Hell, the same woman is everywhere I go, and I have a light-up Christmas tree and a bottle of clairvoyant vodka in my apartment.

I explained this to her. Not the part about her but the other parts. She nodded sympathetically. 'Shall we have an ice-cream?'

'At nine-thirty in the morning?'

'That's somehow worse than a Martini at nine o'clock in the morning?'

She had a point. We ate the ice-cream; ginger for me, strawberry for her. 'Are you at your friends' place tomorrow,' she said, 'or will they come to you?'

'We'll decide later on,' I said, panicking. I mean, I do have friends, but not at Christmas, but I'm not telling her that part either.

She nodded. 'So do you want to come shopping? A few last-minute gifts?'

I shook my head. 'I don't do gifts. It's not a tradition of mine.'

'Didn't you ever make a list for Santa Claus?'

'He's make-believe,' I said.

'Wasn't there ever anything you wanted so badly you wrote to Santa about it?'

'Are you kidding me?'

She wasn't.

'Well, I always hoped I'd get a toboggan, a real wooden one with a leather rein and steel runners.'

'You could get one now.'

I shook my head. 'It was a long time ago.'

'The thing about time,' said Lucille, 'is that it's always there. You didn't do it then, so do it now.'

'Too late.'

'To be a child prodigy, yes, it's too late. To own a toboggan – no, it's not too late.'

I smiled at her smiling at me. I stood up and reached for my coat. 'Happy holidays, Lucille. See you at the office in the New Year.'

She nodded and looked down at the menu. I hesitated. I'm a jerk. But because I am a jerk I didn't say what I wished I could say. I left.

Heavier snow now and fewer cars. Time to go home. I read somewhere that more than half of the people in Manhattan live alone.

At the deli on my corner Farouk was roasting more chestnuts. He gave me a scoop, rattling the tin shovel against the coals. 'We're closing at four. Having a party. Want to come?'

'Sure; what can I bring?'

'You bring nothing – you are my guest.'

I remembered that Lucille had picked up the tab twice now. For coffee, and for breakfast. I didn't even think to pay for my own breakfast this morning. I should call her. I can't call her. I don't have her cell.

I went into my building.

A great big silver bell with a red bow had appeared outside the booth of the Dead Doorman. I knocked loudly on the glass but all I could see was the back of his head and Angela Lansbury running around in 'Murder, She Wrote'.

Am I going to be killed by the Mysterious Christmas-Tree Fairy? I deserve it.

As I tumbled the locks on my apartment door I was both afraid and excited. What now?

Answer: nothing. Disappointment is the default position of my life. There was the tree. There were the lights, but nothing new.

So I caught up on some work emails. They all came back with an out-of-office auto-reply. There's no work ethic in America. It's barely 11am on Christmas Eve.

By noon I was showered and shaved and changed with nothing left to do. I thought I'd take a walk. Get something for Farouk anyway. He liked baseball caps.

I was passing McNally's bookstore. There was a copy of a Hart Crane in the window. I stood looking at it, and I heard myself saying out loud,

'I could never remember
That seething, steady leveling of the marshes
Till age had brought me to the sea.'

Crane wrote that when he was twenty-six. He was dead at thirty-two. My face was wet with rain or snow. I went into the store and bought the book.

The Hart Crane isn't for Farouk but the leopard-skin baseball cap is.

I was sitting with him on the rusty treads of the fire escape behind the building. It's too hot inside now – every Afghan in New York City is at the party. The music's live and there's a lot of laughter. Farouk must have seen me slip out on the fire escape. He followed me with a beer. So I pulled out the cap I bought him.

'Does it fit? Try it on.'

There's a broken fridge with glass doors propped on the gantry of the fire escape. Farouk peers at the makeshift mirror of the glass, using his phone as a light, pulling the baseball cap low on his head, so that the peak is right on his eyes that are deep like black coals. 'I never seen a leopard-skin baseball cap.'

'I guess it's for winter.'

'I feel like a mountain cat in the Hindu Kush. You ever been to Afghanistan?'

'Not me.'

'Most beautiful place on earth. Here, I show you some pictures. My phone. Goats, eagles, the market where my father works – those sacks are rice. He is seventy and he can carry them. Very strong. He thinks I am a taxi driver. He always wanted himself to be a taxi driver.'

'Would you go home if you could?'

Farouk shakes his head. 'What is home? Where is home? Home is a dream. Home is a fairy tale. This Afghanistan does not exist. Not for me. Home is where you make it, my friend. What do you think if I wear this backwards?'

He rearranges his cap. Then he says, 'Your girlfriend – nice girl, big smile; where is she tonight?'

'She's not my girlfriend.'

Farouk looks sorrowful. 'Girl like that – you should try harder.'

It's later now, much later, and I am back in my apartment, staring at the tree and finishing Mrs Noblovsky's clairvoyant vodka. I can see the future and it's just like today. What kind of a future is that?

I throw open the window. Deep breaths of air. The music's still coming from the party. I should get some sleep. One night sleeping fully dressed on the sofa is enough.

But there's something I want to do first.

On top of the wardrobe there's a box in a box. There are other things in the box too, but it's the box in the box I want, a cardboard box and tied with kitchen string.

My mother gave it to me when I was leaving home for college. I smiled, kissed her, kept it for the train.

I opened it like I am opening it now. What had she given me to remind me of home?

Inside was the aluminum butter dish in the shape of a shell.

She never could receive. She never could give.

I should have hurled it out of the train window. Instead I kept it like poison I had already swallowed. Why?

My hands were shaking. I went to the window, leaned back and pitched the dish full pelt, past the air-conditioning units and satellite dishes, away through the night stars. Away into nothing. I didn't hear it fall.

Then I slept.

Morning came. It does.

I went yawning into the lounge in my boxers and T-shirt. There was the tree. There were the lights. Under the tree was a long cardboard box tied with a silver ribbon.

I went back into the bedroom, did the whole yawning and stretching routine again, and returned cautiously to the lounge. The present – it had to be a present, didn't it, because it was under the Christmas tree? – was still there.

Going into my lounge was getting to be as unpredictable as having a wild animal in the house. What was I supposed to do? I made coffee, checked my phone; no messages. I wasn't drunk. Yes, the item under the tree was definitely still there.

All right. Deep breathing. Be calm. Get dressed. Jeans. Shirt. Sweater. Now take the box into the hallway and down the stairs and out onto the street and open it. Whatever is in there needs to be out of there.

I grabbed a knife from the kitchen to split the cardboard. The box was heavy and bulky. In the lobby I saw that the blind was down on the Dead Doorman's booth. Up. Down. So what? Dead is dead.

OK, now I'm outside. It's a beautiful morning. The sub-zeros last night have crisped the snow into a white carpet the length of the block. The moon is still in the sky although the sun is out. The air is sharp as a knife. My knife is not as sharp as the air, but I rip through the cardboard, pulling it away from the object inside.

Objects aren't happiness. But this one is.

Inside the box is a deep-polished wooden sledge with a red leather rein and blue steel runners. But this sledge has articulated joints on the footrests so that you can steer it. Forgetting everything, I sat on it and tried the steering. It's great.

I didn't notice a car pulling up – until the polished hubcaps of the retro VW Beetle flashed the sun in my eyes.

'Do you want to go to Riverside Park and try it out?'

It's Lucille in a bobble hat, the top down on the convertible.

'Did you give me this, Lucille?'

Where didn't we go? Pilgrim Hill in Central Park, Hippo on Riverside. Owl's Head Park. And I was sledding through time or maybe there was no time because Christmas Day comes just once a year.

The sun was going down before we were done. I said, 'Do you want to come back for some lox and cream cheese? It's not Christmas dinner but…I have black bread and some interesting vodka…actually I don't; I finished it last night.'

'I'm taking you to my place,' said Lucille. 'It's small and I share it but the others are gone home for the holidays. And I have dinner for us. But let's go by your place first. I need to drop something off.'

'Haven't you dropped off enough already? The tree, the lights…they were from you, right?'

Lucille nodded. Such soft eyes. I love the way she smiles.

'But how did you get in?'

Back at the building I left Lucille in the lobby while I took the stairs at a bound, changed into dry clothes and packed the lox. I hesitated, then threw in a spare T-shirt, shorts and my electric toothbrush. And something else. Something I knew I had bought for Lucille when I bought it.

'Thank you,' I said to the tree on my way out.

In the lobby Lucille was standing with an elderly man who had the same kind of bright smile that she did. He seemed vaguely familiar. When she saw me she said to him, 'This is Sam.'

'Sure I know it's Sam,' said the vaguely familiar guy. 'Always wants something, so I always ignore him.'

Then he kissed Lucille on the top of her head and went back towards the booth. I recognised the back of his head. 'See you tomorrow, sweetie.' The booth door closed on the not-so-Dead Doorman.

'He's my grandpa,' said Lucille.

We got into her VW. We went to her place, small as an envelope. We ate. We talked. I nearly kissed her, but then I gave her the Hart Crane, and she kissed me. She was in charge, I guess. I said, 'I owe you for coffee and breakfast.'

She said, 'There's all of next year.'

My Christmas Eve
Smoked Salmon
and Champagne

 e *make our own traditions.*
Christmas Eve is frosty. The sky is clear. The stars are like bells. The day is short and the fire is lit. There is peace and anticipation.

In my mind that's how it is. It doesn't matter how it really is. Usually it's raining, or the city is gridlocked, or nothing is ready for Christmas dinner, or the presents aren't wrapped, and it's bath salts again for your auntie.

Some years ago I realised how I wanted to begin Christmas.

I have always loved and always listened to a service on BBC Radio 4 called 'A Festival of Nine Lessons and Carols'. This plays live from the chapel of King's College, Cambridge at 3pm on Christmas Eve – and it has done so since 1928.

The service runs for ninety minutes. It's a time-warp mixture of Bible readings from the Old and New Testaments that prophesy and fulfil the promise of the Messiah. In between these readings the choir and congregation sing carols old and new, and there's specially commissioned music from contemporary composers. The service begins with a single boy soprano carrying a single candle. He enters the chapel singing 'Once in Royal David's City'.

These days you can watch it on TV, but why would you?

The beauty is in the music, the voices, the readings and prayers. And a sense of continuity – religion is good at that.

And a sense of belonging to something more necessary than shopping and party-going. This is a spiritual experience, whether or not you believe in God.

Wherever I am in the world I listen to this service. Everything is put aside and this is an hour and a half of mental relaxation and spiritual concentration. I listen to the readings, though I know them by heart, and I join in with the singing.

If I am at home I light the fire and the candles. I make sure the kitchen is tidy, and I make ready the same food every year, because this is a ritual. The point of ritual is that the sameness of it concentrates and then clears the mind. It's why Jews, even non-observant Jews, light the Shabbat candles on Friday night.

Ritual is a way of altering time. By which I mean a way of pausing the endless intrusion of busy life.

Here's my ritual for Christmas Eve.

Bake some really good dark bread – a rye bread or a sourdough. You can buy this, of course, but making it is part of the pleasure of making this time for yourself.

Get the best butter you can afford.

Get the best smoked salmon you can afford.

Lemon.

And you need pink champagne. I prefer Veuve Clicquot or Billecart-Salmon on Christmas Eve, because there's a richness and an exuberance in those wines without any heaviness. Bollinger is a bit too powerful for me in the afternoon.

OK – so if you can't afford any of the above there are alternatives. I've used them myself.

Stick with the best bread, but try taramasalata, preferably homemade, or get a couple of tins of good-quality sardines.

The oil will mean you won't need butter either way.

Or make a chicken-liver pâté the day before – it's cheap and good if you do it yourself.

Cut the dark bread into small squares and put your topping on nice and thick. It's Christmas!

Smoked salmon and pink champagne look so pretty together against the browny-blackness of the bread.

Lay out a generous plateful.

If champagne's not for you, find a wine you love and have that instead.

Look, you could do this with a pot of tea and a piece of toast.

You could do this with a lovely cup of coffee and a plate of chocolate biscuits – make them yourself.

The reason I suggest making some of this small meal yourself is because ritual has an anticipatory relevance – we prepare for it, practically and psychologically; that's part of its benefit.

It's about making your own raft of time. Your own doorway into Christmas.

You can do this with family and friends, of course, if they're in the zone. And yes, you could do it while wrapping presents, but it wouldn't be as powerful.

Ritual isn't about multitasking.

Ritual is time cut out of time. Done right it has profound psychological effects.

We are too busy and too distracted. Everybody knows that time is speeding up like a car with go-faster stripes and we are running alongside trying to keep pace. Christmas is the busiest time of all – which is crazy. It's lovely rushing around to see family and friends, but how about an hour and a half that belongs only to you?

To begin with it takes a conscious effort – everything worth doing starts with a conscious effort. But you might find this ritual, or your version of something similar, becomes an unexpectedly precious part of Christmas.

*

THE MISTLETOE BRIDE

t is the custom in this part of England to play Hide-and-Seek on Christmas Eve. Some say the custom comes from Italy, where the party draws lots to decide who will be the Devil and who will be the Pope. When this is decided, all the others in the party run away to hide themselves as well as they can. Then the Devil and the Pope search the house looking for sinners. Some are damned and some are saved. Then each must offer a forfeit to the Devil and the Pope. Usually a kiss.

Tonight my husband declares we will play Hunter-and-Hart. The ladies shall hide. The gentlemen shall hunt them.

My husband sits me on his knee, fondly, and kisses me. I am his caught thing but he has not had me yet. There is time for that.

It is my wedding night. It is the custom in these parts to marry on Christmas Eve. It is a holy time, but glowing with strange lights. It is not yet Christ's day; it is still the day of unexpected visits and mummery.

I come from elsewhere. I come from a wild country, though I am gentle-born. My new husband is twice my age at thirty-four. He tells me I am as near a bird as a creature without wings can be. He means it kindly. I am light-boned and fall without a mark. My footsteps leave no print. My husband loves my waist, slender as a rope. He says my hands and feet are delicate as a web. He calls me his spun thing. When we met he gently unwound my hair and kissed me.

'You will learn to love me,' he said.

I am my father's youngest daughter. My dowry is small and I had expected to be sent to the convent. But my new husband is rich and cares nothing for his wife's jewels. I am his jewel. He would rather I shine beside him than glint dully behind the convent walls.

It is the custom here that the husband provides the wedding dress; white, but with a small red stain placed where he chooses to mark the loss of a maidenhead. The maid came to dress me for the wedding. She wished me happiness and health.

'Is he a good man, my husband?' I asked as she fastened the dress tight.

'He is a man,' she said. 'The rest you must decide for yourself.'

I was dressed and I looked at myself in the silver mirror. The maid had a vial of blood. 'For the stain,' she said.

She dabbed the blood over my heart.

My soon-husband and I had travelled from my father's house on horseback. The roads are too rough for a coach. The land is white-covered, bedded down under snow. My horse's bridle is traced with frost.

'Purity,' said my husband. 'This white world is for your wedding day.'

My breath was thick. I fancied I could read the shapes that flew from my mouth. It was as though I was talking to myself in a vaporous language no one else understood. My breath formed words: LOVE. BEWARE. COURAGE. UNSEEN.

This game amused me through the long icicle of our journey. As we rode through Bowland Forest, my soon-husband stood up in his stirrups and cut a low branch of mistletoe from an oak tree. He twisted it into a coronet and hung it on the pommel of his saddle. It was for me, he said, when we married. I would be his mistletoe bride.

I looked sideways at him; so confident and sure he is. I am shy and gentle. I like his certainty and ease.

'She's nervous as a hare,' my father said. 'Nervous as a hare bolted from cover.' My husband said he would cover me. All his men laughed, and my father too. I blushed. But he is not unkind.

As we rode along I fancied that my childhood self rode with me a while. Then, at the first crossroads, she turned her little pony and waved goodbye. For all those miles I had thought only of my home and what I was leaving. I was leaving a part of myself.

There were other selves, too, who disappeared on that bleak road. My free, careless, unconsidered self, the one I am when I am alone on the moors, or reading head down in the dark night by candle-light – she could not come with me, though she tried.

The more my soon-husband talked amiably of my duties as his lady, the more I felt myself caught in a long day of orders to give and people to receive. It would not be fitting for the wife of the lord of the hall to throw a cloak over her shoulders and run out in the rain.

But this was only growing up, and surely nothing to fear? A new self would be waiting to meet me.

Trumpets. Flags. Running feet. Flares.

My Lady, this is your home.

Yes. Here. The castle. Old and walled. His family built it centuries ago. It is as though we are living inside them.

And at the drawbridge – there she is, waiting for me. The self I will become; older, graver, darker. She nodded as I rode over the tongue of the drawbridge. She did not smile.

Trumpets. Flags. Bowed heads. Flares. Music.

We are married.

My new husband held my hand and whispered to me that he would always find me, wherever I hid. He told me he could scent me. He buried his face in my neck as I sat on his knees. He told me he was my gentle hunter, that I should have the run of the house as I pleased. No harm could come to me here.

While he was nuzzling me there was a tremendous knocking at the door. It is the custom on Christmas Eve that a stranger may come unexpected and unannounced, and must be let in with pomp and ceremony.

But it is my wedding day.

The great doors were unbarred. The sound of hooves ricocheted round the vast stone hall as though it were full of invisible horses and invisible riders.

Riding into the hall on a black mare came a lady veiled and dressed in green. She reined in the horse. She did not dismount. My husband went to her, offered his hand, lifted her down. He kissed her hand and welcomed her. He led her to me. I could not see her face but her lips were red and her hair was black.

'My wife,' he said, presenting me to the lady, and yet it seemed to me that those words, hanging in mid-air like my dictionary of frost, would have puzzled a stranger to know which of us that wife was.

The lady inclined her head.

Music struck up. He danced with her, his eyes on her, while I watched in white and waited. Presently he returned and, bowing to me, said, 'A custom – the Uninvited Guest.'

'You do not know her, then,' I said.

'Know her?' he said, and smiled. 'It is Christmas Eve.'

The lady was dancing with another now. The hall was bright and the dancing swift and happy. I drank wine. Ate food. All the guests wished to honour me. I was happy too. The hours went by.

And then...

My husband took his dagger from his belt and banged the table hard with the hilt. The music paused.

'And now for the Hunt!' he said, and there was general laughter.

From his pocket he took a white mask and gave it to me. The ladies began to put on their masks, and the gentlemen also. My husband had a leopard-face, pulled low like a visor. He began his counting.

Now it was time for the ladies, time for me, to run giggling and chattering down the grey corridors as long as a dream.

I knew none of the ways. The tall, heavy candles in the mullion windows stood still and silent as servants, but they hardly lit up the stone passageways. I chased alongside a young girl of my own age, who seemed to follow every twist and stair.

As she ran ahead of me, I noticed a pair of doors that opened into a high chamber. She ran on. I hesitated and went inside.

The bed was carved with a pair of swans. There were petals thrown on the pillows from winter roses kept in hotbeds and grown for the Christmas wedding.

The tapers in the room were not lit. Only the light of the blazing fire showed me the scene.

I knew without knowing that this was the bridal chamber. This is where he would bring me when he found me. This is where we would begin our life together.

Laid on the gold coverlet, laid like sleeping knights, were two garments, both white, though his was embroidered with leopards and mine with harts.

It made me smile to see our images at peace and asleep, and I wondered for how many years we would lie side by side, until time claimed us. On the pillow was the coronet of mistletoe; mysterious, poisonous, white as death, green as hope.

Impulsively I took the pendant from my neck, my father's parting gift to me. I kissed it and laid it on my husband's garment. By this, I gave myself to him. He had no need to hunt me.

Full of happiness, I ran out of the room, light as a shadow. I was deep in the house. I paused to look around and then I heard footsteps, a little way off, echoing on the stone stairs. Quick! Hide! I felt sure it was he.

Under the window at the end of the passage there was a big old chest. I could barely lift the lid. I struggled. Voices now, round and round the turret stair. I heaved open the lid and jumped inside. The chest was empty, and deeper than expected. I could sit quite comfortably while I waited.

Yes. His voice. His footsteps. Soon he would lift the lid and carry me into our chamber. I had to try not to laugh with happiness and anticipation. Perhaps he had instructed the girl to lead me this way.

And then I heard the voice of a woman. I heard her laugh and ask, 'In here?'

He answered, 'Not in there.'

She said, 'Where, then? Or perhaps you have changed your mind?'

It was his turn to laugh. Then silence. Or something like silence, if kissing and touching are silence. I pushed up the lid of the chest just enough to see out.

Against the wall was the lady in green. The Uninvited Guest. In honour of Christmas-tide.

Her dress was undone to the waist and my husband had his hands on her breasts. Her hands were on his back and lower, eagerly, dragging his shirt out of his breeches. He stood back, pulled off his jacket and shirt, heedless of the cold. He was handsome. Strong. Slim. Never taking her eyes from his face, she unbuttoned the flap of his breeches where he sprang and then she was on her knees.

I wanted to stop looking. I had seen this before. In daylight and in my dreams. I had seen the grooms with the servant girls. Now I was watching my own husband. I felt desire, excitement, fear and the fishy taste of vomit in my throat. I was a second away from throwing back the lid of the trunk and confronting them. But my husband pulled the lady to her feet, turned her round and pushed her, frontwards onto and over the trunk. I heard the click of the lid, the rustle of her skirts, then the noise of them at their pleasure.

The box withstood the assault. I put my hand up, right under her belly, an inch of wood separating us. I slid my hand along the underside of the lid to the place where he had entered her. I breathed with them both and waited.

This was my wedding night.

It was not long before I heard them moving away. Their laughter and low voices. Then their footsteps back down the dark stone stairs.

My hands were shaking and damp and had no strength, so I turned on all fours and pushed up at the lid of the chest with my back.

Nothing happened. I was trapped.

My body was sweating. My heart was over-beating. I took a breath of what air was left, and managed to lie on my back to attack the lid with both feet.

The box was yielding but it wouldn't give. The little click I had heard when he pushed her down – that had been the lock, unused for years, and now jammed into its rusty keep.

I shouted. He would hear me. Someone would come. Someone. Breathe. Listen. Breathe. No air. All I could hear was emptiness. Why would he come to his bridal chamber without his bride?

Did I faint? I seemed to be sitting at home on the riverbank waiting for the sun to rise. Had I been there all night? Then I realised in terror that I would never see the sun rising again. My body was like a mist evaporating.

LOVE. BEWARE. COURAGE. UNSEEN.

The words filled the smaller and smaller space of the chest. The smaller and smaller space of my chest. With my last breath I...with my last breath I...

Did not die.

I found myself lying on the floor beside the chest, the maid standing over me.

'I saw what you did,' she said. 'I saw what they did.'

'I will confront him,' I said to her, but she shook her head. 'That lady is his cousin. He is forbidden to marry her by the bishop. He must produce an heir. When you have done that for him he will do away with you and marry her as he wishes.'

'Do away with me?'

'He will poison you with berry of mistletoe. Next Christmas-tide the child you will conceive tonight will be weaned. Your business will be done. And she will come for him as surely as she came for him tonight.'

'Who knows this?' I said.

'We all know this,' she said.

'Then will you help me to escape?'

She did. She found me clothes from his closet. Too big for me but my body was safe inside them.

I threw off my wedding dress and put it inside the chest. I took some gold and silver from his room, and gave the maid the only coins I had brought from home. I left the necklace where it was, on his nightshirt, to remember me by.

The maid led me down a stairwell that took me to a door at the foot of the castle.

The dark and hooded figure I had seen when I first entered still waited, motionless, at the drawbridge. The figure turned to me. I stared, defiant, and shook my head. The future is not fixed unless we allow it to be so.

I walked away from the lit-up castle into the dark of Christmas. I walked through the night as though night were a country I could cross, and at dawn on Christmas Day I came to a convent some miles away and rang the bell and rang the bell, fierce as the beginning of the world.

The nuns came running to the gate and took me in.

At Christmas-tide, they said, always comes some miracle or some mystery that cannot be explained.

They asked for no explanation and I gave none.

And so I remained at the Convent of the First Miracle. I am the brewer here. It is my work to turn water into wine.

*

Two years later, on the shortest day of the year, at the winter solstice, a steward from the castle came to wheel and deal for some barrels of my mead. The lord of the hall was to be married again.

'He is unlucky,' said the steward. 'Only last New Year he married a girl. They were so happy. She had a child, a boy, and then she fell into the moat. Her ghost is seen often, haunting the frosty battlements overlooking the moat where she slipped under the water and felt the ice close about her head.'

I had not heard that he had married. Or so soon. I gave the steward more wine.

'I thought the lord had married already,' I said. 'They called her the Mistletoe Bride.'

'Ah, yes,' said the steward, 'I said he is unlucky. That particular lady disappeared on their wedding night, two Christmases gone. No one knows what became of her.'

Then he leaned forward confidentially, and whispered that there was another story too. The bride's wedding dress had been found in an old chest, her body utterly decayed. When the servants lifted out the dress, there was no trace of a body at all, nothing but dust.

'It is a strange tale,' I said to the steward, 'and, as you say, the lord of the hall is unlucky in love. Who is it that he shall marry now? A young girl from a good family?'

The steward's face reddened, and not with the steam from the mulled wine.

'The lord of the hall has a son and heir now, but no wife, and so the bishop has granted him permission to marry his cousin...'

'Dark hair, a red mouth and a green dress,' I said, almost to myself. The steward looked surprised.

'Yes,' he said. 'People say they are lovers already.'

'Gossip,' I said. 'No doubt.'

'No doubt.'

I had the barrels loaded onto his cart, but before he left I gave him one especially, a small cask for the bride and groom and their Loving Cup. I wove a coronet of mistletoe around it like a wedding band.

'A gift from the convent,' I said.

I did not say that I had added a distillation of mistletoe berries to the brew. There is no taste. Only the sleep from which there is no waking.

☥

*Susie's
Christmas Eve
Gravlax*

In the recipe for Dad's Sherry Trifle, I tell you how my father spent his last Christmas with me and then died before the New Year.

I cancelled all my business for the month of January and that included cancelling an interview I was booked to do with the psychoanalyst Susie Orbach about her new book, *Bodies*.

I had read her for years and I loved the classic *Fat is a Feminist Issue* and *The Impossibility of Sex*. But we had never met.

Looking back, I think it was fateful that we didn't meet that dismal January 2009.

I was just coming out of a long breakdown. I've written about this in *Why Be Happy When You Could Be Normal?* I was better, no longer mentally ill. I didn't feel like you could put your hand right through me – like I was a ghost in my own life; I was solidifying again. But I was still not ready for the outside world. And then Dad died, and, while that didn't set me back, it was significant.

Susie, as I was to discover, was emerging out of a painful divorce at the end of a thirty-four-year relationship with a wonderful man, or, I guess it is fair to say, a man who had been wonderful. Now he was with someone else, and Susie had done the psychologically sane thing and grieved and mourned for two years since the separation, without becoming bitter or broken.

So when we finally met in April 2009 we were both beginning again. What we never expected was that we would begin again with each other.

Love affairs are discoveries of new worlds. The worlds we discovered in each other were far away from our well-known geography. Not least, Susie had always been happily heterosexual. And I wasn't interested in doing further missionary work with straight women.

Fortunately, love is flexible. Sex was the least of our differences.

I am solitary by nature. I live in a wood. I need non-linear time to imagine and to write. I can go for weeks without talking to anyone. I am happiest in my garden. I love sleeping. Beach holidays are not my thing. And Christmas is my favourite time of year.

Susie is social, extrovert, noisy, busy, has a life in New York City (her mother was from NYC, her daughter lives there and Susie lived there for years with her American husband), she loves to be on a plane somewhere, adores a sun lounger in Miami, never sleeps, can't garden (ruins her nails), is ultra-urban and Jewish.

That last bit makes a difference at Christmas.

Our first Christmas together I turned up with a huge home-made wreath of holly and ivy from the wood behind my cottage. 'It's for your front door,' I said.

'Are you crazy?' she said.

But over the years we have found ways of making Christmas-time work. True, it usually involves Susie flying to Miami for a few days with some friends, and me lying by a log fire at home reading books, but Christmas Eve is always a big party at her place done her way.

If you look at my Christmas Eve, you'll discover that I have a ritual of my own to mark the beginning of the twelve days of Christmas. That suits me – and there's plenty of time later for a party.

Loving someone very different – culturally different as well as temperamentally different – is a challenge. What Susie and I have learned is not to mistake a challenge for a fight. We do fight – of course we do – but we try not to pick fights about the fact of who we are.

You know that schtick – you fall in love with someone for who they are and spend the rest of your life kvetching about who they are?

We're different. And either we want to make that work or we don't. This isn't a my-way-or-your-way tug of war – it's shared experience.

Anyway, as the Christmas party gets noisier and later – what do I do? Take a walk round the block and go up to bed. Happy.

So try this great food from Susie's kitchen.

YOU NEED

3 lb (1.4 kg) best quality raw salmon, filleted and pin-boned
Generous cup of sea salt or kosher salt
Teaspoon or less of castor sugar
Small glass of potato vodka – best quality
Horseradish

You also need a long platter for the fish and lots of tinfoil and small bricks or heavy weights.

Susie says: I call this gravlax though it breaks the rules – scant sugar and no dill. I don't use beetroot because, although I like the colour, I don't find the flavour is improved, and it produces too much water. I'm not a dill fan, though I sometimes grate horseradish between the two salmon fillets. It's up to you.

METHOD

Wipe the two fillets with paper towels. Tweezer out any pin-bones. Lay the tinfoil on the platter. Don't cut – you will need to wrap the foil round the fish.

On a big board or wipe-clean surface, lay the fillets skin-down and pour over the vodka. Mix the salt and sugar and spread EVENLY across the two fillets with your hands.

Take one fillet and place on your tinfoil platter, skin-side down. Lay the second fillet on top of the first, skin-side up – so it's salmon flesh to salmon flesh.

Wrap the fillets up tight in the tinfoil. Then cover with another sheet of tinfoil.

Weigh it down with your weights so that there is steady, even pressure right along the fish.

Put in the fridge and leave it undisturbed for twelve hours. Every twelve hours take it out, drain off the liquid, turn it, and reweight. There will be quite a bit to drain off.

Do this four times. The salmon needs forty-eight hours to cure to be at its best.

When the salmon is ready, pat dry the fish with absorbent but not thin paper towels. Or use a clean tea towel. Take a weapon-sharp knife and slice the salmon as thinly as possible, at a horizontal angle. Grate a little horseradish, and add dill sprigs to make it look pretty if you want to.

If you like a sauce make mayonnaise with a little vodka.

Serve with ice-cold-from-the-freezer potato vodka.

AND THE MAYO . . .

Nothing mysterious about mayo. Americans struggle because they keep eggs in the fridge. Eggs for mayo must be at room temperature. If there's a secret – that's it.

Separate 3 organic eggs. Whites not wanted.

In a warm bowl stir or whisk the yolks till viscous, and slowly add excellent, not too fruity olive oil as you stir – maybe a little lemon juice, certainly a little bit of vodka if this is for the gravlax, and a pinch of salt. You can add Dijon mustard if you prefer. Most people add vinegar – for gravlax mayo, I don't.

If this is your first time, like all first times, keep tasting till you like it.

Your own mayo with home-made fries and rib-eye steak is a day-after-the-party dish even J.W. does the way I like it. Try it if you have gravlax for your New Year's Eve party and need something for that hangover.

O'BRIEN'S FIRST CHRISTMAS

nyone could see the ticker tape. It was more frightening than the one that never stopped calculating the national debt. This one said '27 SHOPPING DAYS TO CHRISTMAS'.

It might as well have said '27 DAYS TO ARMAGEDDON'. The frenzy was the same – the rush to buy as many things as you could that you didn't want and couldn't afford. Things so little wanted they were given as gifts – that strange word, a signifier meaning disappointment you can hold in your hands.

And food. Why, at this time of the year, does it become essential to stock up on chocolate-covered pretzels? Why does anyone want instant stuffing? Or drinks blended from cheap whisky and sterilised cream? Or wafer-thin mints?

O'Brien wondered about the wafer-thin mints. What was the important word? Wafer? Thin? Mints? Were these chocolates aimed at anorexics? Waifer-thin mints. Was it all in the fact of the filling? O'Brien had personally tasted the fillings in all of the filled chocolate products. And she had personally tested all of the filled bottles of body lotion. Colour and texture and scent were identical. Somewhere, in a town no one visited, nameless and not on any navigation system, there was a factory dedicated to the manufacture of sticky stuff. Vats of it, made all year, stored at a low temperature and sold to profiteers who traded exclusively in Christmas.

The department store where O'Brien worked prided itself on Never Running Out. Shop as you like, the miraculous shelves were filled with goods the following day. Only too much was enough.

O'Brien didn't like Christmas. If she went home to Cork, a hive of aunts asked her about her marriage prospects. Her father asked her about her job prospects. Her mother asked her about her hair. Her hair had always been lank and brown. She cut it straight across the back and straight across the fringe. 'Why won't you make something of yourself?' said her mother. 'You're no beauty but do you have to look like the donkey at the derby?'

O'Brien wore brown. Her hair was brown. Her soul, she thought, was brown. She had read a book called *How to Sparkle* but she couldn't get past the first affirmation: I AM A SPARK IN THE SPARKLER OF LIFE. Just saying it made her depressed.

All her friends had done better than her. Whatever that meant. She had done nothing that caught in the sieve of the world's esteem.

'And what is it that you do for a living, remind me?'

O'Brien was tired of being the runt of the litter, but the pride she had was fierce enough in its own way. She believed she could do better than nothing – and nothing, so it seemed to her, was all that was left when you took away the wrapping paper of people's lives. They packaged themselves all right – but what was in the box?

But if she didn't go home to Cork, she stayed in London by herself. Not by herself because her landlady never went anywhere on principle. She was a Scientologist and she was waiting to be released from her negative engrams. O'Brien could see that would make it difficult to go on holiday.

'And I am Hungarian,' said her landlady. She never explained why this was significant but it was her default position. If any of her lodgers asked her for something – a new carpet or an extra day to pay the rent – she never said yes, she never said no, she shrugged and shook her head regretfully. 'I am Hungarian.'

O'Brien worked in the pet department at the store and she qualified for a 35% discount on anything alive. It made sense to have a pet and a pet would keep her company, but her landlady would not hear of it. 'Hair carries stray molecules,' she said. 'And what is hairier than an animal?'

O'Brien didn't know if anything was hairier than an animal. Instead she suggested a small tank of tropical fish. Her landlady shrugged her shoulders and shook her head. 'I am Hungarian,' she said.

So O'Brien faced another Christmas alone.

In her lunch break she went online to look at the lonely hearts. There were so many sites to choose from, and there seemed to be extra at Christmas, just as there was extra of everything else. How could it be that so many sane, slim, smart, solvent, sexy men and women, with no obvious perversions and a good sense of humour, would be spending Christmas alone? Like her.

O'Brien had tried online dating already. Her computer profile had matched her to a small, nervous young man who tuned pianos. O'Brien had ticked her boxes as someone who liked to play the piano and didn't like tall, noisy men. So they had sent her the quiet one with the tuning fork. He hadn't said much over supper – O'Brien had ticked the box that said she enjoyed a quiet night in, but she didn't mean she enjoyed a quiet night out where her companion barely spoke.

At the end of the evening her companion had suggested they get married by special licence. O'Brien declined on the grounds that a whirlwind romance would be too tiring after so little practice. It would be like doing an hour's aerobics when you couldn't manage five minutes on the exercise bike. She asked him why he was in such a hurry.

'I have a heart condition,' he said.

So it was like aerobics after all.

Later she had joined a camera club, reasoning that digital had made the days of the darkroom a thing of the past so there would be no hairy hands groping her behind the black-out curtains with their joke-shop gorilla hands. In fact the club had turned out to be a cover for a group of male-to-female transvestites. She had liked them all, and she was given several handbags, but single she remained.

The aunts in Cork offered her advice. 'Don't set your sights too high, girl.'

But she did. O'Brien had loved the stars since she was a tiny girl growing up in a cottage on a country road. There, put to bed, she leaned out of the window every night and tried to count the myriad pins of light.

Now a young woman in a sodium-lit city, she had to imagine the stars more often than she saw them. But she set her sights up there – in the constellations; in the Seven Sisters, romantically alone, and Orion the hunter, his dog-star at his heels. In December, when the stars were bright, she sometimes walked up to Hampstead Heath, just to look into the dark. Just to look into the night and see herself in another life, happy.

Her boss came by. He was whistling 'Climb Every Mountain'. His hobby was whistling. He had a lot of friends because all over the world people love to whistle and since the internet came along they can all whistle to one another.

He gave O'Brien a chocolate elf and told her to cheer up. It's Christmas!

'Find your dream,' he said to O'Brien.

'When did all this start,' said O'Brien, 'this dream-finding?' Her boss looked blankly at her and went away with his bag of chocolate elves to check on the ferrets.

O'Brien wondered if the dream industry had started with Martin Luther King. But he did have a dream and it was a dream worth bringing into daylight. Then she wondered about dreams as messages, the Shaman dream. Then she wondered about dreams as repressed desires, the Freudian dream. Then she thought about Joseph Campbell and his dreams as symbols of the inner life.

Dreams were so tiring that she wondered how anybody ever dared to go to sleep at night.

The store was closing. O'Brien went down to her locker to get her things. She went into the Ladies' and looked in the mirror. Brown, she thought. My life is too brown.

Unable to do anything with the thought except be burdened by it, she set off to the lower lift. To do this she had to walk along a corridor of stars and under a big sign that said FOLLOW YOUR STAR.

Everybody used to navigate by the stars; there was no other way. Did it make a difference if you were looking at the sky instead of a screen? A difference to your sense of self?

'What did you say?'

She was outside SANTA'S GROTTO. Naturally, in a department store, the star led to a merchandising opportunity.

Santa had finished work for the day too. He pulled off his beard and hat. He was young and dark and clean-shaven. 'You said something about looking at the sky, not at a screen.'

'I was talking to myself,' said O'Brien. 'I keep forgetting that if you live in a big city only mad people talk to themselves.'

'I'm a country boy myself,' said Santa.

'Where are you from?'

'The North Pole.'

'What a coincidence, then – that you're playing Santa.' Then O'Brien realised that as usual she hadn't got the joke. She blushed and hurried away, hating herself.

When she returned to her lodgings that evening, her landlady was hanging a holly wreath on the front door.

'This is not for myself, you understand,' said the landlady. 'It is for my tenants. I am Hungarian.'

O'Brien went inside. The entrance hall was filled with home-made paper chains. Her landlady followed her inside and demanded help. Soon O'Brien found herself holding the ends of the paper chains while her landlady creaked up and down the aluminium steps, her mouth full of tacks like teeth like a vampire.

'You are not going home for Christmas?' said the landlady. It was a question but it sounded like an order.

'No. I am resolved to think about my life and change it. My life is meaningless. What is the point?'

'Life has no point,' said the landlady. 'You would be better to get married or start an evening class.'

This was too circular for O'Brien. She had tried to do both.

'Your past is your trauma,' said the landlady. 'If you become a Scientologist you can clear your engrams and eventually you could become a Thetan.'

'Are you a Thetan?'

'I am Hungarian,' said the landlady. And then, perhaps because O'Brien looked sad, perhaps because it was Christmas, perhaps because she was Hungarian, the landlady said, 'Can I offer you a tin of sardines for your supper? They are not in olive oil but tomato sauce.'

Alone in her room, O'Brien made a mental list of the things people thought of as their future: marriage and children – the aunts in Cork were right about that. A good job, money, more money, travel, happiness. Christmas-time swivelled the lens and brought these things into focus. If you had some, all, any of these things you could feel especially pleased with yourself over the twelve days of feasting and family. If you didn't have some, all, any of these things you felt the lack more keenly. You felt like an outsider. And what if you couldn't afford to buy presents? Odd that a festival to celebrate the most austere of births should end up being all about conspicuous consumption.

O'Brien didn't know much about theology but she knew there had been a muck-up somewhere.

'Maybe I'm just not normal,' she said out loud.

'We should all try to be normal,' said her landlady, appearing in the doorway without knocking. 'There is nothing wrong with being normal. Here are the sardines.'

Nothing wrong, thought O'Brien, but what's right for me?

She lay awake through the night, the radio on low, listening to music and talk programmes. There was a story about a princess who was invited to a ball. Her father offered her a hundred gowns to choose from, but not one of them fitted and her father refused to have any of them altered. No dress. No ball. But the princess climbed out of the window and ran all the way to the ball with her hair down, wearing her silk shift. And still she was more beautiful than anyone.

O'Brien must have fallen asleep or she couldn't have woken up with the sense that she was no longer alone in the room. She was right. Sitting at the bottom of her bed was a small, sprite-like woman wearing an organza tutu.

O'Brien didn't panic. The other lodger who lived on her landing worked in adult entertainment. All Vicky's friends wore exotic outfits, and some came to visit late, after their shift was done.

'Vicky's room is by the stairs,' said O'Brien sleepily.

'I'm the Christmas Fairy. I'm here for your wish.'

O'Brien realised her visitor must be drunk. She swung her legs out of bed and sat up. 'Come on, I'll show you the way.'

'This is the address I was given,' said the fairy. 'You are O'Brien. I am here to grant you a wish. You can have love, adventure, whatever. We don't do money.'

O'Brien thought for a moment. This must be a joke from someone she knew, except that she didn't know anybody. She decided to play along. 'OK, what can you offer?'

The fairy pulled out an iPad. What kind of a fairy has an iPad?

Reading her mind, the fairy said, 'Elemental beings run on electrical energy. Humans have begun to make progress. With us, iPads self-charge. You'll get there.'

O'Brien looked at the screen. She read the heading: 'Eligible Men'.

'Choose a pixie,' said the fairy.

'You mean a pixel,' said O'Brien.

The fairy looked annoyed and wiped the screen. 'Here are all the eligible women. It's all the same to me.'

'Shouldn't you be singing this?' said O'Brien.

'Why?' said the fairy. 'Does conversation bother you?'

'No, but you are some sort of singing telegram or singing webpage, or...'

'I am a fairy,' said the fairy. 'Your auntie O'Connor summoned me by mistake – then because she didn't know what to do with me, and I may not depart when summoned until I have completed my task, she sent me to you. Does that explain it for you?'

It didn't. O'Brien looked at the clock: 4.30am.

'Time is running out,' said the fairy. 'What is your wish?'

'OK,' said O'Brien, wanting to go back to sleep. 'I wish I was blonde.'

'That is rather a superficial wish,' said the fairy, 'but it is your wish. As it is Christmas, I will throw in a wash, cut and restyle. When you wake up your wish will be granted.'

'Where are you going now?' said O'Brien.

'Off duty. I have a date with a pixel.'

O'Brien slept deeply. She slept through her alarm and woke too late for anything but a shower and a murky dive into her clothes – at least they always matched, being brown.

In the lift, on her way down to the pet department, she met Lorraine from Lingerie, also in the basement.

'Wow!' said Lorraine. 'I didn't recognise you! Your hair is amazing! Must have cost a fortune!'

Lorraine always spoke in exclamation marks because she had to sell bras and knickers that made women look fantastic!

On her way to her locker, O'Brien bumped into Kathleen from Fabrics and Furnishings. 'It really suits you. You should do more with your make-up now.'

More? O'Brien didn't do anything so even choosing a lipstick would count as more. She could manage that.

She went into the Ladies' and looked in the mirror.

She was blonde. She was blonde as a Viking. She was corn-coloured with honey highlights. Her hair was thick and fashionably floppy. Perhaps it was a wig. She tugged at it. It wasn't a wig.

People went white overnight – but could they go blonde? And in winter? Corn on the cob. Polenta. Madeira cake. Lemons. She hadn't eaten any yellow food. She must be ill. She must have jaundice. That's yellow. But she didn't feel ill. She felt strangely and unaccountably happy.

As she came out of the Ladies' there was Santa, emerging from the Gents', wearing red trousers and braces and carrying his fur-trimmed jacket.

'Can you strap me into my tummy bulge?' he said.

Shyly, O'Brien belted the stuffed pad around his flat stomach, fastening it at the back. She could feel the warmth of him. 'You need a square meal,' she said.

'Are you offering?' he said, but he was turned away from her and he didn't see her blush. When she was done he turned round and looked down at her head. He was at least a foot taller than her.

'Great hair!' he said. 'You did that last night, right?'

'Kind of,' said O'Brien. Then she said, 'Do you believe in fairies?' Immediately regretting it.

'Sure I do! I'm Santa Claus!' He had a nice, friendly smile and a direct look in his blue eyes. 'Listen, I have to blow up two dozen inflatable gnomes for the kids' Christmas Eve party in the grotto. The grotto is made of polystyrene, which is bad for the lungs anyway, so I'm not blowing them up in there. How about we do it together? We can blow them up in Pets. I'll buy you lunch afterwards.'

'How do you know I work in Pets?' said O'Brien, but Santa, whose name was Tony, just smiled.

At the vegetarian café round the corner, where every lentil bake came with its own sprig of holly, Tony asked O'Brien if she'd like to come to a show with him. 'I'm an actor. An out-of-work actor, just now, but my pals are in a show. We can go for free.'

'Can we stay out till after midnight?' said O'Brien.

Tony looked puzzled. 'Sure, we'll be having a drink afterwards. But why?'

'I just want to check my hair, since I had it done by a fairy – I mean, it might go back to brown at midnight.'

Tony laughed. 'I like a girl that can tell a joke against herself. You've got a good sense of humour.'

O'Brien was astonished. Isn't that what everybody wanted in the lonely hearts? GSOH?

They went to the show, and O'Brien liked Tony's friends, and Tony's friends liked her, and at five minutes to midnight they were at the street corner where O'Brien lived and the clock struck twelve.

'Do you think I could kiss you before that fairy comes along?' said Tony.

That next day was O'Brien's day off work. So she went shopping like everyone else. She bought a few new clothes, none of them brown, and some nice food and, in honour of the occasion, a set of fairy lights.

Then the man with a stall on the street corner offered her a cut-price Christmas tree. She shouldered it home. Her landlady saw her arriving.

'I see you are going to get pine needles all over the carpet,' she said.

'It's seasonal,' said O'Brien. 'Thanks for the sardines. Would you like some of these satsumas?'

The landlady shook her head. 'And something has happened to your hair.'

'Yes,' said O'Brien, 'but it's a secret.'

'I hope it is not because of a man.'

'No, it's because of a woman – sort of,' said O'Brien.

'I am open-minded,' said the landlady. 'I am Hungarian.'

She disappeared into her parlour.

*

O'Brien was cooking beetroot linguine in a red T-shirt and red skirt when Tony arrived with a bottle of red wine. He put his arms round her. 'You kept your hair on, then?'

'Looks like it,' said O'Brien.

'That fairy – is she just for Irish folks or would she grant me a wish too?'

'What do you want?'

'To spend Christmas with you.'

'I can handle that one myself,' said O'Brien.

They opened the wine and drank to each other, and to Santas, gnomes and fairies, pixies and pixels, wherever found.

O'Brien strung her little window with fairy lights, and outside the night was strung with stars.

♥

Dad's
Sherry Trifle

y father was born in 1919; a celebratory war baby they soon forgot to celebrate.

He was born in Liverpool by the docks. He left school at twelve and worked alongside the men, when there was any work. This was the Great Depression – not only in Britain, but in the USA too, and Liverpool was a major port. Around one-third of working-age Liverpool men were unemployed.

Those days of casual work were all zero-hour contracts – you went down to the docks at dawn and hoped you'd be picked for a day's paid work, and maybe told to come back tomorrow.

So Dad didn't grow up with much, not even socks – which guaranteed that for the rest of his life he was one of those unusual men who LOVE being given socks for Christmas. Just plain woollen socks. Much better than lining your boots with newspaper.

Christmas brought another treat too: sherry trifle.

This was thanks to Del Monte Canned Fruit Cocktail – the cocktail name coming from the fact that, in the early days of Del Monte, this fruit mix had alcohol in it.

Dad's job down at the docks was unloading cargo of every kind (like Eddie, the longshoreman in Arthur Miller's *A View from the Bridge*), but the best kind of cargo was foodstuffs, and the best kinds of foodstuffs were things you could slip in a poacher's pocket and keep for later; that was cans.

So every Christmas his mother made the family sherry trifle. And when Dad married in 1947 rationing was on, but somehow he managed to eat his annual sherry trifle. My mother was working in the Co-op stores at the time, so that might have been where the tins came from.

My parents were obsessed with tinned food. Mrs Winterson still had her War Cupboard in the 1960s, stacked with stuff that would poison us if it was ever to be opened. But it was never to be opened; it was an insurance policy against Communists or Armageddon, whatever came first.

But we did eat tinned fruit – cheaper than fresh – and, until I got a Saturday job working on a fruit and veg stall on the market, tinned fruit was our treat on Sundays – and tinned fruit always went into the sherry trifle.

For me, growing up in the 1960s, sherry trifle meant Christmas. And Dad made it.

YOU NEED

Old cake
Ratafia biscuits. Optional but nice.
Jelly. Make a pint from a jelly block.
Fruit. Large tin of Del Monte Fruit Cocktail.
Custard. Tin of Bird's Custard.
Double cream (you can use a tin of condensed milk)
Harveys Bristol Cream sherry
Tube of hundreds and thousands

About the old cake: fancy cooks want you to make a sponge specially – and I understand that shop-bought sponge fingers aren't for everyone. The point about food is that a lot of it used to be left-overs and recycling. Same here. A dry, old cake is just what you want for a trifle because a fresh cake has moisture in it and gets soggy once you pour in the sherry. A dry cake soaks up the sherry and sits firm and content at the bottom of the bowl. So now you know.

*

METHOD

Get out your best cut-glass bowl from a dusty shelf at the top of the cupboard. Or find one in a charity shop for the right look. Wash it.

Single-layer the old cake in chunky slices on the bottom of the bowl and a little way up the sides as with bread-and-butter pudding – another great pud made from a base of stale left-overs.

Crumble in some ratafia biscuits for an almond taste – you can use fancy Amaretti.

Pour over the sherry – standing back a little, as the fumes from a fresh bottle of Harveys Bristol Cream are quite heady. Leave for 5 minutes to soak in. Do not drink the rest of the bottle until you are desperate.

Pour in the fruit cocktail. One tin or two is up to you.

Pour the liquid jelly over the fruit and sponge and leave in the fridge to set. In our case no fridge was needed as the house was so cold (see 'Mrs Winterson's Mince Pies').

When the jelly is set you can spread the custard in a thick layer on top.

Then, for the true triumph of a sherry trifle, pipe the cream in peaks on top of the custard. (You can just spoon it on if you prefer, but a piping bag was a big part of wartime England and beyond.) This is the moment where a couple of tins of condensed milk can substitute for cream, but I don't recommend it.

Decorate with hundreds and thousands – these look like mini multicoloured ball bearings.

Put it all back in the fridge and serve when you are ready.

Modern people use fresh or frozen raspberries, make their own custard and usually leave out the jelly. They top it with flaked almonds and truly it is a thing of beauty.

But one day you may find yourself with some old cake, a tin of custard, a tin of fruit cocktail, a few cubes of jelly, some sweet sherry and a bit of cream – or maybe even a tin of condensed milk if you are camping. These things happen.

And you will know what to do.

In 2008 my father died – but not before he had spent his last Christmas on earth with me.

If you've read my memoir *Why Be Happy When You Could Be Normal?* you'll know something about that last Christmas.

Dad was eighty-nine and too weak to sleep upstairs – I had him on cushions in front of the fire and I was sure he would die that Christmas night. He had stopped eating, except for…yes, he wanted a sherry trifle, and not the fancy kind.

I made it for him and we watched *Toy Story* on TV.

Three days later, back up north, he died.

I think about that time and, without being sentimental, I am sure that if we can find reconciliation with our past – whether parents, partners or friends – we should try and do that. It won't be perfect, it will be a compromise, and it doesn't mean happy families or restored bonds – there is often too much damage, too much sadness – but it might mean acceptance and, the big word, forgiveness.

I have learned, painfully, over the years that the things I regret in my life are not errors of judgement but failures of feeling.

So I am glad of that last Christmas with my dad – not because it rewrote the past, but because it rewrote our ending. The story, for all its pain and sometimes horror, did not end tragically; it ended with forgiveness.

THE SECOND-BEST BED

re there things that cannot be explained?

And if there are, how do we explain them?

My closest friend, Amy, left the city this summer to live three hours out of town in a rambling old house that had no heating.

She and her husband, Ross, want to have children. Ross is ten years older than Amy; he had his own place and a good IT business when they married, and his dream has always been to bring up his kids in the country – the way he was brought up.

Amy's a midwife, and the local hospital is glad to have her. Ross can mostly work from home as long as he has a satellite connection and, while Amy has been fixing up the house, the summer for him has been about installing the mast.

By Christmas-time, they were ready for guests and parties, and so I packed up my car and set off. I was glad to go. My own relationship hasn't worked out so well. I know Amy hopes something will happen between me and Ross's younger brother, Tom. I've met Tom and I think he's gay.

*

I was the last to arrive. Directions aren't my USP, and my car is too old and too cheap to have a navigation system. The twisty, frosty roads didn't leave any scope for speed, and I had to slow down at every junction to follow the printed-out route on the passenger seat.

When I finally reached the house, Amy was pulling dinner out of the oven, so Ross showed me upstairs to dump my bags and freshen up.

'We've put you in this room. We call it the Second-Best Bed. Ours is the master bedroom, just down the hall. I've put the boys on the next landing, out of our way.'

The room was big and square with a bay window overlooking the rear of the house. It was warm and well-lit, with a fluffy rug on the polished wood floor and a desk under the window. The bed was a four-poster.

'The bed came with the house,' said Ross. 'Been here since 1840, so I'm told. We bought a new mattress, don't worry.'

A gong sounded downstairs. 'That came with the house too,' said Ross. 'She loves it.'

He left me while I washed my face, brushed my hair and put on a lighter shirt. It was almost hot in here. Not what I expected from a country house. I looked round the room and smiled. I was being looked after. I started to relax after the drive.

At dinner Tom and Sean hugged me and wanted all the news. Tom works in TV, and Sean is Amy's college brother studying to be a doctor. Their whole family is medical. Amy didn't go down the doctoring route – not because she isn't smart, but because she loves so much of life. She's a potter and a cook and she wants to be a mum, and she knows, because she's seen both her parents do it, how much of you it takes to be a good doctor.

I love Amy. She was starting her biology degree while I was in my final history year. We hit it off straight away. Amy leaving the city is difficult for me. It was difficult for me when she married Ross. But we're fine. Ross can be prickly sometimes – he's possessive – but mostly, we're fine.

In the kitchen, Amy stretched up to hug me; I am nearly a foot taller than her. It was wonderful to see her again. She's like a part of me.

At dinner, everyone talking at once, we made our Christmas plans – the movies we wanted to watch, the games we wanted to play. Some people from the village were coming round in a day or two – get to know the neighbours.

By 11pm I was yawning my head off. I needed an early night. 'I've put a hot-water bottle in your bed,' said Amy.

'Just like old times,' I said, thinking about when we shared a flat before Amy moved in with Ross. Everybody said goodnight as I left the room. Except Ross.

I was half dozing when I heard the others making their way upstairs. There was no sound outside. No main road. No people. I fell deeply asleep.

What time was it when I woke? My watch and phone were on the desk where I had left them. All I knew was that the house was still.

I had been lying on my back, and I turned over in the bed.

There was someone next to me.

I put out my hand. Yes. There was someone else in the bed.

The body lay still. Whoever it was wore thick flannel pyjamas or a heavy nightdress. And whoever it was was cold. I could hear breathing. Slow, low, irregular breathing.

The light switch was on the wall. Easy to find when I had slipped into bed and put out the light. Now my hand was slithering over the wall, but I couldn't find the switch.

My heart was beating hard but I felt in control. Whoever it was, they were asleep.

I got out of bed carefully. Immediately I was shivering. The room was so cold. I went to the window, opened the curtains and looked out over the garden. I hadn't seen it before, but there was Ross's mast, and the earthworks around it. A half-moon gave some light.

Not wanting to, I turned back and looked at the bed. Yes, there was a shape, lying on its back, I thought, though the bed covers were pulled up and the head was in shadow. The figure was long and narrow. Not a woman.

Was it Sean? Tom? Had one of the boys stayed up and got drunk and stumbled into the wrong room?

This was my room, wasn't it? Yes, I could see my bags. I hadn't sleepwalked, then. Had my visitor?

But the awful temperature of the room propelled me away from the window, to my dressing gown flung on a chair, and then I was out of the door and down the stairs.

The house was silent. No sound came from the corridors except for a little bit of snoring. I went to the kitchen and put the light on. Normal. Everything normal. The hum of the fridge. The dishwasher light flashing its finish. The table cleared. The big ticking clock on the wall that said 4am.

I opened the fridge, heated milk. Ate chocolate biscuits. All the things you do in winter, in the middle of the night, when you're sleepless or scared.

And then I curled up on the battered sofa under somebody's coat and fell asleep.

This is what I dreamed.

I'm in an apothecary shop. The shelves are lined with glass jars filled with herbs, powders, granulations, liquids. There's a set of brass weighing scales with weights piled up like counters. An old man is weighing a substance on the scales. He tips it into a paper funnel, twists the ends and hands it to the woman standing before him. She's young, well-dressed, with a bonnet and an anxious face.

'Is that all there is?'

'That's all you can afford.'

'For pity's sake!'

The old man looks at her, leers. 'What will you give me in kind?'

The young woman shudders, takes the paper and leaves the shop.

I was woken by Amy, gently shaking my shoulder and standing over me with a mug of coffee.

'Sally? What happened?'

I sat up, stiff and groggy. 'Someone got into bed with me last night.'

Amy sat on the edge of the sofa. 'What?'

'Whoever it was wrapped themselves in their flannel pyjamas and didn't so much as say hi. But it was weird. I think one of the boys must have wandered into the wrong room. Were they up late drinking?'

'Let's go up,' said Amy.

Together we went back upstairs. Someone was filling a bath.

I opened the door into my room.

'God, it's cold in here!' said Amy. 'I'll get Ross to check your radiator. We had a new boiler installed.'

We looked at the bed. It was empty.

My side had clearly been slept in, the covers thrown back where I had got up in the night. The curtains were half-open, as I had left them. My things were in the room. The other side of the bed was undisturbed. The covers were neatly pulled up. The pillow was plump.

Amy walked round the three sides of the bed not against the wall.

'I hate to tell you this, love, but I think you've been dreaming. Was it about Tom?'

'No!' I said. 'How embarrassing.'

We were laughing. She gave me a hug. 'Come on, night-walker. Bacon sandwich?'

'Let me shower; I'll be down in fifteen.'

I went into the bathroom. Everything was as I had left it. There was no sign of any human presence but my own.

At breakfast, Amy told the others about my night-time adventure. There was a lot of laughter at my expense, but I didn't mind. It was a relief to be in daylight and with my friends. We were going for a crisp winter walk to cut boughs to decorate the house.

All I had seen of the countryside last night was through my head-lights. Now, in the dazzling winter sun, I can see why people like this kind of thing. It's clean, the air smells of pine and woodsmoke. The wood itself is just a little way down from the house. Amy has baskets and string, and she wants us to cut holly and whatever we can find.

The boys are with Amy; they're going to do a bit of tree-climbing and get some mistletoe. Amy starts unskeining ivy from ancient trees.

'Get some pine cones, will you, Sally? There's loads at the edge of the wood.'

I go towards the wood and start foraging on the forest floor.

It's pleasurable work, and I'm absorbed. I can hear the others a little way off, but I can't see them.

Soon I'm moving deeper into the wood on my quest.

It's so beautiful. The branches of the trees are hung with last night's frost. It's a winter wonderland and I feel like I'm in a Christmas card.

I must have wandered, because ahead of me, through the trees, there's a small building, like a hut made of stone. I go towards it, out of curiosity, my boots leaving crisp, clean prints in the snow. I can easily find my way back again.

The hut is a tiny cottage, long since abandoned, the chimney stack fallen into a pile of bricks by the rotten window. The roof tiles were still intact, and there was a wooden front door, now silvered with age and damp. I looked in through the dirty window. A cast-iron cooking range was set into one wall, still with two ancient implements hanging on hooks above it.

I walked round. Another window. This time into a bedroom. The iron bedstead was in the middle of the room, and on the wall a mouldered picture of a figure kneeling in front of the cross. The lettering said FORGIVE US OUR TRESPASSES.

I shivered. The Victorians loved shade, and this little house was built in the shade of two enormous spruce trees. It must have enjoyed little light, even in summer.

Enough. Time to pick up my basket and join the others.

I retraced my steps. They were easy to follow, though it seemed further than I remembered. But I have no sense of direction. Still, I felt that I was walking away from the house.

The bright day had faltered. The crisp, sharp air had softened, dampened. Above me the branches dripped wet gouts of ice. I was chilled to the bone.

In front of me I saw a pair of rusted iron gates, one swinging from its hinges like a broken gibbet.

I went forward. Through the gates. The ground was overgrown with thorny, leafless brambles and crumpled brown bracken. Either side of the smashed stone path was a line of yew trees, long since surrounded by birch and sycamore that no one had planted.

It was a graveyard.

I ran back out – how had I come here? As I ran, I saw that there was only one set of footprints on the ground – and they led towards the graveyard. I stopped to get my breath, to try to understand. I had followed my own prints and I had made a second set of prints. Where were they?

Whose track had I followed?

I was moving quickly, jumping over fallen logs, hoping to hear any noise that would help me. At last I heard a car going by. The sound led me to a fence that bordered the road. I climbed over the fence, feeling relieved and ridiculous. What was I frightened of? The others would soon have found me. It was only an abandoned graveyard.

Then I thought about the footprints.

Rounding the bend of the road, I saw a stone bridge and said Thank God, out loud. I had driven along this road. The turning for the house was less than a mile away.

At lunch-time over lasagne I tried to explain to the others what had happened. The boys thought it was funny – is it a male thing to turn the unexplained into a joke?

Ross was more sympathetic. He had explored the wood. He knew about the derelict cottage.

'This was once a proper estate,' he said, 'with land and staff. That cottage belonged to the gardener. But no one has lived there since the 1930s. That's when the estate was broken up. Death duties, I think. The place has no services, and the water came from a well.'

'It isn't ours,' said Amy. 'The woodland belongs to the Forestry Commission.'

'There's an abandoned graveyard in there,' I said.

Sean whistled low. 'I'd like to see that. I love old, spooky places.'

'I didn't love it,' I said.

'Did you look at the headstones? Loving Wife of Albert, that kind of thing?'

'I ran – like I said, I ran!'

'You really scared yourself, didn't you?' said Amy. She put her arms round my shoulders. 'This afternoon we'll go into the village – stock up for Christmas. And we'll all stick together.'

'Is there a pub?' said Tom.

'Of course there's a pub,' said Ross. 'Why do you think we moved here?'

It's so easy with them; their warmth, their pleasure in their new home and in each other. And I want to be here at Christmas. I don't want to be behaving like a Victorian hysteric with the vapours.

But while Tom is clearing the table and I am stacking the dishwasher, and Sean and Ross are bringing in more firewood for this evening, and Amy has gone to get the car out of the garage, I have only one thought in my head: I didn't scare myself. Something, or someone, scared me.

*

'I'll show you the village,' said Amy as we pulled up outside the pub. 'It's a real olde-worlde street, with little shops. There's a butcher, a baker — '

'A candlestick maker...' said Tom.

'No, but look at this old chemist's shop. You ever see anything like it? Sally? What's the matter?'

I had let out a small cry.

I stood staring at the curved bay glass front with its etched lettering on the window. Through the window I could see the high-stacked glass jars.

'There's a big brass weighing scale in there, isn't there?'

'Yes...' said Amy.

'But don't you see? This was my dream. I told you. The apothecary shop.'

'You looked up the village on the web, that's all,' said Ross, 'and you dreamed this because we live in a big, strange house in the middle of nowhere. The mind plays tricks.'

'I didn't look up the village, Ross.'

I went inside. The bell tinkled as I opened the door, and I thought I would see the small, leering, whiskered herbalist. Instead I saw a plump woman in a white coat. She was measuring out cough sweets from a jar.

Amy came in behind me. 'I sent them to the pub,' she said. 'We'll pick up the food. Sally, what's wrong?'

'There's nothing wrong,' said Ross to Amy when she went to get him an hour later, and the two of them were together at the bar while Sean and Tom played table football. 'I wish she'd calm down. I don't want ghosts and ghouls all over Christmas.'

'You didn't want her to come, did you?' said Amy.

'She's your friend. You can invite who you like.'

'Yes, she's my friend, and I wish you'd accept that.'

'I've been doing my best. But she always wants attention.'

I came out of the loo. I could see them arguing. I knew it was about me. Ross never liked the way Amy and I were together. We used to sit up talking non-stop in her big bed, or lie around in our dressing gowns at the weekend watching movies. He was desperate for Amy to move in with him – to be together, of course. And not to be with me, that was part of it.

I'm not being fair.

When we got back to the house Ross tramped us round the back to see his satellite mast. They had dug a huge hole to set it in the ground. It was twenty feet tall with a two-metre dish.

'What's this?' said Tom. 'Your phallic symbol?'

'There's absolutely no signal,' said Ross. 'I'm getting it from some sputnik in the sky.'

'You might get more than you bargained for,' said Tom. 'You could run your own TV station with this.'

By the side of the huge mound of excavated earth was a stone staircase leading nowhere.

'We uncovered it,' said Ross. 'Must have been cellars down there. Maybe an ice house.'

'Help me.'

'What? You said *help me.*'

'No, I didn't.'

Ross was staring at me. 'Yes, you did, Sally. Whatever it is, drop it, OK?'

He walked off. Tom was standing awkwardly to the side. 'Take no notice of him. He's always been moody.' He put his arm round me. 'Hot chocolate?'

The rest of the day and evening was easy enough. Tom and Sean's high spirits made up for Ross's mood and Amy had decided to ignore him. At bedtime she offered to come up with me to check the room.

We opened the door. Lying in the bed, clearly outlined, was a figure under the covers.

Amy drew back. I was rigid. The motionless figure of who? Or what?

Amy took my hand and we went straight back downstairs into the kitchen – where Tom and Sean couldn't keep their faces straight any longer.

Tom held up his hands. 'OK, OK, we put a bolster in the bed. Sorry.'

Amy threw a cushion at him. Ross looked up. 'Enough attention for the day yet, Sally?'

I said to Tom, 'Did you do that last night too?'

He shook his head. ''Course not.'

I got into bed. Amy kissed me goodnight and closed the door after her. The room felt fine. Absolutely fine. And I fell asleep.

I dreamed I was in my bedroom, standing at the window. There was a figure lying in the bed and the young woman I had seen in the apothecary shop was standing over the bed with a small glass.

'Sit up, Joshua; you must drink this.'

The figure tried to raise himself. I saw his emaciated arm. His face was waxy.

'You must get stronger. We must get away from here.'

The figure did not speak. With difficulty he swallowed the tincture.

I woke. Turned over, terrified. There was no figure in the bed. I lay on my back, my heart thudding. What was going on?

The next day Sean proposed I show him the graveyard. I didn't want to do it but I was feeling silly and hysterical and I thought it would be good for me – like holding a spider when you hate them.

We set out, and after an hour or so of aimless wandering we saw the gate. Sean's bluff ordinariness was reassuring. He went straight in, deeper than I had done, brushing moss and frost off the pitted headstones to read the inscriptions.

'I always visit graveyards,' he said. 'It's my way of dealing with death.'

My throat was tight and my lungs resisted the cold air. I was light-headed. Breathe deep. Breathe deep.

Sean was up ahead now. The morning was clear. There was nothing here but my lurid imagination. And then, on the ground, I saw footprints. Not ours.

The footprints led towards a mausoleum. Some sort of family vault. The vault must have been handsome in its day. Now it was broken, weather-beaten and colonised by ferns. The lintel bore the inscription: WILLIAMSON. MAY THEY REST IN PEACE.

There was the usual roll call of names – Augustus, Loving Husband of…Evangeline, Devoted Wife. Arthur, Killed in Action. And then what caught my eye: Joshua, Aged 22, Died 1851, Also His Sister Ruth, Aged 25, Died 1852.

Sean came over. He was intrigued. His presence bolstered me, and I walked a little further, to a row of small headstones, children's graves no doubt. As I bent down I saw a stone tablet lying to one side. Someone had carved on it – hand-carved, with a chisel, crudely – HE IS NOT HERE.

I jumped back. 'Sean?'

He came over and took a look. 'It just means they're with Jesus or in heaven. What's the matter?'

'There's another set of footprints in the snow.'

Sean went back the way he had come. 'No, Sally, just yours and mine.'

He was right.

Hallucinations and diseases of the mind.

What's the matter with me?

'You know what's the matter with Sally?' said Ross angrily, in Amy's face. 'She wanted you for herself.'

'We were never lovers,' said Amy. 'And so what if we had been? So what? Can't you cope with intimacy between women?'

'It's classic,' said Ross. 'She's repressed, she's resentful. She's always hated me.'

'She likes you,' said Amy simply. 'It's not her fault she's taller than you.'

Ross banged down his glass. 'She wants to ruin our Christmas because we've ruined her life.'

'Of course we haven't ruined her life!'

They didn't see me coming in at the kitchen door. They didn't hear me overhearing them.

My cheeks burned with shame and anger. I should go home. Christmas in my flat with a can of soup would be better than this.

To avoid crossing the kitchen I walked round the house to the back door. There was Ross's mast and the Piranesi-nightmare stone stairs leading nowhere.

I stood at the top of the stairs, looking down, still numb from what I had heard. Was Ross right? Was I jealous of them? I am happy that she is happy. I do believe that. But deep down? Did I want Amy for myself? Do I not know myself at all?

Help me

I turned round. No one there. Who said that? A woman's voice. I heard it earlier. In my mind I saw a picture of the footprints – first from the ruined cottage to the graveyard, then in the graveyard itself, the footprints that had led me to the Williamson vault.

Help me

They were a woman's footprints. That is why I had mistaken them for my own.

I went down the stone steps leading nowhere. But they did lead somewhere. I had a terrible feeling that beyond the bricked-up entrance to what Ross thought was an ice house or a disused cellar of some kind was some secret, awful to know. Some secret hidden through time, intended to be hidden forever, until Ross had sited his mast.

And I could imagine what they would say if I asked them to un-block it.

No. Let it be. Pack. Leave. Never come back.

I went into the house. At the foot of the stairs I met Amy. She looked pleased to see me. 'I've made mince pies. Come and have a cup of tea.'

'Is Ross there?'

She frowned. 'I don't want it from both of you. It's Christmas, for God's sake.'

'I was about to pack my things,' I said. 'It's better if I go. I heard you... earlier... I was at the door.'

Amy let out a big sigh. 'I'm sorry. I know it's not you. Except that, well, you have been behaving a bit strangely. I told him you're just tired and this is a big old house in the middle of nowhere. It's easy to imagine things. Even Sean got spooked in the graveyard.'

'Did he?'

'Don't make me spend Christmas with three idiot males, even if I do love them all in different ways.'

'I really think I should leave.'

'Give it one more night. If you absolutely want to go, go in the morning. You'll only get lost in the dark. And we've got some people coming tonight.'

She put her arm round me. I nodded.

Ross must have decided to make an effort because dinner was pleasant enough and David and Rachel from the village were jolly and easy. As we were heading back towards the fire in the sitting room, I asked them if they knew the history of the house.

'She wants to know if it's haunted!' said Sean.

Everybody laughed. 'We'll have to disappoint you,' said Rachel. 'There's no headless horse or ghoulish vicar. The Willamsons had the house built around 1800 and occupied it for about fifty years when the line died out.'

'Joshua Willamson,' I said.

'She's been studying her gravestones,' said Sean.

'Yes, that's right,' said David. 'The estate passed to another branch of the family, and by the 1960s there was not much land left, and what you have here, this house and generous garden, has been bought and sold ever since. I know my local history, so if there was more to tell you, I would.'

'There you are, Sally,' said Amy, throwing her legs over mine on the sofa. 'You'll sleep well tonight.'

And I did. Until about 3am. I woke with my teeth chattering in my head. My body was frozen numb. I rubbed my thumb and index finger together and felt nothing. I had to get out of bed.

With all my strength I sat up and forced my feet onto the floor. I had no feeling. The bedroom was shrouded in ice. Icicles hung from the ceiling, pointing down at me like baleful spears. The floor shone with cold. Chattering and shaking, moving on rigid legs, I went to the window. The curtains were frozen apart like caught waterfalls. I looked out.

Down below, by the mast, on the abandoned stone steps, a figure was being wrestled into an opening that lay in shadow. I knew this was the tall figure I had seen in my bed. Two men fought with him. At the top of the steps, on her knees, begging, was the young woman I had seen in my first dream.

She looked up, straight at my window. She saw me.

Help me.

But the world is darkening. It's too late.

Amy woke, not knowing why. Ross was asleep beside her. The house was still. She lay for a few moments, her eyes on the ceiling. She was afraid and she didn't know why. She got out of bed, found her dressing gown and went out onto the landing. She went to Sally's room and opened the door.

The cold was like a burn.

SEAN! SEAN!

Sean and Tom carried Sally out of the bedroom and down to the fire. 'She has barely any pulse – she's freezing to death – we have to get her core warm – Amy! Rub her feet! Tom, her hands! Ross, call the ambulance. Sally! Can you hear us? Sally? Sally?'

It took the ambulance an hour to arrive and by that time I was conscious. My pulse had quickened. I had some colour. Amy was making me drink warm water. Tom was holding me tight against his body, the living warmth of him bringing me back from the dead – or so it seemed.

'What has happened here?' said Amy. 'I don't understand.'

'He is not here,' I said.

'The graveyard,' said Sean.

'We have to open the room at the bottom of the stairs,' I said.

The next morning Ross, Sean and Tom went at the bricked-up arch with mallets and chisels. The lime mortar and the soft clay bricks were old and damp and yielded easily. A couple of hours later there was a hole big enough to step through. Ross got his searchlight and went inside. Tom and Sean followed. Amy and I sat huddled together at the top of the stairs.

I heard Sean say, 'Both are women.'

It was an ice house. An ice house that had been turned into a room – if a burial chamber can be called a room.

There was a rough bedstead. A table and chair. A candlestick. Two candles left unburned. An empty jug, a notebook. And two bodies, rapidly disintegrating in the air.

*

The notebook told the story.

Joshua Williamson was a woman. She had been raised as a male as the heir to the Williamson estate. She was unusually tall for a woman – especially in the 1840s – and no one but the immediate family had any notion of the truth. Her father had married for the third time – determined to produce the heir he needed to stop the estate passing to his cousin. What would have happened to Joshua if he had succeeded is unclear. But Joshua's fate came sooner than that.

Joshua fell in love with the gardener's daughter and announced his intention of marrying her. 'I have lived as a man; should I not love as a man?'

To prevent this his father began to poison him with mercury. Not to kill him, it seems, but to weaken and sicken him and break his will. But the mercury doses proved fatal, and in the last stages of his wracked dissolution Joshua had determined to tell the truth about his situation. His sister, Ruth, had gone to fetch the lawyer.

She was overtaken and brought back to the house.

Joshua, it was put about, had died of TB. His father, desperate that no one should examine his body, walled him up in the ice house to die. His little lover, the gardener's daughter, was forcibly taken and walled in with him. Then the site was earthed over and levelled. It had lain undisturbed for more than a hundred and fifty years.

Only two people alive at the time had known the true story – Williamson himself, and Ruth. Ruth died the following year.

Tom drove me back to the city. 'I don't see how they can stay in that house – do you?'

I didn't answer. If you don't answer the speaker will speak again. 'I thought I might make a documentary about it – find out the whole story. What do you think?'

I didn't answer.

'None of this would have happened except for Ross and his bloody mast.'

'It was me,' I said.

'Any of us could have slept in that bedroom.'

'It was me.'

'Don't blame yourself, Sally. Would you like to go out for a Chinese on Christmas Day?'

Tom reached over and patted my hand. I took it.

'My grandmother was a Williamson,' I said.

-

Shakespeare and
Company's Chinese
Dumplings

hristmas is about community, collaboration, celebration. Done right, Christmas can be an antidote to the Me First mentality that has rebranded capitalism as neo-liberalism. The shopping mall isn't our true home, nor is it public space, though, as libraries, parks, playgrounds, museums and sports facilities disappear, for many the fake friendliness of the mall is the only public space left, apart from the streets.

I think we can all reclaim the spirit of Christmas – less shopping, more giving, less spending, more time for friends, including the joyfulness of cooking and eating together, and sharing what we have with others.

There's a sign over the entrance to Shakespeare and Company: Be Not Inhospitable To Strangers Lest They Be Angels In Disguise.

Shakespeare and Company has been a bookshop in Paris since 1919. Begun by the legendary Sylvia Beach, from Pennsylvania, the bookstore became a second home to all those famous pre-war Americans – Gertrude Stein, Hemingway, Ezra Pound, F. Scott Fitzgerald. Beach was the first publisher of James Joyce's *Ulysses*.

The store closed during the Second World War, and eventually re-opened under its original name, opposite Notre Dame, run by George Whitman, an ex-GI who loved books and Paris in equal measure.

George never closed the store on Christmas Day; usual opening hours of midday to midnight were observed, and George cooked a meal for anyone who wanted to eat – that has included Anaïs Nin, Henry Miller and a batch of Beat poets. Ginsberg read 'Howl' with his clothes off and Gregory Corso particularly liked the holiday fare on offer one year: ice-cream, doughnuts and Scotch.

And they kept coming back – in 1982 George's daughter, Sylvia, spent her second Christmas on this earth with Allen Ginsberg, Lawrence Ferlinghetti and Gregory Corso, eating a supper of baking-powder biscuits and cheese soufflé.

George believed that books were a sanctuary for the mind. His bookshop became a sanctuary for body and soul. There is a library for anyone who wants to sit and read out of the cold or the sun. In George's day, as many as twenty-four impoverished writers and readers were sleeping in the store as well.

Now George is dead. He made it to ninety-four and died in his tiny apartment over the shop. His daughter Sylvia (born when George was sixty-eight) runs the ever-expanding bookopolis with her partner, David Delennet. The bookstore has finally become a business (George refused a computer or a telephone, or even a cash register), though the spirit hasn't changed. The store is no longer open on Christmas Day, but Sylvia and David cook a meal for staff and volunteers, and any lost writers fighting with their masterpieces.

Sylvia wrote to me:

> *One Christmas when the only thing left at the butcher's was a piglet, I cooked it for twenty-five people. Its teeth came out and it looked terrifying. When I presented it to the table, there were gasps of shock from the display and then lots of giggles because half the table was Jewish and didn't eat pork!!! Disaster.*
>
> *Then there was another Christmas when Hong, the Chinese caretaker who helped with Dad, made dumplings – actually she called them DUMPINGS; this was when she first arrived and barely spoke a word of French or English. The Irish writer Ulick O'Connor was there, and as he was about to put a dumpling in his mouth he asked if there was any onion in them. Hong shook her head. He popped the dumpling in his mouth and said, 'Good, because if there's onion I die.'*

I googled an onion, showed it to Hong and she suddenly
changed her mind and said yes, yes, there's definitely onion
in there. Nightmare.
He was OK, though. Dad said he mustn't be allergic to
Chinese onions.

Soon after Christmas in 2007 I made my way to the bookshop in a
bad state of loss – that summer my partner had left me abruptly; it
felt like a death. That loss had triggered something deeper and scarier,
but I was trying not to let anyone know.

I was coping by writing – in fact, the story in this collection 'The
Lion, the Unicorn and Me' was written that December. I wrote it
straight through one night, too unhappy to sleep. Its hero is a runty
little donkey who gets a golden nose. I am the donkey.

Sylvia and David gave me the bookstore to roam in, their dog, Colette,
to keep me company, a radiator to sit beside and all the meals I could
eat. Later on, as things got worse for me, they bought me pyjamas and
nursed me through a chest infection.

I had been to Shakespeare and Company many times before. I had
met George, already ninety.

He didn't look pleased to see me. In fact he threw a book at my
head.

George: What's she doing in my apartment? Who's she?

Sylvia: She's a writer, Daddy. Jeanette Winterson.

George looked pleased and he put down the next book he was
preparing to launch at my person.

George: Did you show her the writers' room? No? Goddam, do I
have to do everything myself? She can stay as long as she likes – let
me show you the writers' room. You read Henry Miller? He…'

George loved writers. All writers. His home was our home. To be made welcome. To be acknowledged. To be fed. To sleep soundly. To feel safe. To read. To put words on a page that others will read.

My mind was in free fall. Going mad is a risk. A journey not to be made if you can help it. Sometimes it is a journey that has to be made. But like all desperate journeys, there will be helpers along the way.

So at Christmas I raise a book and a glass to the star that led me to Shakespeare and Company and the refuge I found there, and the creative kindness of a way of life that has never reckoned money as the bottom line.

If you want to read the whole story of Shakespeare and Company, past, present and future, they have just published a book about it: *Shakespeare and Company: A History of the Rag & Bone Shop of the Heart* (I wrote the foreword).

And here is the recipe for Hong's Dumplings.

YOU NEED

1 lb (450 g) flour
1 lb (450 g) pork
1 lb (450 g) Chinese cabbage
Bunch of scallions
Fresh root ginger – not too much
Tablespoon of white wine
Salt and pepper
Water
Egg – if you like a richer dough. Not necessary.

METHOD

Hong says: Make the dough in the usual way, kneading the flour and water. Less water if you are adding an egg. The dough must be not too soft, not too hard. If it is too soft, add more flour. Too hard and dry, add more water. Making the dough takes about 15 minutes by hand, depending on the quantity you make.

Cut the dough in half or thirds, depending on the quantity you make, and roll each portion out thinly, but not too thin, or it will break when filled. Use a cup to cut out rounds like little full moons. Each of these full moons will be the dumpling parcels when filled.

For the filling, chop everything up separately, and small as a fingernail. This is important. Then mix all your filling ingredients together in a big bowl. Season to taste. And maybe you like more onion, maybe you like more ginger – up to you. As you experiment you will know.

Now fill your dough parcels with about a tablespoon of filling. You have to learn just how much filling so that the dumplings are plump, but not so fat that they come apart when boiled.

Today you will fold your full moons into half-moons for the filled dumplings. That is simple to do. If you like making dumplings you can experiment with different shapes and fancy folds later on.

My grandmother makes beautiful shaped and folded dumplings while she watches TV; her hands know what to do and she never even looks down once.

When the dough is filled, fold it into the easy half-moons and seal the edges all the way round by dipping your sealing fingers and thumb in a bowl of water. Seal must be tight. No gaps, or the filling will escape, and your pan water will be a messy soup of pork and cabbage bits.

While you are making the dumplings, bring to the boil a big pan of water, like for pasta.

Add the dumplings, stirring so that they don't stick.

Now add another big cup of cold water – enough to take the water off the boil, and bring back to the boil.

Repeat this step.

You are boiling the dumplings 3 times.

After 6 or 7 minutes, take one out and slice open to see if the filling is cooked.

If you cook from frozen, it takes a bit longer. Remember to tip the dumplings straight into the hot water; do not defrost first.

You can use different meat. Doesn't have to be pork. Or shrimp. You can add carrots to the cabbage. Cooking times vary a little depending on the filling.

In China people were poor when I was growing up. Dumplings were made with what you could get. We kept pigs, like many Chinese. Once you have the feel for dumplings, use for your filling whatever is in the kitchen, fresh at the market, or in the garden.

My friend JW made rabbit, carrot and leek dumplings and they were very good. She has a lot of rabbits in her garden. I think because she grows a lot of carrots. But it is well-known that rabbits do not eat the onion family so she grows her carrots behind an armed guard of leeks. Still, sometimes, a rabbit has to be taught a lesson and the dumplings were the result.

Dip your dumplings in any sauce you like – a simple, good quality soy sauce with added ginger or scallions is delicious.

CHRISTMAS CRACKER

hristmas Eve at the Cracker Factory. Boxes labelled 'Trumpets', 'Drums', 'Stars', 'Robins' and 'Snowmen' were stacked on either side of the long tables where the crackers were assembled. Sheets of gold cardboard were piled against the cutting machines. Waterfalls of red streamers ran down the walls.

The spitting, snapping, banging, firing, pistol-shot strips that made the crackers crack were safely in tubes on the shelves. Three giant vats, of the Ali Baba kind, marked 'Hats', 'Jokes' and 'Balloons' sat under the funnels that automatically topped them up as more and more crackers were filled, packed and dispatched.

The cracker factory operated all year round but at Christmas-time everybody worked harder to fulfil the orders: Cheap crackers. Economy crackers. Family packs. De-luxe boxes. Sets for children, sets for grown-ups, and some boxes marked 'Adult', because they contained very tiny briefs. Most of the crackers had long since been dispatched to stores and from stores to tables as everyone made ready for Christmas Day.

But there was one cracker left to be made. The very last, the very special, the giant charity Christmas cracker, long as a crocodile, fat as a pudding, an enormous golden tube lying on its side, waiting to be stuffed tight as a sausage.

But for now the factory is empty, because it's early morning, the bus is just arriving at the gates, and Bill and Fred and Amy and Belle are coming in, special shift, cheerful because it's Christmas now, and they'll have a drink when they're done.

The factory is empty. Or is it?

The dog is still asleep in a dream of warm tissue paper, where he crept last night, cold and wet, because somebody left open a small window, and he is only a small dog.

In he crept, under the red safety light that shone on the gold card beneath the paper angels. He rolled on his back to get dry and ate a marzipan donkey – bad for his teeth, but what can you do? – and fell asleep.

In they come, neon lights, radio on, and before the dog can say 'woof' a golden tunnel opens right before his brown eyes and a pair of firm, spade-like hands shoves all the tissue paper and all the dog right inside one end of the cracker and seals it with a plastic lid.

He can still see out the other end. He buries his nose deeper, the hair in his ears twitching, as an avalanche of chocolates crashes round his head, followed by an army of teddy bears, an arsenal of pop-guns, a barrage of balloons, beads like hailstones, a string of yo-yos, a peal of whistles, a masked ball of false noses and beards, a plague of clockwork mice and a huddle of evil-looking finger-puppets dressed in black.

Somebody says, 'Make it good with the explosives, then – this one has to go with a bang!'

A fuse-rod of gun-powdery stuff is poked past the dog's nose (sneeze) and past his tail (twitch), and out through a hole in the lid.

The dog thinks of all those circus animals fired out of cannons, or the ones dropped by parachute behind enemy lines. He thinks of Laika, the Soviet dog shot into space, never to come down, and he thinks of the star-dogs, Canis Major and Minor, tracking the dark fields above, glittering guardians of their rougher kind below.

Perhaps he's going to join them, sky-set, a new-burned star, Canis Fugit, the flying dog.

But he doesn't want to be a flying dog!

He wants all four paws on the ground.

Too late!

They are tying the ribbon at both ends round the giant charity Christmas cracker. He feels himself lifted up and carried out like a canine Cleopatra in a roll of carpet, and there he is on a gilded barge – no, it's the back of a battered truck – driving towards a large hotel with a green-coated doorman at the door, and a white Christmas tree behind the door in the chandeliered lobby.

The dog and his cracker are carried in by specially chosen elves on the minimum wage, to the wonderment and applause of all.

This is the children's charity party – rich parents have paid a lot so that their children can help children in need without having to meet any of them.

The dog can hear announcements being made – special prizes, and the best prize of all is for the one who wins the cracker.

The dog is worried about what will happen when they find him wrapped up inside. He isn't anyone's idea of a free gift; not anyone's idea of a gift at all. He is a stray. He knows no one will want him. He lives in the park and drinks from the fountain. He came with the fair when he was a puppy, and ran round the rides in his criss-cross mongrel colours, until one day the fair packed up, and the caravans pulled away one by one, and he went to sleep for a bit because he didn't know what was happening, and when he woke up everyone had gone.

He ran sniffing after them at first, following the scent of diesel and hot dogs, but his paws were slower than their wheels and, though he ran and ran till his pads were raw, at night-time he had to give up and, limping and frightened, through the dark and noise he found his way back to the park.

He was glad of the rustle of the trees and the soft leaves.

Sometimes people feed him sandwiches and sometimes they don't. Sometimes they try to catch him. He knows the sound of the van and he runs down the street where he can slither under a gate until they have gone. Sometimes a human sleeps in the park too, and makes a fuss of him, but the humans move on. You can't rely on people; he knows that.

Last night was very cold. He was out scavenging for food. The kebab man had gone back to Turkey for Christmas. The dog likes kebabs. He sniffed a bit round the bins but the streets had been cleaned for Christmas.

As he trotted down the road, keeping to the wall, he saw a window ajar, and the red light inside. It looked warm. The rain had turned to sleet.

But now...

What will happen when they find him in the cracker?

He can hear a lot of noise. He'll keep quiet.

The hotel ballroom is crammed with children waving raffle tickets. It's time for the prizes to be given away – dolls, games, toy guitars, remote-control cars. There's a man in a spangly jacket with a microphone. He's on the stage and he wants the children to sing 'Jingle Bells'.

Then it's time. The Big One. The Cracker. The elves push it on stage.

What's the winning number? Yes! It's 999.

Two children rush forward – a fat boy in a red Elvis suit and a slim girl in a fake-fur coat. Has there been a mistake? There are two winning tickets. The children glare at each other and take up combat positions at either end of the cracker. The room fills with feral energy as the kids in the room take sides:

'PULL! PULL! PULL!'

The fat boy wraps his fat hands round one end, and the slim girl digs her heels in and just holds on, like she's seen her mother do in the sales.

But then a pale, quiet boy comes forward and gives the master of ceremonies his ticket. He's got 999 too.

The master of ceremonies scratches his wig. 'Whatever is inside this bumper, giant, gigantically exciting cracker, you'll just have to share.'

The children in the ballroom boo.

'Sharing is for suckers,' says the slim girl.

'It's Christmas!' says the master of ceremonies, as though repeating the obvious will make the unexpected happen.

The pale, quiet boy stands back while the boy in the red suit turns redder than his suit as he pulls and pulls at his end of the cracker. The girl throws her whole body weight on top of the cracker to stop her new enemy, the fat boy, winning the bang. The pale, quiet boy standing in the middle, holding his ticket, wonders why he can see a paw beginning to poke through the rip.

BANG! There it goes like somebody split the atom and up in the air is a mushroom cloud made of chocolate and yo-yos and false noses and finger-puppets, and for a second it hangs in perfect space, then, as the contents of the cracker scatter over the ballroom, it's every child for itself, fighting over silver coins and plastic spiders, and nobody notices that free falling back through the smoky, acrid air is a small terrier with a paper hat round its neck.

'Where's the big present?' demands the fat boy. 'I won the cracker. I want the big present.'

The dog lands at his feet.

'What's that dog doing in the cracker?' shouts the slim girl.

The dog is used to being chased and shouted at, but this time he knows he's in trouble, so he thinks on his feet, all four, as fast as his doggy brain can, and he says, ' Hi! I'm a magic dog, like the genie in the bottle.'

'What genie? What bottle?' says the fat boy, suspicious that he's missing something. 'Who stole my genie?'

'If you're a MAGIC DOG, yeah, right, where are my three wishes?' says the slim girl.

The pale, quiet boy says nothing. He's looking at the dog.

'OK! One wish each,' says the dog, pointing at the children with his snouty nose. 'One. Two. Three! Your wish is my command!'

'I want a Ferrari,' shouts the fat boy.

'Righto,' says the dog. 'Give me ten minutes.'

The dog dives under a long table-cloth and races to the end of the ballroom. He is thinking only of escape. He skids across the polished floor, over the carpet, past the cloakroom, sees the zigzag sign for the emergency stairs and reckons that must be for him.

This is an emergency! Go, dog, go!

He helter-skelters down the narrow concrete stairs and lands on his head in the underground car park.

'Move that Ferrari in Bay 16, will you?' shouts the valet, winging the keys through the air towards his assistant.

And it must be said that for all our planning and plotting, and deliberating and deciding, the moment that changes everything comes when it will, and cannot be coaxed, or invoked, and should not be missed.

The dog didn't miss. He stood on his hind-paws and leapt. He leapt out of his scraggy, raggy, tooth-and-nail past and caught the future as it whipped by his jaws.

There he is, back up the whirl of the concrete stairs, through the emergency exit, past the cloakroom, into the ballroom, just escaping concussion from a hundred yo-yos, but with one bound he's on the stage by the remains of the exploded cracker, and there are the car keys at the feet of the fat boy in the Elvis suit.

'Underground parking, Bay 16,' says the dog.

The fat boy's eyes gleam with greedy happiness. He doesn't bother to thank the dog, just grabs the keys in his fat fist and waddles off, shoving the smaller children out of his way.

'Me now,' orders the thin girl. 'Me, me me! I want a real fur coat.'

'That's unethical,' replies the dog, who has never heard the word before, but finds it on the tip of his pink tongue.

'I want one!' shrieks the girl with such force that all the glass baubles on the Christmas tree shatter to powder.

'OK!' says the dog. 'Your wish is my command.' He's about to turn tail, but the pale little boy has knelt down and given him a drink of water and a ham sandwich, from which he has carefully removed the lettuce.

The dog is grateful, and hopes that, whatever happens, he can bring the little boy his wish. But first there is the matter of the fur coat.

He's lucky, because the parents are arriving to collect their children, just at the moment when gentle tinsel snow begins to fall in the bar next to the ballroom, and wouldn't a drink be nice, and what's five minutes in a lifetime, especially at Christmas? But these are the minutes some good angel has earmarked for the dog, who can't believe his soft brown eyes as coat after coat is passed over to the girls working in the padded cloakroom, and if he just sits quietly, and just waits – yes, it's a mink!

The girls are busy hanging up the coats in the pile and chatting about best-value turkeys, so they never notice the mink silently sliding away under the counter and across the floor, dog underneath it, twenty times his size, but he's a terrier and born with the Holy Law of the Jaw – Don't Let Go.

'Darling, there's a coat running across the floor on its own,' says one very drunk man to his very sober wife.

She doesn't even look round. 'Don't be silly, darling.'

And so the sleek mink coat, piloted by the rough-coated dog, makes its way across the carpet, into the ballroom and towards the bottom of the steps of the stage.

There's a muffled, 'Woof!' The girl is on her mobile phone and doesn't notice that her heart's desire has arrived. The pale little boy has been waiting, really a bit anxious about the magic dog, and when he sees the coat like a rug on centipede legs slinking across the floor he knows the dog must be underneath, and runs to pull him out.

'Are you all right?' asks the boy.

'Bit hot,' says the dog. 'Tell her the coat's here.'

The girl covers her face in her hands, then starts clapping, the way she's seen winners do on TV talent shows. She pulls on the coat, and sashays off the stage and falls flat on her face, just as the master of ceremonies reappears with a microphone in his hand. He looks grim. He looks serious.

It seems that the winning ticket 999 has not been multiplied by three after all. It wasn't the Christmas elves; it was two felt-tip pens. The holders of ticket numbers 9 and 99 each added the required 9s to their stock. The big present will go to the real number 999 only.

The pale little boy still has his ticket in his hand. The master of ceremonies examines it through a magnifying glass – yes, it's the one.

The organ strikes up 'Jingle Bells', but not loud enough to drown out the terrific crash in the hotel lobby.

Everyone runs to the doors to see a red Ferrari, driven by a red-faced boy in a red suit, stalled in a shatter of plate-glass, with the white Christmas tree jammed through the sunroof and the green doorman sprawled over the bonnet.

'The dog made me do it!' screams the boy as the security guards drag him out.

The girl in the fur coat is laughing so much she can hardly hold her phone still enough to take the snap to send to all her friends. As she holds both hands above her head a pair of handcuffs slots securely round her wrists.

'That girl has stolen my coat. She's wearing it!' The Russian model is unhappy. 'I am a friend of President Putin.'

'The dog gave it to me,' wails the girl. 'Arrest the dog!'

But the dog is nowhere to be seen. The dog has crept behind the blow-up reindeer in the ballroom and he's not coming out.

As the row in the hotel lobby reaches custard-pie proportions, the master of ceremonies takes the pale, quiet boy to a gold box with a red ribbon and tells him to open it. Hesitatingly the boy pulls the ribbon, because he isn't used to big presents. He and his mother don't have much money. Inside the box is a mountain bike.

'And it's all yours,' says the master of ceremonies. 'You won it fair and square.'

Left alone with the bike, the boy runs his hands over the clean cogs and smooth gears, the lightweight frame and the drop/raise handlebars. It's the best bike in the world.

'Well, you won't be needing a wish, then,' says the dog invisibly, from behind the blow-up reindeers. 'Probably for the best, under the circumstances.'

Another shriek comes from the hotel lobby as the Ferrari owner is reunited with the remains of his car. He's shouting something about a golf course and Donald Trump.

The boy sits on the edge of the stage, swinging his thin legs and looking at the dog's eyes looking at him. He holds out another sandwich. The dog's brown eyes dart left, then right, then he trots out, takes the sandwich and sits next to the boy.

'I'm not a magic dog,' says the dog. 'I'm a stray. I got trapped in that cracker. It was so cold last night, and I usually sleep under the wheelie bins in the park, but they had taken them away, and I was shivering, so I went for a walk to get warm and I saw a light in a window and I found a bench full of coloured paper, and fell asleep, and, well, here I am.'

'I came on the bus,' said the boy. 'I live with my mum. She cleans at the hotel so they have to invite me to the party.'

'What were you going to wish for?' said the dog. 'If I had been a magic dog?'

The boy thought for a bit because he was that kind of boy, then he said, 'If I had a wish, my wish would be to take you home with me and keep you forever.'

'What?' barked the dog, his ears going round and round like satellite dishes picking up an alien signal. 'What? Woof! What? Woof! What? WO-OO-OOF!'

'I'd wish for you,' said the boy. 'My name's Tommy. What's yours?'

'Haven't got one.'

'Then I'll call you Magic,' said Tommy.

And Tommy asked his mother if he could take Magic home, and she said yes, he could keep the dog, as long as he knew that a dog is forever and not just for Christmas.

That was all right, because Tommy was a forever sort of boy.

Then Tommy and Magic ran round and round and helped Tommy's mum to collect the streamers and burst balloons and all the things that Christmas leaves behind. And they were happy because they weren't leaving behind each other.

At last Tommy's mother finished work, and off they went, all three into the frosty streets to the bus stop.

The dog trotted beside the boy, and looked into the clear sky at the star-dogs, cold and fine, and he knew that, whatever you wish, you can't wish for better than love.

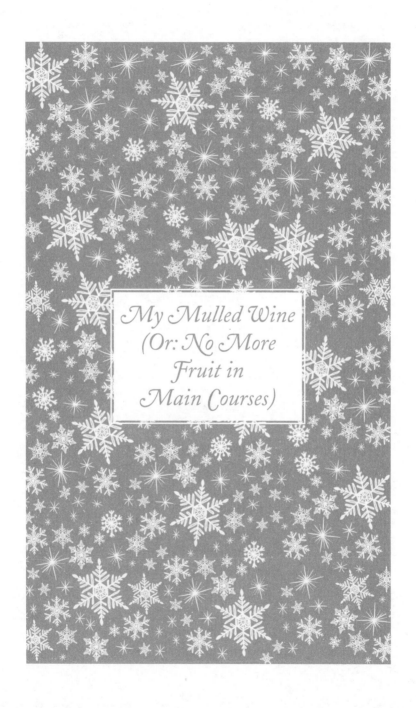

My Mulled Wine
(Or: No More
Fruit in
Main Courses)

ver Christmas-time nobody escapes without eating dried figs, satsumas, pomegranates, cinnamon, cloves, marzipan, gingerbread, all kinds of fruits and spices, often made into stollen, lebkuchen, mulled wines, hot punches, stirred puddings, and candy sticks whirled out of sugar and orange oil and hung on the Christmas tree.

If there is a stocking for Santa to fill on Christmas Eve, tradition has it that an orange is put into the toe. An orange studded with cloves in the bottom of the pan is the basis for all mulled wines.

In cold countries fresh fruit in winter used to be scarce. The orange, with its bright colour, sweet taste and injection of vitamin C was a welcome Christmas treat.

Christmas is a midwinter festival.

For most of humans' time on earth the dead of winter has been the hardest time for food, especially fresh food. The dead of winter is also the most difficult time psychologically. The days are short. The weather is harsh.

Imagine no electricity, poor roads, little travel, the daily toil to keep the fire and cooking stove going. Damp clothes, damp beds and numbing cold. None of that changes until the 20th century.

Imagine the joy of twelve days of feasting, warmth, relaxation, cheer, contemplation, singing, charity, kindness and some kind of point to life. Religious faith can protect the mind from depression and despair, not least because of the story it tells; of hope and new beginnings. And because communities are essential for mental health. The loneliness that so many people experience now at Christmas is a consequence of our loss of community – including the community provided by belonging to a church and a faith.

At a time when religious extremism hasn't been so deadly since the Crusades or the Inquisition, it is difficult to think about faith as hope, or belief as kindness to others. But Christmas, in the Christian tradition, begins with gifts – the gift of new life in the baby Jesus, the gifts of the kings to the Christ Child and the gift of God to us. There is no need to believe this to see its basis and purpose. Christmas-time is about giving.

As a festival, then, when food and warmth was harder to come by, sharing with your neighbours – loving your neighbour as yourself – could be life-saving.

And it would cheer you up.

When I was growing up we had a cherry tree on our allotment. Every year my dad covered the ripening fruits with old nylon net curtains to stop the birds stripping them. Later the fruit was bottled for Christmas.

Some of our bottled cherries were bartered for other things we wanted to eat at Christmas. Everyone we knew worked on the same system – stored apples for apple sauce swapped for sticks of Brussels sprouts, chestnuts traded for walnuts, gingerbread men exchanged for mince pies.

The story goes that in England, Elizabeth I had gingerbread men given out in her own likeness. I suppose they were gingerbread queens, and you'd think the gay community would have revived them by now.

My German friend tells me that the gingerbread houses so popular in Germany, and in the USA, started as a craze in the 19th century, after the Grimm brothers' fairy tale of Hansel and Gretel. The witch's house in that story is made of gingerbread – and we know that Christmas traditions are a bizarre mix-up of influences. That is part of their charm.

Talking about gingerbread with Nigella, she drew my attention to her gingerbread stuffing (find it in *Nigella Christmas*). This is perfect

Christmassy, spicy, fruity fare, with the zest of satsumas included. And, as she says, if you don't stuff the bird with it, you can eat slices of it cold as a kind of savoury cake.

Dried fruit and spices came to the colder northern countries from the Middle East via Spain, with its Moorish connections, and later from India. One of the many drawbacks of the British Empire was Britain's obsession with foreign food – cooked the British way. Think coronation chicken.

Throwing in dried fruit or ginger felt racy and modern at the same time as being imperialist and colonial – so it was a perfect combination for a dwindling power more comfortable with Mrs Beeton than the Beatles.

Mrs Winterson made her own Boxing Day turkey curry, which I cannot reproduce here, but which was a version of coronation chicken, fried up with curry powder, crystallised ginger and sultanas.

It is no wonder that in England in the 1970s there used to be a political party called No More Fruit in Main Courses.

This was at a time when anyone could stand for parliament – the financial outlay being low, and eccentricity still being a British virtue.

Too many of us were being forced to eat prunes and mashed potato, duck à l'orange made with tinned mandarin segments, or tinned tuna and sliced apricot halves. Curry sauces made using lime or mango jelly mixtures were common.

At Christmas things only got worse as some vague idea of Bethlehem being in the East took hold of the nation's kitchens.

Two other recipes in this book – one Pakistani and one Jewish – handle fruit and spice with the deftness you'd expect, but for now I'll leave you with a mulled wine – it's got fruit, it's got spice, and you don't have to eat it.

*

Imagine yourself a hundred years ago arriving at an inn in the snow and the cold and wanting something warming with a boozy, snoozy effect. There you are, standing by the log fire, your chilled hands round a cup of warm wine that is aromatic and pleasing.

To me, drinking mulled wine in a party dress in an overheated room is a bit odd.

Mulled wine is great to decant into a flask and take on a winter walk with a slice of Christmas cake and a hunk of cheese in your pocket.

Author's note: mulled wine is more of a spell than a recipe. A steaming pan of dark liquid looks and smells like a witchy brew. Use your nose. Taste as you go along. Experiment.

YOU NEED

Bottle or two of decent red wine

A couple of glasses of ruby port

Fresh orange studded with fresh cloves. I know this takes ages to do, but small children and old people like doing it. Good moment to listen to another chapter of that audiobook...

Small piece of peeled root ginger

Cinnamon stick

Fresh bay leaf

Raw cane sugar

About the wine: don't believe anyone who tells you that any old red will do. A headache is a headache. Buy a good, straightforward claret. A wine merchant's everyday claret will serve you better here than a dash to the supermarket wine lake. If you wouldn't drink the wine from the bottle, why would you drink it from the pan?

About the port: nothing fancy, but my maxim is: one liver, one life. Some people throw in a dash of brandy, and if I don't have any port I just use claret.

METHOD

Put the studded orange in a heavy-bottomed pan and pour in the wine and port. Add the other ingredients, except for the sugar, and heat slowly and gently. Once the mixture is warm, add sugar to taste. The level of sweetness is entirely up to you.

Don't let the mixture boil or you will boil off the alcohol.

You can gently reheat the wine later.

I like mulled wine at eleven o'clock in the morning, when I've finished my winter jobs outside, or at four or five o'clock in the afternoon, when the day is done and it's not time for drinks or dinner. Enjoy it with gingerbread and cheese.

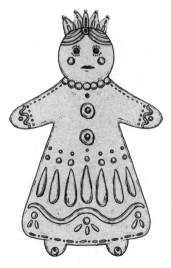

A GHOST STORY

n the Bernese Oberland of Switzerland is the famous ski resort of Mürren.

Mürren cannot be reached by road. You must arrive by train at Lauterbrunnen and from there take the cable car to the village.

Three peaks stare you down: the Eiger, the Mönch and the Jungfrau.

The British started going to Mürren in 1912.

That was the year Captain Scott died at the North Pole. There was much talk of him that year, talk of his heroism and his sacrifice, talk of how the British must bear their burden of Empire, half the world coloured pink like a tin of salmon.

Then the war came.

When the British returned to Mürren in any number the year was 1924. Arnold Lunn pitched up with his father, Sir Henry, a minister who had failed to convert the Indians in Calcutta to Methodism, and who had decided, instead, to evangelise the British to the glory of the Alps.

It was young Arnold who fell in love with skiing and who established downhill skiing as a competitive sport – rather than just the fastest way to get to the bottom of the hill.

Although it *was* the fastest way to get to the bottom of the hill. In 1928, Arnold and some friends climbed to the top of the Schilthorn, above Mürren, and skied the fourteen hair-raising, eyebrow-stripping, gut-churning, knee-wrecking, leg-breaking, mind-numbing, heart-soaring kilometres down to Lauterbrunnen. They enjoyed it so much they did it again. And again. They called the race the Inferno.

And every year the world comes here to do it again too.

My friends and I are not Inferno material. Rather we rag-bag along at the start of each New Year, putting aside our lives around the world and meeting to share old times. We've worked together, or been at college together, or been neighbours, until one or the other moved away. Wives and husbands are not allowed on the trip. This is a friendship club. It's pleasingly old-fashioned in the age of Facebook. We don't upload. We don't really keep in touch that much over the year.

But if we're alive we'll be here, in Mürren, every New Year.

We stay at the Palace Hotel and organise the first dinner for ourselves on January 3rd.

It was after a good dinner of trout and potatoes, sitting in front of a blazing log fire, drinking coffee or brandy or both, that one of our number proposed that we tell ghost stories, real ones – supernatural happenings that had happened to us.

Mike was like that – a larger-than-life type with an appetite for anything new. Since last year, he said, he'd been researching the paranormal.

When we asked him why, he claimed it had started here, in Mürren. So why hadn't he told us about it before?

'I wasn't sure. And I thought you'd laugh at me.'

We were laughing at him. Who believes in ghosts except kids and old ladies?

Mike leaned forward, holding up his hand to stop the flow of quips and comments about ghostbusters and so many drinks he was seeing double.

'I wasn't drunk,' said Mike. 'It was daytime. You were all on the chairlifts for the slalom. I decided to go cross-country, clear my head – you know I was having difficulty with my marriage last year.'

Suddenly he was serious. So we listened.

Mike said, 'I was alone, skiing pretty fast on the pass above us. I saw someone else, higher up, frighteningly high up, like he was skiing on a tightrope. I waved and hollered, but the figure went on. It was like he was airborne. I got myself going again, thinking I'd try and find this guy who skis in thin air, later, in the bar, and then about an hour afterwards I saw the same man. He seemed to be looking for something.

'I skied across to help him out. I said, "You lost something, buddy?"'

'He looked at me – I'll never forget that look; eyes milk-blue like the blue of the sun on the snow in the morning. He asked me the time. I told him. He said he was missing his ice axe. I thought maybe he was a geologist, you know? He had a knapsack that looked specialist.

'He was dressed real strange. Like he'd just gone out in his clothes with his skis on. Thick seaman sweater – no hi-vis microfibre. He wore boots – but they were old leather things with those long wrap-around laces they used to have. And his skis – I'm not kidding you, they were wooden; can you believe that?

'But it wasn't just those things. I had the sensation that I was looking through him. That he was made of glass or ice. I couldn't actually see through him, but the feeling was real. He didn't seem to want company so I skied off a little way and then I turned back. And there was no one there.'

We had listened in silence. Then we all butted in at once. We all had our own explanations to offer: they do historic skiing demonstrations here sometimes – the old skis, the heavy clothes, that kind of thing. And Mike admitted he had been tired and more than a little strung-out. The air can do that to you.

None of that equalled ghost. Mike shook his head. 'I'm telling you, I saw something. I've been trying to understand it all year. There's no explanation. A man comes out of nowhere and goes back into nowhere.'

While we were arguing, one of the managers here, Fabrice, came over, offered us drinks on the house and asked if he could join us.

'It's ghost night, Fabrice,' said Mike. 'You ever heard anything like this here?'

Mike started to repeat the whole thing. I got up and excused myself. I wanted a little air. When you first arrive here it takes time to adjust. The fire and the brandy were making me sleepy but I didn't want to go to bed. So I went outside, intending to walk round the hotel.

I like looking back into rooms filled with people. I like the silent-movie feel of it. I used to do it when I was a girl, watching my parents and sisters, knowing they couldn't see me.

Now, in the crisp, starry air, I looked in and saw my party, my friends, laughing, animated. I smiled to myself. Then, as I was watching, another guest came through the library. No one I recognised. You get to know the usual faces. This one was young and strong. He carried his body well.

Judging from his clothes, he was British. He wore wool trousers, khaki shirt and short tie, fitted tweed jacket. The timeless look the

Brits do well. He didn't even glance at our group; took a book from one of the shelves and disappeared through a door set in the panelling. The library is modelled on a gentleman's club of about a hundred years ago: leather, wood, warmth, books, animal paintings, old photos in frames, newspapers.

I went back inside – the others were having a good time, but I still wasn't in the mood. Tiredness, I think. On impulse I followed the man the way he had gone. The hotel had had some renovations recently. I thought I might have a look at what they had done.

But when I went through the door I realised I was in the oldest part of the hotel. Probably the service side.

I could see the man's legs disappearing up a narrow staircase. Why did I go after him? I wasn't trying to pick him up or anything. But I experience a freedom here – actually a recklessness. It's the air. The air is radiant here; it's like breathing light.

I followed him.

At the top of the stairs a low glow came from a room with a small door under the eaves. The room looked like it had been tucked in as an afterthought. I hesitated. Through the half-open door I could see the man with his back to me, turning over the pages of a book. I knocked at the door. He looked round. I pushed the door open.

'Did you bring the hot water?' he said.

Then he realised his mistake.

'Don't apologise,' I said. 'I'm the one who's disturbing you. I'm with that noisy group downstairs.'

The young man looked puzzled. He was broad-shouldered, rangy, built like a rower or a climber. He had taken off his tweed jacket. His trousers were held up with braces. He stood in his shirt and tie, touchingly formal and vulnerable in that formal and vulnerable way that Englishmen can be.

'I was going to settle down to read this book about Everest,' he said. 'I shall be going there later in the year. Come in. Please. Would you like to come in?'

I went in. The room was not at all like a hotel room here. There was a low fire burning in the grate and a single divan pushed against one wall. There was a wash-jug and bowl on a nightstand. A heavy leather case lay half-unpacked in the middle of the room, a pair of striped pyjamas rumpled on the top. Two candles dripped on the mantelpiece. There was an oil lamp on a desk by the window. An upright chair matched the desk, and a pink velvet armchair was drawn close to the fire. There didn't appear to be any electricity.

He followed my gaze. 'I'm not rich. The other rooms are better. Well, I'm sure you know that. But this is cosy. Would you like to sit down? The armchair is quite comfortable. Please…Miss…?'

'Hi, I'm Molly,' I said, holding out my hand.

'Sandy,' he said. 'You must be American.'

'Why?'

'You don't sound American, but you seem very sure of yourself.'

I laughed. 'I knew I was intruding… I'll go.'

'No! I mean it, please…my terrible manners. Sit by the fire. Go on. Please.'

He rummaged in a knapsack that seemed to be made of canvas and pockets, and came out with a hip flask. 'Will you have a brandy?'

He poured us two generous amounts in tooth tumblers.

'I've never seen this part of the hotel. It's so quaint. I guess they never restored it. Is it part of their historic?'

Sandy looked puzzled again. 'Historic what?'

'You know, the demos they do – skiing the Arnold Lunn way, all of that.'

'Do you know Arnold Lunn?'

'I know of him – if you stay here, who doesn't?'

'Yes, he's quite a character, isn't he? Do you know the Sherlock Holmes connection?'

I didn't know it, and I could see he wanted to tell me. He was so eager and enthusiastic. He leaned forward, pushing up his sleeves. His skin was bone-white.

'The old man, Sir Henry, Arnold's father, loved those adventures, read them aloud round the fire at night – said they're made to be read aloud, and I agree. At any rate, Conan Doyle was in the Bernese Oberland with Sir Henry, on one of his Alps tours, and Conan Doyle was mooching around in a pretty mournful state because he wanted to kill off Sherlock Holmes so that he could devote his life to paranormal research. Can you believe it? Paranormal research! And stop writing bloody detective stories.'

Sandy was nodding, laughing at this. He took a big gulp of his brandy and poured us both an extra shot. His hands were big, strong, and the whitest hands I have ever seen on a man.

'It's pleasant to have company,' he said. I smiled at him. He really was good-looking.

'I didn't know Arthur Conan Doyle believed in the supernatural.'

'Oh, yes – he converted to Spiritualism. Absolutely believed in it. So Sir Henry, though he didn't want to see the back of Sherlock Holmes, wanted to help his friend out, so he said, "Push Holmes over the Reichenbach Falls." Conan Doyle had never heard of the Reichenbach Falls, had no idea where they were. Sir Henry, a great expert in the Alps, took Conan Doyle to the falls and Conan Doyle knew he had found his answer. And that's how Holmes and Moriarty died. I so enjoyed that story: "The Final Problem".'

'If you have to go, you might as well do it sensationally,' I said. 'And you might even stage a comeback.'

His face changed. Pain and fear. 'Hold on to the rope.'

'What? I don't follow.'

Sandy passed his hand across his head. 'Sorry. I'm rambling. That is, I mean to say, the English prefer to live well rather than live long.'

'Really?'

'There were so many chaps, just too young to fight in the war, who never forgave themselves for not making the ultimate sacrifice. Those chaps would take on anything, go anywhere, do anything.'

'Why would anyone needlessly risk their own life?'

'For something glorious? Why would you not risk your life?'

'Would you?'

'Certainly. It's different for women.'

'Because we have children?'

'I suppose so. Though now you have the vote…'

'Exercising your democratic rights doesn't interfere with child-birth.'

'I suppose not.'

He looked into the fire. 'Would you like to come skiing with me tomorrow? I know some interesting routes. You look strong enough.'

'I'll take that as a compliment. Yes, why not? That would be a pleasure. When you talk about the war, Sandy, you mean…'

'The Great War.'

I guessed he must be following the centenary coverage. I said, 'I wouldn't risk my life for anything. Death is too final.'

He nodded slowly, his eyes on me like blue lasers. 'Do you not believe in the Afterlife?'

'Not at all. Do you?'

He was silent. I liked his earnestness. He hadn't checked his smartphone once. And he read books. Old ones. I could see the one he had borrowed, open on the little desk where he had put it down.

'It's not a question of belief,' he said, finally. 'It is what it is.'

I didn't want to get into another debate about what happens when we're dead, so I changed the subject.

'Did you say you are going to climb Everest?'

'Yes. It's an official British expedition. I'm in charge of the oxygen cylinders, nothing glamorous. I don't expect I'll get to the summit, but it's an honour to be chosen. Everyone else is much more experienced than me. I've always been fascinated by mountains and wilderness. Cold mountains. Cold wilderness. When I was a boy I devoured all I could get my hands on about Captain Scott and the Antarctic – and that cheater Amundsen.'

'Amundsen used dogs not ponies. That wasn't cheating.'

'He should never have run against Scott to start with. Ours was a scientific expedition. He was just going for glory.'

'Welcome to the modern world.'

'Cheap. I don't want to be cheap.'

'Why do you want to climb Everest?'

'Mallory said it better than I can: "*Because it's there.*"'

He was white and monumental like marble. Perhaps it was the fire dying down, or that my face was flushed with brandy, or perhaps it was the moon shining in through the bare, bright window. He might have been carved from moonrock, this boy.

'How old are you, Sandy?'

'Twenty-two. I can't ask you the same question because it's not done to ask a lady her age.'

'I'm forty.'

Sandy shook his head. 'You're far too handsome to be forty. I hope you don't mind me calling you handsome. Rather than beautiful.'

I didn't mind at all.

'I'm leaving for the Himalayas in April. By way of Darjeeling. Then to a monastery right at the foot of the mountain. Rongbuk. We'll stay there. The monks believe that the mountain – Everest – sings. That the music is too high-pitched for us to hear, but certain of the Buddhist masters can hear it.'

'That's a bit too mystical for me.'

'Is it? When you're here at Mürren, don't you feel light-headed?'

'Well, yes, I do, but that's because of the thinness of the air. It's physiological. It's—'

Sandy interrupted me. 'People feel light-headed on mountains because the solid world dematerialises. We are not the dimensional objects we believe ourselves to be.'

'Are you a Buddhist?'

Sandy shook his head impatiently. I was failing him, I could tell. He tried again, looking directly at me. Those eyes...

'When I am climbing I understand that gravity exists to protect us from our lightness of being, in the same way that time is what shields us from eternity.'

When he spoke I felt a chill. Something cold entered me like sitting in a room where the temperature is dropping. Then I saw that there was ice on the inside of the windowpane.

Sandy was looking past me now. As though he had forgotten I was there. And I noticed something odd about those eyes. He doesn't blink, I thought.

When he spoke again it was with a wild despair in his voice. 'I never sought to avoid the overwhelming fire of existence. It's not death that's to be feared. It's eternity. Do you understand?'

'I don't think I do, Sandy.'

'Death – it's a way out, isn't it? No matter how deeply we fear it, isn't there relief that there will be a way out?'

'I've never thought about dying.'

He got up and went to the window. 'What if I told you that dying isn't a way out?'

'I'm not religious.'

'You'll find out. When it comes to it, you'll find out for yourself.'

I stood up. There was no clock in the room. I checked my watch. The glass had broken.

'Broken, is it?' said Sandy. His voice was far-off, as if he was talking to someone else. 'You should put it in your pocket.'

'I must have banged it.'

'This bloody shale. The mountain is rotten.'

'What mountain? The Eiger?'

'Not the Eiger – Everest. I always thought that name was a joke – that pitiless, relentless rock, no pause, no sleep, wind speeds of a hundred and fifty miles an hour if you're unlucky, and you are always unlucky – and the British called it Ever Rest. Do you suppose he was thinking of the dead?'

'Who, Sandy, who was thinking of the dead?'

'Sir George Everest. You don't think a mountain in the Himalayas was named Everest by the Tibetans or the Nepalese, do you? Royal Geographical Society 1865 – named after the Surveyor General of India, Sir George Everest. To his credit he objected – said it couldn't be written or pronounced in Hindi. To them Everest will always be the Holy Mother.'

'Strange kind of a mother who kills so many of her children,' I said.

'There are sacred places,' said Sandy. 'Places we should not go. I didn't know that until we stayed at the monastery in Rongbuk.'

'You've already been there? I thought you were going.'

'Yes. Yes. What time is it? The sun has gone down.' He seemed confused. I decided to carry on the British way, as though nothing had happened.

'The Chinese destroyed the original Rongbuk Monastery in the Cultural Revolution back in '74, didn't they?'

Sandy wasn't listening to me. He was on his knees searching in his knapsack, his big body curled over like a child's. 'I have lost my ice axe.'

I knew I had to get out now. I stood up to put on my coat. My feet were numb. I was colder than I realised. The room was slowly petrifying. Whitening. The warm tones of polished wood had bleached, like a bone in the sun, like a body left on a mountainside. The fire had gone out, its ash a mountain of its own, grey and useless. The curtains looked like sheets of ice framing the frosted window.

I was shivering now. The back of my neck felt wet. The pink velvet chair was spotting darker. As Sandy kneeled I saw his khaki shirt had snowflakes on it. Frightening. Beautiful. Can they be the same thing? It had begun to snow inside the room.

'Sandy! Get your jacket. Come with me.'

His eyes were such a pale blue.

The wind started up. Like the snow, the wind was inside the room. The wind was raising and dropping the lid of the leather suitcase on the floor. The room was rattling. The wind blew out the candles on the mantelshelf. The oil lamp was still alight but the clear flame was faltering now, and the inside of the glass canopy was fogging with carbon dioxide. The air in the room is too thin. The wind is blowing but there is no air. Sandy was standing motionless by the window.

'Sandy! Come on!'

'May I kiss you?'

Absurd. We're about to die and he wants to kiss me. I don't know why, but I went towards him. I put my hand on his chest, stood on tiptoe, as he bent his head. I will never forget that feeling of his lips, the burning cold of his lips. As I opened my mouth, just a little, he breathed in through his mouth, like I was an oxygen cylinder – that was the picture in my mind.

He breathed in and I felt my lungs contract with the force of the air rushing out of me. His hand was on my hip, gently, resting there, so cold, so cold. And now my lips were burning too.

I pulled away, gasping for air, my lungs ballooning with the effort. He was less pale now, his cheeks stung with colour. He said, 'Hold on to the rope.'

I was at the door. I had to use both hands to get it open against the drift of snow piled against it. I half-ran, half-fell down the steep stairs, stumbling in the dark. I found my way, somehow, back to the main part of the hotel. I had to get help.

The bar was closed. The library where we had been sitting after dinner was deserted. The fire had long since gone out. I ran through into the lobby. The nightman was on the desk. He seemed surprised to see me. I said, 'Where is everyone?'

He raised his eyebrows and spread his hands. 'It is four-forty in the morning, madam. The hotel is in bed.'

I had hardly been gone an hour. But this was not the time to argue. 'The young man who's staying in the old part of the hotel – he's going to freeze to death.'

'There is no one in the old part of the hotel, madam.'

'Yes! Through the door at the end of the library – I'll show you!'

The nightman picked up his keys and his torch and came with me. We went back through the library to the door in the panelling. I turned the handle. The door didn't open. I was pumping the handle up and down, shaking it. 'Open it! Open it!' The nightman gently put a hand on my arm.

'That is not a door, madam; it is for the decoration only.'

'But there is a staircase on the other side. A room – I'm telling you, I was there!'

The nightman shook his head, smiling. 'We can look again in the morning, perhaps. May I escort you to your own room?'

He thinks I'm drunk. He thinks I'm crazy.

I went to my bedroom. 5am. I lay down wide-awake and woke with a start, the sun on my face, slanting through the open blinds. Outside I could hear the noise and bustle of the day. And I was in agony.

I looked in the mirror. My lips were frostbitten.

I showered, changed, coated my lips in Vaseline and went downstairs. Some of our party were standing in the lobby with their skis. 'Hey! What happened to you last night? You just disappeared!'

Mike was there. 'Did you see a ghost?'

General laughter.

I asked Mike to come with me. First we went to the door in the panelling.

'It's faux,' said Mike. 'For the olde-worlde look.'

I made him come outside with me, around the back, where the window should have been.

But there was no window. I tried to explain. I was babbling like a fool. The kiss. The rope. Everest. The boy was going to climb Everest. Mike's face changed. 'Come and talk to Fabrice,' he said.

Fabrice was in his office surrounded by paperwork and coffee cups. He did not seem surprised by anything I said. When I had finished he nodded, glancing first at Mike, and then at me.

'It is not the first time this young man has been seen on the mountain, but it is the first time he has been seen at the hotel. The room you describe – it used to exist, nearly a hundred years ago; look, I will show you the photographs.'

There was the Palace Hotel in the early days of the Alps tours. A party of men holding wooden skis stood outside, smiling. Fabrice pointed them out with his pen.

'Sir Henry Lunn. His son, Arnold Lunn…'

As he was talking I interrupted. 'That's him! That's Sandy.'

'*Voilà,*' said Fabrice. 'That is Mr Andrew Irvine. You know the name perhaps?'

Mike's voice was low and not steady. 'The guy who climbed Everest with George Mallory?'

'That is the one. Irvine and Mallory failed to return from their attempt to reach the summit on June 8th 1924. Unlike Mallory, Irvine's body has never been found.'

'And he stayed here,' I said.

'As you see. Staying in a third-class room in the hotel. He was a remarkable young man. Born in 1902. A gifted mechanic and engineer. The story goes that Mallory chose him as his partner for the final fatal climb because only Irvine could fix the oxygen cylinders.'

'How did he die?'

'No one knows. Mallory's body was not found until 1999, the rope still round his waist.'

Suddenly I can see Sandy, in the white-out. 'Hold on to the rope!'

'Excuse me?'

'Nothing. Nothing.'

We were silent, all three. What can you say?

Eventually Fabrice spoke. 'Irvine's ice axe was found in 1933. No clues since. But if they do find his body some day, there'll be a camera round his neck, and the people at Kodak say it is likely that the film will be able to be developed. So perhaps we will know if Mallory and Irvine reached the summit of Everest.'

I took my broken watch out of my pocket and put it on the desk.

'That's strange,' said Fabrice. 'Mallory's watch was found in his pocket, broken. Broken perhaps at the moment when time stopped for him.'

'Look at this,' said Mike. He handed me his iPad.

And joy is, after all, the end of life. We do not live to eat and make money. We eat and make money to be able to enjoy life. That is what life means and what life is for.
George Mallory. New York City. 1923

Like everyone else I douse my spirit in materiality, weight my ankles like a deep-sea diver. Refuse the call, because to answer it would be to live in the see-through air, to step off the mountain, to go and not come back.

The overwhelming fires of existence.

And the snow is falling round them. And the sky is over their heads. And in their eyes the old stars, lighting cold and bleak, in different skies.

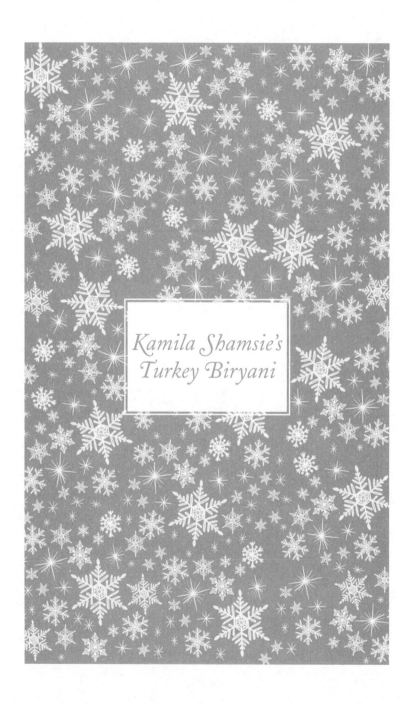

Kamila Shamsie's
Turkey Biryani

or the holiday season last year my wife, Susie Orbach, was thinking about preparing her usual feast.

I said, 'Why don't I cook this year?' She looked horrified. Susie is an excellent cook. When we met I was an enthusiastic cook, but I soon realised that she didn't want to eat any of my food – roasts, stews, pies, casseroles, sausage and mash, that kind of thing. I bought a Yiddish dictionary to find out what goyishe chazerai meant.

Our friend, the Pakistani writer Kamila Shamsie was visiting Susie and me that December, and I asked her about Christmas in Karachi, her home city of twenty-five million people. She told me a wonderful story, heard on American news, about the great support for the Taliban in Karachi, as evidenced by stick-on Taliban beards being sold at traffic lights.

Kamila had called a friend in Karachi to verify this interesting detail – it turned out that the beards in question were the usual Santa Claus beards popular at the time of year.

Kamila Shamsie is many things, including a wonderful writer, and she diplomatically managed the shoot-out between Susie and me last Christmas by offering to cook her own Pakistani version of a Christmas-time meal.

Not to be left out, I made pheasant casserole from the Mary Berry Aga cookbook. I am glad to say that lots of our guests ate it, but there is no doubt that Kamila's turkey – don't call it curry – was the best.

This recipe came out of our discussion about fruit in main courses (see my recipe for mulled wine on page 193). As Kamila said, 'The British colonised half the world and still ate boiled cabbage.'

So for those of you who like dried fruit and fresh spices and have too much turkey on your hands, try this – reproduced by kind permission of the cook.

Kamila says: Turkeys are not birds you're likely to see in Pakistan so I can't explain why there were two of them at a farm in Punjab, which belonged to family friends, that Christmas in 1980 when I was seven years old.

The first turkey made its way to our plates on the day my parents and sister and I arrived, and, having never seen it in living form, I had no qualms about eating it – roasted, 'English-style'. But the next day five of us – my sister and I and the three siblings of the family we were staying with – heard an extraordinary noise, which we followed to an even more extraordinary sight: a puffed-up beast, all feathers and wattle and beak. We named him Aha!. (There were also, on the farm, two ducks whom we had named Déjà Vu and Voulez-Vous. We didn't speak French but there was a café, recently opened, in Karachi named Déjà Vu and we all knew the ABBA song 'Voulez-Vous'. And because the chorus of that song went '*Voulez-vous*...aha!' it gave us the name for the turkey.)

This Aha! was soon discovered to have a characteristic that provided us with endless delight: if you raised your voice and spoke or sang to him in tones of a certain pitch he would reply, in 'Turkish', for exactly the length of time that you had addressed him. '*Voulez-vous*...aha!' we would sing. 'Gurgle gobble yip,' he'd reply. 'The hussy! – Ought to be ashamed of herself!' we'd say (a favourite line from the musical 'Oklahoma!'). 'Gurgle yip gobble yip-bark gobble gurgle,' sent back the turkey.

This story doesn't end well, of course.

One day, Aha! disappeared. 'He's run away with a wild turkey,' we were told and, to give this story credence, children and adults set off to try and find him. 'A wild-turkey chase,' we all cried out as we set off on foot, and in Jeeps, past the cotton fields and sugar-cane fields and orange groves and onto the sand dunes, which mysteriously bordered the verdant farm.

Aha! was never found, and it wasn't until well into adulthood that two of the children who had been on the farm told me the terrible, inescapable truth: Aha! hadn't eloped romantically into the desert; he had ended up on a chopping block.

But what happened after that?

'We ate the turkey that night,' the siblings insisted, and continue to insist.

'No,' I said. 'We had turkey the first night, before we knew Aha!. I wouldn't have held on to the turkey-elopement story for all these years if he'd appeared on our plates for dinner.'

Looking back, I can only surmise that we must have eaten the turkey in disguise. At the end of that day of searching, something would have appeared on our plates, presented as chicken, and I would have munched down on it thinking the darker flavour was the taste of my sorrow.

I dislike a plot with holes and so I'm compelled to imagine that in-disguise meal of Aha!.

I like to think it was turkey biryani.

That seems a fitting send-off for a bird of panache, one who offered so much by way of delight – down to the last morsel.

Overleaf you will find my left-over turkey biryani recipe (gobble gobble gobblegobble).

*

YOU NEED

Left-over turkey, diced (or if you want to start from scratch, roast a couple of turkey legs and then chop up the meat into cubes. The skin you can discard or devour as you choose – fowl skin never finds its way into Pakistani cooking.). I'll suggest 500 g, but really it depends how much turkey meat you have left. You can adjust other quantities in this recipe as need be.

500 g rice. Only basmati will do. Please believe me on this point. (I use Tilda.)

2 large onions, chopped finely

1 tablespoon grated ginger

3 garlic cloves, crushed

Red chopped chilli or 1 teaspoon chilli powder (or more, depending on your tastebuds)

1 teaspoon turmeric powder

1 teaspoon salt (can be adjusted, as can all ingredients here, to suit your particular needs/desires)

8 green cardamom pods

6 cloves

1 teaspoon whole black pepper

1 cinnamon stick

1 tablespoon coriander seed

3 medium tomatoes, diced

100 ml milk (if feeling extravagant – and why not? – infuse a little saffron in the milk when you start preparing the biryani)

Handful of large raisins (optional)

Handful of cashew nuts (optional)

*

METHOD

Do this well ahead of time, if it makes life easier:

Rinse the rice until the water runs clear. Place in a pan and add 500 ml water. Cook on a high-ish heat until the water is absorbed (approx 8-10 minutes). The rice should be parboiled. If you think the rice is cooking too fast and the water hasn't been completely absorbed, just strain out the excess water. I get the rice-to-water quantity right about two times out of three – possibly because I don't actually measure out the water before placing it in the pan. The parboiling is what matters most here – if you press down on a grain of rice it should be mostly yielding, but with a hard centre. Fluff it all up with a fork to prevent the rice kernels from sticking together as it cools.

In a separate pan, cook the onions over a high heat until they are golden brown. This is an important step. The heat should really be high and nothing less than golden brown will do. Of course, you'll need a generous quantity of oil so that the onions don't stick to the bottom. Remove a tablespoon of the fried onions and set aside to use for garnish later.

Add all the spices to the onions that remain in the pan. Stir them about for a minute or two – they should start to release a fantastic fragrance. (Not everyone loves the fragrance of frying onions and spices – one way to counter it is to place a stick of cinnamon on the stove in boiling water. That will absorb the scent.) Add the diced tomatoes to the spice mix, and turn down the heat to low. Cook until the tomatoes and spices form a thick paste (you may need to add a tiny bit of water if the mixture appears to be sticking to the pan). This should take 15-20 minutes (trust your eyes more than you trust the timing I'm giving you).

Add the turkey and cook for around 10 minutes, still on a low heat, so it can absorb the flavours.

If necessary at the end, turn the heat up high for a few minutes to absorb any excess liquid.

Do this 40 minutes before you're ready to serve:

Grease a casserole dish. Spoon a third of the rice onto the bottom of the dish. Sprinkle milk on top. Layer half the spiced turkey mix on the rice. Add another layer of rice. Sprinkle milk on top. Add the rest of the spiced turkey. Then cover with the remaining rice. Sprinkle milk, the fried onions you had set aside and a generous quantity of shredded coriander leaves on top. Cover with foil or a lid. Place in the oven at 180°C for about half an hour, maybe slightly more.

Final optional step – depending on how deeply you've been scarred by fruit and nuts DONE WRONG in Christmas food:

Fry the raisins in a little oil until they swell up. Set aside. Fry cashews for a minute or so.

Before serving the turkey biryani, scatter the raisins and cashews on top.

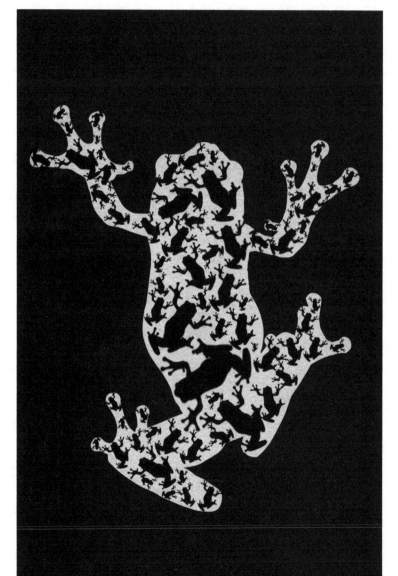

THE SILVER FROG

rs Reckitt's Establishment for Orphans was preparing to celebrate Christmas.

In the spacious entrance hall stood a mighty spruce tree soon to be decorated with impressive ornaments.

On the front door hung a holly wreath the size of a lifebelt. That the front door was black was perhaps unfortunate, as the combination of the sombre colour and the wintry wreath had something of the funeral parlour about it.

Yet the brass knocker was polished to a shine and the brisk bell-pull gleamed for visitors. And visitors there were: the great and good of Soot Town were coming to Christmas dinner.

Soot Town had paid for the dinner, in honour of the day, and in charity towards the poor, parentless children who had taken shelter under Mrs Reckitt's ample wings.

Had she been a bird it is unlikely that Mrs Reckitt could have flown far – or indeed flown at all – for in most respects Mrs Reckitt resembled a giant turkey. Not a wild turkey. No. A bred bronze bird with a substantial breast, a folded neck, a small head and legs – but no one had ever seen Mrs Reckitt's legs, the fashion of the times being for concealment. Suffice to say that her legs, assuming she had them, were of the turkey type. That is, not designed for travel.

If in most respects the lady resembled the celebrated bird of the Christmas feast, in one singular respect she bore another resemblance. Mrs Reckitt had the face of a crocodile. Her jaw was long, her mouth was wide. Large teeth lurked inside it. Her eyes were small and crêped and protruded from her face with an expression of watchful murderousness. The skin on her neck and décolletage had more of handbag than human about it. But she was not green. No, Mrs Reckitt was not green. She was pink.

And, as everyone in Soot Town agreed, a delightful and compassionate pink-flushed widow.

The cause of the late Mr Reckitt's end is unknown. It is enough to know that he is dead and that the couple had no children.

Mrs Reckitt said it herself, often, with crocodile tears in her crocodile eyes. Her orphanage therefore became that happy collision of chance and charity, allowing her the family denied her by fate.

Orphans were collected from near and far and hospitably housed in the large villa paid for by subscription from Soot Town.

That Christmas the house was full of children. Orphans were the core business, but certain parents, having obligations elsewhere, from time to time boarded their offspring with Mrs Reckitt. The fees were considerable, but, as she said herself, remark the service.

Visitors to the Villa of Glory, as Mrs Reckitt liked to call her establishment, were regularly impressed by the cheerful, bright parlour where the girls did their sewing in front of a warm fire.

In the garden stood a workshop where the boys made and mended useful objects. There was a schoolroom, an allotment, a lily pond and two dormitories. Each little metal bedstead had a warm quilt on top and a button-eyed bear perched on the nightstand.

And Christmas – ah, well, Christmas. 'Tis the season to be jolly.

That morning the children were decorating the Christmas tree. It stood in the hall, a gift from the lumber-yard on the edge of town. Strong men had cut it down and put it upright again. Its lower branches were deep as a forest. Its feathery top was far away like a green bird.

The children, in their brown overalls, stood looking at the tree. Mrs Reckitt looked at the children.

'Any child who breaks a glass bauble will be locked in the coal house without dinner,' said Mrs Reckitt. 'And why is the ladder too short to reach the top of the tree? Do I keep you idle boys to sit in woodwork classes learning to make ladders that are too short?'

Reginald put up his hand. 'Please, Mrs Reckitt, it isn't safe to make a stepladder taller than this one. A stepladder is an A-frame, Mrs Reckitt, yes, and...'

Mrs Reckitt's pink face was deepening towards red. She came forward and regarded Reginald through her pearl eye-glass. Reginald realised that Mrs Reckitt didn't blink. 'Well, then,' she said, 'if that is the tallest ladder you can make, you will have to balance a chair on top of the ladder, and then you shall balance yourself on top of the chair, and you will PUT the FAIRY on top of the tree. Do you hear me?'

It was impossible not to hear her. The children were silent. The chair was fetched. Reginald could hardly lift it. Maud stepped forward. 'Please, Mrs Reckitt, Reginald can't climb the ladder with the chair. He has a twisted foot.'

Mrs Reckitt looked down at Reginald's heavy black boot. 'If there is one thing I dislike more than orphans, it is crippled orphans,' she said, inspecting Reginald as though she might be considering eating him. 'Ronald, are you a crippled orphan or an orphaned cripple? HA HA HA HA HA.'

Then she turned to Maud. 'Very well, Mavis. I see you are the smallest child we have here – failure to thrive is always disappointing, but in this case useful. Climb the tree.'

Maud looked at the tree stretching upwards towards the ornate plasterwork ceiling. The topmost top of the tree was directly underneath the chin of a cherub.

'Up you go, straight up the middle, and place this fairy at the top.' Mrs Reckitt got out the fairy. She was made of cloth with raffia hair. 'Carry her between your teeth. Like this.' There was a terrified and disbelieving OOH and AAH sound from the orphans as Mrs Reckitt put the hapless fairy in her mouth. Holding it there, she carried on talking without any difficulty. 'In my day orphans climbed chimneys twenty times higher than this silly tree, and it never did them any harm.' She removed the fairy from her mouth – its presence had reminded her that she was hungry. 'It is time for my mid-morning sausage roll. When I return this fairy had better be on the top of the tree. And mind what I said: if you break one single, solitary glass bauble, it's the coal hole for you!'

Mrs Reckitt swept off towards her sausage roll. Reginald put the cloth fairy between Maud's teeth.

Maud realised that she had to get to the centre of the tree and climb up the trunk. The tree smelled of resin and winter. The lower branches were so thick that it was like being inside her own private forest. The world was green. Maud couldn't see the other children any more. She was lost in the wood like Gretel.

The tree was scratchy and the pine needles were well-named. Soon her hands and feet were bleeding and big red marks criss-crossed her face. She daren't open her eyes or look up. She was getting cold and her face was wet. She had the strange sensation that it was snowing inside the tree.

Up she went. She was thinking about her mother, who had died when Maud was a baby. Her father had given her to an aunt, the aunt had given her to a cousin, the cousin had given her to a neighbour, the neighbour had given her to a rag-and-bone man. The rag-and-bone man, collecting old clothes and broken pans in Soot Town, had sold her for a drink at the Baby in Half. The landlord had never seen such a small child. He thought she might live in a bottle on the bar, next to a stuffed owl. Good for business.

But Maud had other plans and she ran away. She was caught stealing eggs to eat, taken to prison and rescued by one of those well-meaning old gentlemen who imagine that all a child needs is bread and butter and discipline.

At Reckitt's Academy for Orphans, Foundlings and Minors in Need of Temporary Office, there was discipline. And occasionally bread and butter. But there was not play. And there was not hope. And there was not warmth. And there was not love.

Maud was nine when she came here.

'Stunted,' said Mrs Reckitt when she inspected her for the first time. 'Useful for drains and retrieving small objects from gratings.'

Maud was given very little food – but she was a skilled thief and usually managed to get extra rations for herself and some of the other children.

The MINTOs (Minors in Need of Temporary Office) had plenty of good food – steamed sponge, dumplings, egg custard and so on. They had nice beds and nice bears, and their accommodation and bill of fare was offered as the standard. In truth, it was far from it. Parents of MINTOs paid handsomely to abandon their offspring for sudden necessary trips to Monte Carlo or urgent visits to dying wealthy relatives.

Mrs Reckitt depended on repeat business and glowing reports. And so the orphans and foundlings who had no parents, rich or poor,

lit fires, blacked boots, combed hair, swept, dusted, mopped and polished, while the MINTOs, who were as selfish as the adults who had
raised them, imagined all this to be their due.

Today, on Christmas Day, the MINTOs had their own dining
room and Santa Claus. Lavish presents from neglectful parents were
waiting to be piled under the tree.

The orphans and foundlings queued up later to take the discarded
wrapping paper and string so that they could draw pictures or play
cat's cradle.

Maud had reached the top of the tree. Her head suddenly popped
up beneath the fat plaster cherub. The children far below cheered.
Maud looked down; that was a mistake. She looked down just in
time to see Mrs Reckitt returning from her appointment with the
sausage roll.

Hands on hips, Mrs Reckitt bawled, 'MARGARET! THE
FAIRY, IF YOU PLEASE!'

Maud took the fairy's arm out of her mouth, then secured the
snap-clip sewn into the fairy's back onto the topmost branch. Maud
was as red and green as Christmas, what with her hands all bloody,
and pine needles sticking out of her body like a hedgehog.

She was wondering how to get down when the branch under her
left foot snapped. CRACK!

There's Maud, tumbling, swinging, catching, falling, dropping,
scraping, sliding, bumping, catching, missing, down and down
through the dark green tunnel of the tree until she lands safe, on her
bottom, on the piles of straw baled up at the base for the Nativity.

There was no harm done.

All the children clapped and cheered.

'SILENCE!' shouted Mrs Reckitt. She walked over and grabbed Maud by her arm, pulling her out of the straw. 'Ow, ow, ow!' cried Mrs Reckitt. 'Wretched child, you are stuck through with needles – look what you have done to me!'

But before Mrs Reckitt could further catalogue her woes, she saw what she saw, and what she saw was a glass bauble broken on the floor. Her fat eyes gleamed. 'What did I say? WHAT did I SAY?' She tried to bend down and pick up the broken bauble but her corset would not allow it.

'Hand me that bauble!' she shouted.

Trembling, Maud picked up the broken glass, cutting her hands further, but as she did so she realised that inside the bauble was a tiny silver frog. She managed to conceal it.

Mrs Reckitt ordered Maud into the coal house for the rest of the day. Then, shuffling out of the wings in his customary white coat and rubber gloves, came Dr Scowl, her lieutenant responsible for child welfare. He regretted to say that it was not possible to place Maud in the coal hole; there were four children lumped in there already.

Mrs Reckitt looked unhappy.

'May I suggest outdoors, madam?' said Dr Scowl. 'It is bracing and healthful for a child to be outdoors. We may be sure that the careless young person can reflect upon her delinquency without the distractions of coal. The other day the children imprisoned in the coal house, for the purposes of moral improvement, were using lumps of coal to build castles. Imagine that!'

Mrs Reckitt imagined it. When she had done imagining it, she turned to Maud. 'You! Outside! No coat, scarf or gloves. Goodbye.'

Reginald limped forward. 'Please, Mrs Reckitt, I'll go outside. Maud climbed the tree for my sake.'

There was little Mrs Reckitt liked less than human kindness. She regarded Reginald down the long, unevolved lifetimes of her reptile brain. Why eat one child when two are available?

'In that case, Rodney, you may join Marigold in the garden. Fresh air! I am too kind – but it is Christmas Day.'

There was a gasp from the gathered orphans. Mrs Reckitt swept round her skirts to face them.

'And one single, solitary, stray, sad little slipped-out word from any other meaningless orphan – and you will ALL spend Christmas outdoors. Do you hear?'

The orphans did not have parents but they did have ears. They heard. The hall was silent.

Then…

'DING DONG! MERRILY ON HIGH,
IN HEAV'N THE BELLS ARE RINGING;
DING DONG! VERILY THE SKY
IS RIV'N WITH ANGEL SINGING…'

'The carol singers of Soot Town!' cried Mrs Reckitt, who, like all unfeeling people, was sentimental. 'I must welcome them in for hot punch and melted jelly babies.'

To the front door she went, face flushed redder than any berry, heart colder than the snow that swept through the door. The lanterns were lit and the sound of singing filled the hall. The air was beeswax and green spruce and brandy and cloves and sugar and wine, and the tree shone.

Outside in the garden the pond was frozen solid. Reginald and Maud ran round and round to keep warm, but Dr Scowl saw them through the drawing-room window, where he was warming his sizable bottom at the sizable fire. Running looked too much like a game and too little like a punishment, so he yelled at them to stand still.

Maud's grey overall was thin and her dress was thinner. Reginald wore grey shorts and the regulation mustard-yellow jacket made of felt. Soon the children began to turn blue.

It was then that they heard a tapping beneath the ice on the pond. Yes, it was quite clear. TAP TAP TAP.

They wondered what this could be, and momentarily forgot their chilliness.

'Over there!' said Reginald. 'Look!'

Leaving a trail of prints the size of a saucer where he sat between leaps, hopped a large frog.

Silver. Not bright. Unpolished. His eyes, though, were bright as silver stars and steady in their unblinking gaze.

'Greetings, children,' said the Silver Frog. 'My own children are trapped under the ice.'

TAP TAP TAP.

'Who has imprisoned them?' said Reginald.

'In the past,' said the Silver Frog, 'the gardener always put a log in the pond in the winter. At a slant. Lying through the water and against the bank. This made a bridge and we frogs could come and go, hiding under the ice to keep warm, returning to land to feed. But now no one considers us.'

'No one considers us either,' said Maud. 'All the orphans here are trapped under the ice of Mrs Reckitt's heart but, though we can never escape, we will help you if we can.'

The Silver Frog listened, and his eyes, which were always moist, because, after all, he was a frog, grew wet. Amphibians don't cry. But it was Christmas.

'We can smash the ice to bits!' shouted Reginald. 'I can stamp on it with my twisted foot! Look, the boot has an iron sole.'

The Silver Frog shook his body. (A frog cannot shake his head.) 'Too dangerous. You will fall in and drown. No, there is another way. She has the answer in her pocket.'

Maud fiddled around in her overall pocket. There was a bit of bacon rind she had saved from breakfast, and something hard, like a pebble. Maud fished it out. It was the tiny silver frog she had found inside the broken bauble.

'Yes,' said the Silver Frog, 'that is the Croak.'

'The Croak?'

'The Croak is the Queen of Frogs. No one has ever seen her in the skin and bone, or web and slime, but no one doubts that she watches over us. That solid silver frog is her sacred image. Now, do as I tell you to do and place it on the surface of the pond.'

Maud had little confidence that an inch-scale silver frog could do much good in this frozen world, but she did as she was asked, and slid the frog onto the smooth ice.

Nothing happened. Maud shivered.

'This is never going to work,' said Reginald. 'Why don't I just smash it all up?'

'Behold,' said the Silver Frog and, as it was Christmas, 'behold', though ornate, was acceptable.

A dark patch was spreading under the little tiny miniature weight of frogness. The dark patch bubbled. There was a sigh and a crack. The surface of the pond was wet and crazed.

'It's melting!' said Reginald, who had forgotten to shiver.

And it was. And, as the melting melted, the little frog slid ahead of the breaking ice, and where the frog slid the ice cracked, and the soft water spread over the hard surface.

And if this was not remarkable enough, something more remarkable happened next. The surface of the pond was alive with identical silver frogs.

'They are tiny!' said Reginald.

'They are new,' said the Silver Frog. 'Like the moon.'

The children looked up. The moon looked down, bladed and beautiful and silver.

'I'm not cold now,' said Reginald.

And neither was Maud.

The Silver Frog said, 'My friends, you have helped my children; now my children shall help you. Come along but tread carefully!'

Maud and Reginald followed the Silver Frog, and all the tiny frogs flowed round their feet like a river. The moon lit them up and the children seemed to be carried on a silver stream towards the house.

Through the long windows into the dining room the children could see the final touches being laid to the table for the Christmas feast. How beautiful it looked: red candles and red crackers, damask tablecloth and napkins. Maud knew all about the tablecloth and napkins; she had ironed them with a flat iron heated on the range. It had taken her four hours.

'In we go!' ordered the Silver Frog, and magically the tiny frogs streamed through the glass and suddenly the children were inside too.

'Glass is ruled by the moon,' said the Silver Frog as though this explained everything.

Once inside, two tiny frogs climbed into every cracker. Twenty-four tiny frogs dropped themselves into the bottom of the crystal water glasses. There was a beautiful trifle in a glass bowl in the centre of the table. The trifle was decorated with tiny silver beads that were soon replaced by tiny silver frogs.

'Now, then, my dear little froglinos and froglinas, scatter yourself like balls of mercury wherever you please and be sure to cause trouble from the moment you hear the first scream.'

'What will you do?' asked Maud.

'I have a particular task but that is not yet. In the meantime, Maud, you and a dozen froglissimos – the fastest I have – will hide behind the Christmas tree in the hall. They will know what to do – and they will do it to Dr Scowl.

'Reginald! Under the table with you – crouching, frog-style – and be sure to tie together the gentlemen's bootlaces, and when the ladies take off their shoes – as ladies always do when their feet are out of sight – move the shoes from one to another so that no one has a matching pair. Do you understand?'

The children nodded.

'Excellent!' said the Silver Frog. 'And now help yourselves to that ham on the sideboard. We have a little time.'

The great and the good of Soot Town were arriving in the hall, as carriages with steaming horses queued for their place at the steps, by now lit up with flares.

Dr Scowl had put off his white coat and rubber gloves and stood resplendently stuffed into white tie and tails.

Mrs Reckitt was wearing an evening gown that had taken its inspiration from a large pink blancmange. Around her shoulders lay a pink fox-fur that fastened itself by means of its fox-teeth to its fox-tail.

'Such an interesting clasp!' said Lady Fleas, putting her finger to it. 'Ow! I declare I am bleeding!'

'Ha ha ha ha ha!' laughed Mrs Reckitt. 'My little joke of the season. Not quite dead.'

In they came, one and all, great and good, self-satisfied and vain, and they enjoyed their usual tour of the accommodation: they were shown the rooms where the MINTOs slept, where indeed there were eiderdowns and bears, but they were not shown the rooms where the orphans slept, where the bedclothes were made of sacking and the pillows stuffed with straw, and never a fire blazed in the boarded-up hearth.

And they were shown the children's dining room, set out with delicious food – jelly and cakes and a steaming bird – but they were not told that all this food would soon be whisked away and that Christmas dinner for the orphans was a thin soup made of bones and peelings and some beef spread on coarse bread.

'Somewhat cold in here for small children,' remarked a kindly gentleman with a gold watch. He was new to Soot Town. Mrs Reckitt realised she had forgotten to have the fire lit.

'Oh, my! Yes! Bless me! We have all been so busy playing Christmas games and decorating the tree that I quite forgot! It shall be lit at once.'

And with that she firmly closed the door.

'Where are the orphans?' enquired the kindly gentleman. 'I should like to give each one of them a silver sixpence, in honour of the day.'

'They are putting on their best clothes,' said Mrs Reckitt, 'after all the excitement of the games. But do not worry. If you give the sixpences to me I shall give them out in my happy guise as Mother Christmas.'

'They are indeed fortunate children,' said the kindly gentleman.

The fortunate children were at that very moment shovelling coal from the coal house into iron wheelbarrows to be wheeled to the great furnace that warmed the house and heated the hot water.

The children were so black that they could not be seen at all against the black sky and the black coal.

'Ah, listen to them singing!' cried Mrs Reckitt as upstairs Dr Scowl put on the phonograph recording of a long-dead children's choir singing 'The Holly and the Ivy'.

And, warmed and touched by happiness and deception, the great and the good of Soot Town went in to dinner.

It was not long into the first course of jellied eel that one of the ladies took a drink from her water glass and screamed and threw the contents over her neighbour. Her neighbour stood up in silk-drenched fury to find that her shoes were missing. The gentleman on her left agreeably got up to help her and fell flat on his face into the trifle – out of which exploded like the plagues of Egypt dozens of tiny frogs.

A lady clutched at the curtains and found her hand shimmering with frogspawn. She fainted. A gentleman bent to help put her head on a cushion and saw that her wig was leaping alive on her head.

Mrs Reckitt, reaching to ring the bell for reinforcements, saw, or thought she did, a determined frog clinging to the clapper. Ring as she might, mightily, no sound sounded. She threw the bell in a rage onto the fire and did not see the agile frog leap out of the bell and onto her fox-fur, where he sat quiet as a brooch.

The ladies were all hysterical by now, especially without shoes, and, thanks to Reginald, there was not a gentleman whose shoes were not tied together, except for Dr Scowl.

'Those evil orphans!' shouted Mrs Reckitt. 'This must be their idea of a joke! I'll give them a joke! I'll bury them up to their underfed necks in stinking sewage.'

The kind old gentleman new to Soot Town was taken aback by this outburst, and privately wondered if all at the Villa of Glory was as it was advertised. No one else seemed to care about Mrs Reckitt's threats to her charges; the guests were too busy fighting off frogs and managing their footwear.

At length, and after being served copious amounts of champagne, everyone was at last settled again and tucking into the excellent roasted meats, without incident.

All except Dr Scowl, who had taken it upon himself to tour the orphanage.

In the quiet of the hall, he heard a loud croak. Croak? Surely not? Then he heard it again, coming from the Christmas tree. Perhaps there were frogs living in the tree? Tree frogs? Did tree frogs live in Christmas trees? Perhaps the orphans weren't responsible after all. They would still be punished, of course. But perhaps Mrs Reckitt could sue the lumber-yard. Misfortune meant money.

Dr Scowl poked himself deep into the tree.

'Now!' said the Silver Frog, who was sitting on Maud's lap surrounded by a hundred-thousand froglissimos.

As one, they LEAPT, and the doctor, in his black tails, found himself with a frog tail, and a frog body and froggy arms and legs as the rapid froglissimos covered him like pins on a pin-board.

Dr Scowl fell on all fours, unable to see as two determined frogs held down his eyelids. He opened his mouth to cry out and five warm, wriggling frogs jumped inside and sat on his tongue like a lily pad.

'Take him to the pond and throw him in!' said the Silver Frog.

And, by a miracle of frog-motion, the doctor began to slide along the polished wooden floor on what looked like silver castors.

'Ho, ho, ho,' said the Silver Frog. 'Now, Maud, go and find every orphan you can and bring them out of their dark, damp, shivering holes and sit them around the Christmas tree.'

Back in the dining room, the guests declared themselves so exhausted by unexpected events that they elected to take their crackers and Christmas pudding into the warm, comfortable sitting room that opened off the dining room.

No sooner had they vacated than a thousand froglets whisked away the ham and turkey and roast potatoes and conveyed all these to the orphans gathered in the hall.

The frogs grouped themselves into what looked like shining silver plates – on legs – and in this way everything was easily managed.

Reginald crawled out from under the table, several silver shillings richer from where the guests had upended their pockets.

In the hall the children tucked into such food as they had never eaten before and felt the good, wholesome warmth in their empty stomachs. They started to smile, and some laughed, and they talked to each other, not in whispers any more, and everyone shared what they had and no one took too much and the smaller children hoped that when they grew up they would marry a roast potato dressed in gravy.

In the comfortable sitting room the guests were calmed by pudding and Mrs Reckitt comforted herself with thoughts of punishment and revenge. No child would be given food for a month and all would be required to sleep in the garden until at least half were dead – as an example to those who remained.

It occurred to her that she had been too kind to the children. If they were dead they would be cheap to feed. From now on she would only take dead orphans.

As she ate her sixth helping of Christmas pudding the kind old gentleman new to Soot Town proposed a toast, followed by crackers pulled in the traditional way – in a circle, hands crossed to your neighbour.

'To the founder of the feast – Mrs Reckitt!'

'Mrs Reckitt!' returned the company, glasses high and brimming with port.

Mrs Reckitt blushed, one imagines – her face was too red to allow blushing – but she did murmur her thanks, profoundly, while hinting that further funds would allow her to expand – not referring to her waistline; the iron-corseted ladies tittered.

'But where is Dr Scowl?' wondered Mrs Reckitt.

The doctor, who had trained as an undertaker, taken a course in body-snatching, made money and returned to civilised society with a title he did not own, was stationed by a kind of levitation at the edge of the pond.

Frogs from every garden, every woodland, every bog, every stone, every ditch, every heap, every cellar, every fairy tale were gathered round in silent, crouched concentration. They were gathered in the name of the Croak.

The pond had frozen over again but that would be no challenge to a mortal as fleshed-out as Dr Scowl.

'Dispatch him,' ordered the Silver Frog.

It was just at the second when the crackers were to be pulled that Mrs Reckitt heard what sounded like a very large object entering water. But her grip was tight round her own and her neighbour's cracker and, as she was determined to win whatever was inside both, she closed her little eyes and pulled with all the strength in her fat fists.

WEE – KE-BANG – POP – CRACK – OW!

And in a flare of gunpowder everyone laughed and then SCREAMED!

The little frog-bombs leapt from the crackers square into eyes, nostrils, mouths, décolletages, trouser bottoms, trouser tops, and wriggled and squirmed and jumped and waited and waited and jumped.

The great and the good of Soot Town ran out of the parlour into the hall, and there their yelling stopped, as it must, because sitting around the tree, cross-legged and ragged, were the orphans, the real ones, not the postcard offerings and exhibits.

They were lost. They were neglected. They were broken-hearted. They were dirty. They were thin. They were tired. They wore tatty clothes and odd shoes and their hair was either not cut or all cut off. They were children.

Their eyes were big through staring at the dark and they no longer expected something to happen. But today something had happened.

And the kind old gentleman said, 'How dare you, madam?' And some of the ladies started to cry.

And Maud stood up and said (as the Silver Frog had told her to say), 'Please come this way.'

And the Christmas guests saw the peeling dormitories and the bare beds. And the cold rooms and the empty toy box. And there had been a bear, but the smallest children had shared him, so that one had a leg, and another an arm, and his head was passed round to anyone who had been punished that day so that they could hold his gentle head against their hurt hearts.

And they found the children still shovelling coal into the furnace. And the children asleep in the straw in the hen-house. And the children outside under the moon.

Mrs Reckitt was packing a carpet bag with valuables. She didn't notice the brooch on her fox-fur twitching or the frog's legs stretching. She didn't know that this frogarina, a princess among frogs, was a tiny live alarm for a cohort of silver soldiers.

And they came. And they waited. And as she set off, cloaked and secret on her turkey legs, the frogs were like ball bearings, everywhere at once, random, underfoot, and Mrs Reckitt was sliding and falling and clutching and rolling, and the Silver Frog opened the front door and out she rolled, bang, bang, bang, down the steps.

And she was never seen in Soot Town again.

Is that the end of the story?

No! It's Christmas.

The kind old gentleman took over the orphanage and the children were looked after, and fed, and they had lessons and playtime, and warm clothes and beds and bears.

And every year the Christmas tree decorated the hall, and instead of a star or an angel they put a silver frog on top – though this one had wings.

Maud grew up and became the matron of the orphanage, and every child who went there, sad though the circumstances might be, found a home, and love, and was never shut out in the cold.

Reginald ran the woodwork classes, and taught all the boys and girls how to look after their home from home, and he even built a special ladder that could reach right to the top of the Christmas tree.

And some time later Reginald and Maud got married, and the Croak herself came to their wedding and gave them, so the story goes, a bag of silver coins that never ran out.

And in return Reginald and Maud dug a series of ponds for the frogs, who were never again trapped under the ice in winter, and who sang with the best of us on Christmas Day.

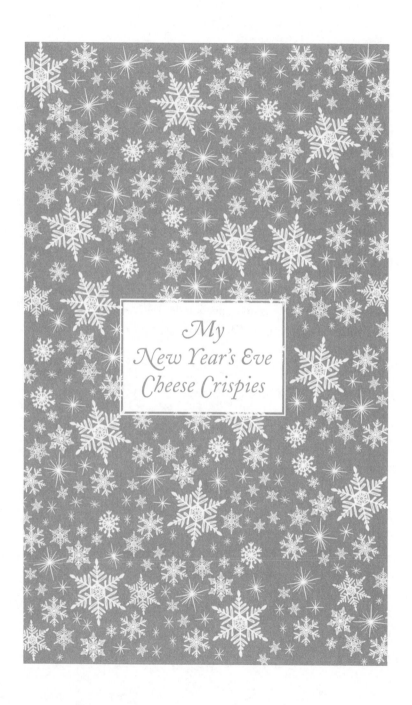

My
New Year's Eve
Cheese Crispies

ew Year for most of us means the calendar new year that starts on January 1st.

The Romans named January after Janus, god of doorways, deity of time and transitions. He has two faces because he looks backwards and forwards.

I don't make New Year resolutions – instead I have a psychic clear-out. What would I prefer not to repeat?

It's not just History with a capital H that repeats itself; it's our personal history too. It's hard to shift negative patterns and negative thoughts. It's hard to do things differently, to stop destructive and self-destructive behaviours, to stop colluding with our own worst enemy: ourselves.

I prefer to have a New Year's Day party than a New Year's Eve party where everyone gets drunk and sings out of tune.

For me, New Year's Eve, like Christmas Eve, is an opportunity for reflection.

And it's a time to remember.

Memory doesn't happen chronologically. Our minds are less interested in when something happened than in *what* happened, and *who* happened. Getting the year or the month wrong seems less important as time goes by. We can't always say *when*, but we can always say, *'This is what happened.'*

Memories separated in time are often recalled side by side – there's an emotional connection that has nothing to do with the diary dates and everything to do with the feeling.

Remembering isn't like visiting a museum: Look! There's the long-gone object in a glass case. Memory isn't an archive. Even a simple memory is a cluster. Something that seemed so insignificant at the time suddenly becomes the key when we remember it at a particular time later. We're not liars or self-deceivers – OK, we are all liars and self-deceivers, but it's a fact that our memories change as we do.

Some memories, though, don't seem to change at all. They are sticky with pain. And even when we are not, consciously, remembering our memories, they seem to remember us. We can't shake free of their effect.

There's a great term for that – the old present. These things happened in the past, but they're riding right up front with us every day.

A bit of self-reflection on New Year's Eve is no substitute for the all-over detox that going to therapy makes possible, but a bit of self-reflection on New Year's Eve can help us look at our mental and emotional map – and see where some of the landmines are.

And some bad memories are really other people's baggage but we drag them along as if we're working for a diva who always packs several trunks but can only be seen carrying a purse.

Why am I portering this shit? It's a good New Year question.

In the Jewish tradition Yom Kippur, the Day of Atonement, falls ten days after Rosh Hashanah, the Jewish New Year. I am married to a Jew, who tells me that the whole period between the New Year and the Day of Atonement is a period of reflection – a time for starting again, and a recognition of what needs to be atoned for. Judaism is a practical religion. You don't just wring your hands and wail 'oy vey'; you do something about it.

I like the idea of atonement – a practical response to where we know we've done wrong. Maybe others won't atone for the wrong they've done us, but maybe we can atone for the wrong we do ourselves; the self-harm.

And, as Freud so brilliantly understood, you can go back in time, you can heal the past. It may be fixed as a fact – what happened happened – but it isn't fixed in the ongoing story of our lives.

Memories can be tools for change; they don't have to be weapons used against us, or baggage we have to drag around.

And memories, sometimes, are places we go to honour the dead. There's always that first, terrible New Year when our loved one won't be here.

It's good just to sit quietly in that place of loss and sadness, and let the feelings be the feelings. Those memories are liquid; we cry.

And good memories, happy memories also need to be honoured. We remember so much of the bad stuff and we are so careless with the good stuff. Remember the year for what it brought. Even if there was precious little, that little is precious.

But, you may say, *what has all this got to do with cheese crispies?*

Whether it's for a New Year's Day party or a little personal party for you and the cat and dog on New Year's Eve, these biscuits are the best.

I love them with a cold, dry, salty sherry from the fridge or a vodka and soda with chunks of lime. If you want red, try a light red you can chill, like a Chiroubles, a Gamay or a Zinfandel or, if you are adding extra Parmesan, a Dolcetto d'Alba. Just lovely.

I started to make my cheese crispies when I noticed my favourite Dutch brand were putting palm oil in their biscuits. Palm oil isn't good stuff, for humans or for the planet.

My golden rule is: don't buy foodstuffs that contain ingredients you'd never use yourself if you were making the same kind of thing.

Cheese crispies don't need shelf-life – they get eaten in ten minutes max.

So try these. Quick. Simple. Fun. And a bit of self-reflection deserves a biscuit.

*

YOU NEED

½ lb (225 g) good salted butter
½ lb (225 g) organic plain flour
½ lb (225 g) cheese mixture
Salt to taste

About the cheese mixture: unpasteurised cheddar should be your staple here – but I also mix in Gruyère and Parmesan. Yes, all unpasteurised. I could write a long essay here about bacteria, but it's Christmas, and bacteria aren't that festive. I don't blame them; it's just not their way. So look up the pros and cons of pasteurisation once we're past Twelfth Night, and see if I ain't right…

On the choice of cheese, well, you can't use blue cheese or cream cheese, but if you have a hard cheese you like, one that's local, or some old thing in the fridge you need to use up, then experiment. You'll soon find the flavour you like best, and I bet cheesy biscuits were invented the usual way – needing to use up a surplus of something – or because something was past its eat-me date. In this case, whiffy cheese.

(Author's note: dogs are also a good way of using up whiffy cheese.)

METHOD

Rub the butter and flour in a bowl until it looks likes breadcrumbs – you can whizz it in the food processor if you want to.

Add the cheese until the whole thing is a nice, doughy mixture. If it's too dry add a bit of milk or an egg.

Knead it all out till smooth and firm.

Roll the mixture into logs about 8 inches long – too short and it's fiddly, too long and it's unwieldy.

Put the logs in the fridge to stiffen up (I know you've made a sex toy but we won't go there).

When you want your cheese crispies, heat up your oven to 180°C or whatever. HOT. I have an Aga and I don't really understand other ovens – the noise makes me nervous – but we can work it out.

If you too have an Aga, it's top oven, obviously.

Lightly oil a baking tray to prevent STICK – or use baking paper (useful as a firelighter afterwards).

Slice your logs into thin slices – imagining the biscuits you want to eat – and stick them in the oven for 15 minutes.

These logs freeze well.

And that's it! Even if you make these for your ungrateful party guests, keep a few for yourself, the cat and the dog, and that time of reflection.

THE LION, THE UNICORN AND ME

Before it happened, an angel lined up all the animals –
every one, of every kind, because this angel had the full
list left over from the Ark.

Most were eliminated at once – spiders, monkeys, bears,
whales, walruses, snakes. Soon it was clear that four legs on the ground
at the same time would be necessary to reach the qualifying round.
That left some serious competition – horses, tigers, a stag with antlers
that branched into an unknown forest, a zebra painted black and white
like an argument.

The elephant could carry the world on its back. Dogs and cats were
too small, the hippopotamus too wayward. There was a giraffe in jigsaw
graffiti. The camel was wanted elsewhere, as were the cattle. After a
long time, it was just the three of us: the lion, the unicorn and me.

The lion spoke first. Present position: King of the Jungle. Previous
history: worked with Hercules and Samson, also Daniel in the lions'
den. Special strengths: special strength. Weaknesses: none reported.
The angel wrote it down.

Then the unicorn spoke. Present position: mythical beast. Previous history: in Hebrew I am Re'em, the creature that cannot be

tamed. Special strengths: known to be good with virgins. Weaknesses: tendency to vanish. The angel wrote it down.

Then it was my turn.

'He'll make an ass of himself,' whispered the lion. I did. I am. A proper ass. Present position: under-donkey. Special strength: can carry anything anywhere. Weaknesses: not beautiful, not well-bred, not important, not clever, not noticed, not won any prizes…

The angel wrote it down, and down, and down. Then the angel gave us a tie-breaker: could we say, in one sentence, why we were right for the job?

The lion spoke first. 'If He is to be King of the World, He should be carried by the King of the Beasts.'

The unicorn said, 'If He is to be the Mystery of the World, He should be carried by the most mysterious of us all.'

I said, 'Well, if He is to bear the burdens of the world, He had better be carried by me.'

And that is how I found myself trotting quietly along, the red desert under my hooves, the sky rolled out like a black cloth over my head, and a tired woman nodding asleep on my back, towards the little town of Bethlehem.

Oh but it was a musty, rusty, fusty pudding of a town turned out for a show, its people cussed and blustering, all buy and sell and money, taking their chance while the going was good before the goods got going again. Taxes, and everyone here to pay up, and everyone had to be put up for this one night, so that even the mice were renting their mouse-holes, and there were travellers hanging out of birds' nests, their beards full of twigs and old worms, and the anthills were full up, and the beehives had three families apiece, and there was a man tapping on the frozen lake asking the fish to let him in.

And every bed and every under-the-bed, and every chair and cushion and curtain and carpet, and every ledge, nook, shelf, cranny, gap, rack, cupboard and cart squeezed and popped with arms and legs. When we arrived at the inn, there were two large, empty pots on either side of the door.

Being a donkey, I poked my head into one of them to see if there was anything to eat. At once, a stubbly face popped out of the pot, and warned us that the inn was so full that he and his brother had had to uproot the olive trees from either side of the porch. Sure enough, there was the brother, head like a melon, scowling in the other pot.

My master Joseph was an optimistic man.

He knocked at the door. The innkeeper opened it, and the boy who had been sleeping in the letterbox fell out.

'No room,' said the innkeeper.

'For my wife only?' asked Joseph. 'Tonight she will bear a Son.'

'Then she must do it by starlight,' said the innkeeper, closing the door. Joseph put his foot in the way.

'Listen,' said the innkeeper, 'you think I'm joking?' He pointed upwards, into the beams, where five spiders were looking gloomily at six infants whose father had knotted the webs into hammocks.

Joseph nodded and was about to turn away, when the innkeeper said, 'But go round the back to the stables, and see what you can find.' Now, the animals that night knew that something strange was going to happen because animals always do know when something strange is going to happen.

They were murmuring among themselves: the ox had seen a star glowing brighter and brighter, and the camel had had a message from his brother, who worked for a king, that kings were travelling to Bethlehem that night.

Mary, Joseph and me pushed our way into the crowded stable. It smelled of sweet, warm dung and dry hay. I was hungry. Straight away, Joseph swept some straw into a heap, and spread out a blanket from the saddlebags. He went outside to fill his leather bottle with water from the well, and because he was a kind man, he brought in fresh water for the hot, crowded animals too. Mary was glad of the heat of the animals. She fell asleep for a while.

When I was unsaddled of all my burdens, Joseph turned me out into the yard to eat my supper. It was cold, sharp, biting weather. The stars were bright as bells. The deep black sky had the new moon cut in it and the fields beyond the town were visible under that moon, but as a dream is visible to one who sleeps, and not to one who is awake.

'Something will happen tonight,' said the ox. 'I can feel it in my shoulders.'

'I can smell it,' said the dog.

'It's quivering my whiskers,' said the cat. The horse pricked her ears and looked up. I carried on eating because I was hungry. Eating as only an ass can eat, I saw the light flash across my hooves, and wipe from grey to bright the turned-over, trampled and frosted clods of earth around the stable. I looked up; the back of the inn was ramshackle and dark, but the stable was shining. Two creatures in bright array were sitting on the slipped clay tiles of the ridge, their feet clean and bare, their hair flowing like a fast river, and each carried a long trumpet slung across his back.

Above them was a star whose edge was so close I thought it would cut the roof in half, and wedge its brightness in the wormy purlins, so that the stable and its star would be solid together, hay and dung and another world.

There was a great commotion, and three camels, jewelled and brushed, stood steaming in the yard. At a word, the camels bent and kneeled, and the kings who rode them each unpacked a precious box of great price.

In all of this light and motion, I trotted quietly through the little door and pushed my way through the other animals to where Joseph was kneeling with Mary. She was on all fours, just like us. There was a rushing sound, like water, and a cry, like life.

It was life, bloody and raw, and wet and steaming in the cold like our breath, and the Baby, its face screwed up and its eyes closed, and Joseph's hand bigger than its back, and suddenly there was the blast of trumpets, and the front blew clean off the stable, and I looked up and saw the angels' feet pushed through the sagging roof and their bodies taut on the ridge-line, heralding the beginning of something, the end of something, I don't know what words to say, but beginnings and ends are hinged together and folded back against each other, like shutters, like angels' wings.

I tipped back my head, and I brayed and brayed to join the trumpets. My nose was so high and the roof so low that the angel's foot brushed me as I sang.

The kings came inside even though there was no inside left now that we were blown inside out, time past and future roaring around us like a wind, and eternity above us, like angels, like a star. The kings kneeled and one of them, the youngest, began to cry.

Then four shepherds, dressed in sheepskins and smelling of sheep dip, came with hot mutton in a broth and poured it into wooden bowls, and Joseph fed Mary as she leaned against him, the Baby under her cloak, its body lighting up her body, so that even in the gold that was the angels, and the silver that was all the stars of the sky, the Baby shone brighter. They wiped Him. They wrapped Him up. They laid Him in the manger.

Some time in the night, the lion on soft paws crept in and bowed his head. Some time in the night, through a gap in the wall, no bigger than thought, the unicorn touched the Baby with his horn.

Morning came, a stretching, yawning, sniffing, snorting, shuffling sort of a morning. I trotted round to the front of the inn, and there were the scowling melon-heads sitting on their pots by the porch, drinking thick coffee from tin cups.

'Look at that donkey's nose,' said one.

'What's he been eating?' said the other.

I squinted down the velvety barrel of my nose, but I couldn't see anything strange.

All around, the town was waking, merchants and herdsmen, camel-drivers and bankers, and the whispering news was that something wonderful was happening.

The innkeeper came out of the inn. He was the first with the news: King Herod was coming to Bethlehem – what an honour, what a compliment, that must be the meaning of the star, and the babbling portent of the raving drunk asleep in the empty wine barrel – angels on the stable roof, he'd said. He looked at me.

'What happened to your nose?'

The three kings had left before dawn, warned in a fitful dream to return by another route. I had seen their dromedaries moving like music out to the fields where the shepherds were already lighting their morning fire.

There was nothing to show for the night just gone, except three boxes of precious stuff, a hole in the roof where the angels had dangled their feet on the rim of time, and the fact that the stable door had been blown off. Joseph paid for the door with a piece of gold from the box, and showed the innkeeper the Baby Boy, and they talked about the star seen in the East, and the innkeeper gave his opinion, boasting about Herod, and some fool-talk about angels, and then I trotted back round the corner, nose-first.

'Well I'll be blowed,' said Joseph.

The truth is that when the angel's foot had rested on my muzzle as I brayed, my muzzle had turned as gold as a trumpet that proclaims another world.

We didn't wait for Herod. We set out for Egypt, not telling anyone where we had gone, and I carried Mary and her Baby, many days and nights, into safety.

Sometimes, when the sky is very cold and clear, and I have done my day's journey and stand half-asleep, half-awake in the warmth of my stall, I think I see the bowl of a trumpet, and its long funnel, and a foot, clean and white, dangling over the ridge-line of the stars, and I lift up my voice and I bray and I bray, for memory, for celebration, for warning, for chance, for everything that is here below and all that is hidden elsewhere. Hay and dung and another world.

My
New Year's Day
Steak Sandwich

have never been good at New Year's resolutions. New Year's Eve, like Christmas Eve, is a time of contemplation for me. It's a good moment to look back – not with a view to doing things better; that only works with practical stuff, like practising your swimming stroke or improving your French. No, the important stuff has to be done not better, but differently.

It might be the way you relate to your partner or your kids. It might be to bring more joy into your life. It might be to make time. It might be to let something go.

Doing things differently is difficult. We like habit. I guess that's why people resolve to kick their habits at New Year. Some do that, through willpower; most of us fail. Actions and behaviour – habits – are on the surface. Why we act or behave in certain ways is usually buried deep – and so it's hard to change our behaviour unless we change something more fundamental about ourselves.

My old Jewish friend Mona says you go through life carrying two bags, and you have to know which bag to put your problem in. One bag is time and money. The other bag is the life-and-death struggle.

The life-and-death struggle includes having any kind of conscious life at all beyond the effort to meet your material needs. And it includes coming to terms with death.

Mrs Winterson celebrated New Year with a mixture of gloom and anticipation. This was a woman for whom life was a pre-death experience. Somewhere there was a better world but it wasn't on the bus route and she had never learned to drive.

Every year she wondered – out loud – if this would be her last. She wondered too if it would be the Year of the Apocalypse.

Our drill went like this: in the middle of the night, while I was sleeping and Dad was on the night shift, Mrs W stood at the bottom of the stairs blowing her version of the Last Trump. We didn't have a bugle so it was usually a mouth organ or comb and paper. Sometimes she just banged a pan.

I had to run downstairs and get in the cupboard under the stairs, where there were two stools and an oil lamp. And lots of tinned food. Then we read the Bible and sang. When the End came we were going to wait under the stairs till an angel liberated us. I used to wonder how the angel's wings were going to fit under the stairs, but Mrs Winterson said there would be no need for the angel to come in.

I don't know where Dad was supposed to be in all of this, but he still had his tin helmet from the war, so perhaps he was supposed to wear that and wait outside.

We were living in End Time. If you live that way you live on high alert. I did. I do. There's so much we carry with us from our past. And if we can't change it then the next best thing is to recognise it.

At least that way you can laugh about it or maybe make something of it for yourself.

We had a ritual at home of burning the calendar on the fire on the stroke of midnight. I still do that. I like going round the house collecting the old calendars. I realise that few people have open fires these days, and a shredder doesn't have the same poetic intensity.

A friend of mine writes a page of regrets and sets fire to it in the kitchen with a candle. Other friends let off fireworks, each one a wish for what might happen.

Fire is celebratory and defiant. Light and fire have always been symbols of the spirit against the relentlessness of time.

Nearing midnight I turn on the radio. Hearing Big Ben chime the hour on the BBC has a solemnity to it and a sense of tradition.

On the first stroke of the great bell I open the back door to let the Old Year out, and I stand with her as she goes. Goodbye! On the last stroke I open the front door to let in the New Year, welcoming her as she comes.

This is all pretty busy because I have to make it past the fireplace with the calendars on the way.

And usually, because everybody gets a bit sentimental sometimes, I'm reciting Tennyson to myself:

> *Ring out, wild bells, to the wild sky,*
> *The flying cloud, the frosty light:*
> *The year is dying in the night;*
> *Ring out, wild bells, and let him die.*

The rest of this part of the very long poem 'In Memoriam' is pretty terrible tea-towel stuff so I stick with the first verse. Being a great poet doesn't mean that you always write great poetry.

In itself, that's a lesson for New Year.

We're humans, not machines. We have bad days. We have mental difficulties. We are inspired, yet we fail. We are not linear. We have hearts that break and souls we don't know what to do with. We kill and destroy but we build and make possible too. We've been to the moon and invented computers. We outsource most things but we still have to live with ourselves. We're pessimists who believe it's too late so what the hell? We're the comeback kids in love with second chances. And every New Year is another chance.

What is New Year anyway?

Until 1752 Britain and her colonies (sorry about this, America) had two new years a year because the legal new year began on March 25th, Lady Day, so-called because if you're going to have Jesus born on December 25th Mary has to be bang on time and conceive on March 25th – a date conveniently close to the spring equinox of March 21st, when our pre-Christian ancestors celebrated New Year. New life, the return of the sun, all very sensible.

Britain has been celebrating a new-year festival on January 1st since the 13th century, but until the 18th century the legal new year on March 25th forced the custom of double-dating for nearly three months of every year depending on whether you reckoned you were in a new year or not.

To add to the fun, in 1582 Roman Catholic Europe ditched the Julian calendar, invented by Julius Caesar in 45BC, and started to measure the year by the Gregorian calendar, still used today.

The problem was that Caesar's solar year was eleven minutes a year out, which added a day to the calendar every hundred and twenty-eight years. By the time we had reached the 1500s, the calendar pinned on the wall (OK, so there wasn't one but you get the point) bore no relation to the two equinoxes and the solstices. Pope Gregory decided Europe needed a new calendar, named after him, of course, and because he was Pope everybody had to agree. Except England.

England was busy splitting forever with the Church of Rome – this was our first Brexit from Europe. Naturally we weren't buying their calendar with a different picture of the pope for every month.

So we carried on being eleven days different from the rest of Europe. And we did this, not just Britain but America too, once the Puritans had made it to Plymouth Rock, right up until 1752.

You can hear the old calendar in the names of the months: September – the seventh month; October – the eight month; November – the ninth month; December – the tenth month.

Adjusting to the new calendar in 1752 involved 'losing' eleven days. And so September 2nd 1752 was followed by September 14th 1752.

Time is a mystery.

*

Here is my New Year's Day steak sandwich.

YOU NEED

Best sourdough bread you can buy

Sirloin steak. Buy a wedge and slice it thinner than usual – think sandwich not slab.

Winter salad greens and reds – radicchio, chicory, romaine lettuce

Horseradish

Home-made mayo (see 'Susie's Christmas Eve Gravlax')

METHOD

Slice the bread not too thin. Spread with mayo. Not butter.

Pile on the greens and reds – both pieces of bread.

Fry or grill your slices of sirloin the way you like them – bloody or burnt – and put one or two on top of one slice of bread.

Spread the steak slice with horseradish.

Slap the second slice of bread on top of the first – the lettuce will stay put.

Cut in half with a lethal knife.

Eat at once.

Drink with a slightly chilled Gamay whatever the time of day, including breakfast. This is New Year's Day and millions of people will be detoxing, dieting and proclaiming Dry January. Take a stand.

If I have guests who are vegetarian I make them an omelette sandwich, same bread, spread with HP sauce, no butter, and served with a glass of champagne. Or a cup of strong tea. That's the best I can do.

Happy New Year.

THE GLOW-HEART

hristmas Eve.

Marty was leaving his friend Sarah's house after supper. Sarah always threw a party on Christmas Eve and, like all the other Jews they knew, went to a Chinese restaurant on Christmas Day.

Marty was the last to leave. He stood looking out of the window of the apartment. The snow was falling contentedly. The street was quiet.

'Christmas Schmistmas,' said Sarah, leaving the pile of plates she was stacking in the dishwasher and coming to stand beside him and leaning on him a little. 'Jesus was a Jew born in Bethlehem. Why is it always snowing?'

'Well, it is snowing, no arguing with that,' said Marty. 'I like a white Christmas. Bing Crosby, Judy Garland, "Have yourself a merry little –" et cetera.'

'Don't be so sentimental,' said Sarah.

'What's the matter with schmaltz?' said Marty. 'We invented it.'

'We invented Christianity and what good did it do us? Hundreds of years of persecution.'

'We invented it but we didn't believe in it – we were too practical; as a story, it's ridiculous, the woodworking Messiah raised from the dead and heaven at the end of the runway. But think if we'd kept the copyright.'

'Yeah, it was a lousy deal, but you can't rewrite history.'

'What do you think I do all day in my office? "Hey, can we break this contract?" "Hey, can we stop these people breaking the contract?"'

'That's just business. I'm talking life. The life of us all.'

'Wait a minute – aren't you a shrink? Did I miss something?'

'No, you didn't miss anything. If you want to talk about inventions of the mind – and to me that's what religion is, an invention of the mind – then the Jews invented psychoanalysis because every Jew would like to change the past: *Oy vey! She ate the apple… Sure, the food's nice, but you should have eaten here before the flood… You're telling me that's the Promised Land? Can we share an Uber back to Egypt?* Maybe everyone would like to change the past – the regrets, the failures, the mistakes, but you can't do it.'

'But you can change the past,' said Marty, 'not big history but small history. As a mass we're doomed and disappointed, I agree with you. Individually, things can change. I know you believe that.'

'Home is where the heartache is,' said Sarah. 'My job is always a challenge around Christmas. People get worse, not better. But what about you? How are you doing? I'm sorry we didn't have time to talk tonight – so many people, and we're all so noisy. Want a Scotch?'

Marty shook his head. 'I'll get going.'

'Sit next to me tomorrow at Chine-Ease.'

'I'm not coming. I want to be with David. He loved Christmas.'

'Marty…this isn't good…'

In reply Marty kissed Sarah on the cheek and took his coat. He forgot his gloves.

How quiet it was. Had everyone gone to bed already, waiting for Santa Claus? What an inspired mess is Christmas. Santa Claus, spruce trees, elves, gifts, coloured lights, decorations, magic, a miracle birth. And the winter solstice shortest day just gone, and the need of something like hope, just now.

Marty started singing Judy Garland – was it from *Meet Me in St Louis*? "*Someday soon we all will be together, if the fates allow. Until then, we'll have to muddle through somehow…*"

David was dead. This was the second Christmas Eve he'd walked back from Sarah's alone.

The first Christmas Eve he'd stayed the night with her, on the couch, under blankets thick enough to keep out the cold air but not the cold in his heart.

Love is regret, he thought. The ultimate 'if only'. The seductive swerve in time where life changes track twice. When you meet. And when you part.

David had been the dreamy one, the gardening one, the sporty one, the outdoor one. Marty preferred a movie and a meal with friends. David didn't eat hot food unless someone else was cooking it. Left to himself, it was cheese sandwiches or sardines from the tin, with a bottle of the best wine. He ate handfuls of salad and carrots raw from the garden. Marty protested and tried to bring the produce indoors to try a new recipe. David thought you should cook intuitively – 'That's because you never cook,' said Marty.

David believed in signs – 'Look for the signs,' he said, whenever there was a decision to be made and Marty, sighing, was trying to weigh up the odds.

'Good thing we didn't try to meet on a dating site,' said Marty, 'or we never would've.'

They weren't opposites; more like different time zones. Marty working late into the night. David up early in the garden. David sleeping without waking. Marty staring at the ceiling for at least two hours of every darkness.

Marty liked to be on time. David was always running late. There was an acceleration in him, thought Marty. His body couldn't keep up with his mind. His mind raced ahead. His body ran out of time.

The city had finally stopped counting down to Christmas as though everyone was their own personal space rocket and Christmas their own personal star.

That afternoon the shops had closed. The assistants had gone home. Marty knew that millions of people were still buying online but at least they were out of his way and he could walk the streets – if not in peace, in quiet. He liked walking. He liked city walking. He didn't want to have to go to that place called the countryside to take a walk. He wanted to stuff his hands in his pockets, set his internal compass vaguely east or south and wander till he was tired enough to get the bus home. He'd done a lot of that since David's death. It was a way of being with him.

What Marty hated about death was the fact that you thought about the other person nearly all the time – it was overwhelming and invasive. Exhausting. What you didn't do any more was arrange to meet at 6pm and try a restaurant. You didn't rush to finish up at work so that you could get away early for the weekend together. There wasn't the glorious muddle of forgetting someone completely – because you had that luxury – and then looking up, seeing the clock, feeling the jolt of anticipation, sexual, emotional, knowing you would be with them soon, leaving work, flowing down the street with thousands of others, but moving in the certainty of the two of you together.

And always that same smile, hello, kiss, his hand on your shoulder, what a day, what will you have, oh, it's good to see you. And not going home apart later. The silence of the night where he's turned from you, sleeping, and you touch his bare back unseen, and this bed is your raft of time.

They had walked through London together, and now the walks were a way for Marty to spend time with the man he loved.

As if he were there. And at the door, at home, Marty said goodbye – sometimes he left his dead David at a bus stop, kissed him, walked on, without turning round.

Then, when he got in the house, poured a drink or made tea or sat with a book, then just for a little while it felt better. But he still woke up too many nights, even after all, and turned over into the emptiness of the bed.

'You should try to meet someone,' said Sarah.

'I'm not ready.'

Sarah lived in Camden Town. Marty lived in Shoreditch in an old Georgian house that had belonged to his parents. They had never sold it – it wasn't worth anything back then. Instead, they had moved out to the suburbs from the rough city streets, and rented the house, room by room, to students, all sharing the single bathroom.

Marty had inherited the house, gone on renting out the rooms, living in the basement that only had a cold-water tap, until he could afford to let the tenants go.

He renovated the house year by year, doing much of the work himself.

He lived alone because he liked it. He had men, but not relationships. David was the first person he had fallen in love with.

David had never moved in with him – there was more than enough room, but David liked his small bright rented studio in King's Cross.

Marty suspected that David saw other men for sex but he didn't ask. David liked to go clubbing. He was braver, more flamboyant. 'What exactly is flamboyant about holding hands?' he had said to Marty, who was nervous about it at night, walking home, and embarrassed about it by day.

David worked out, liked his body, had a pieced ear. Marty bought him a diamond soon after they met.

'That's flamboyant,' said David. 'The word means wavy like a bouncing flame – and look at the light bouncing off me now!'

Marty had waited, unseen, outside David's studio one evening. He saw an older man going in with David. About an hour later, the man came out. Marty was meeting David that night for a late movie. He sent David a text to cancel. He didn't give a reason. He never told David what he'd done, but he realised that night that either he would have to start spying on his lover, or he would have to stop right now.

David was David. Why do we fall in love with someone because of the glory that they are, and immediately try to change them?

It wasn't until after David died that Marty started haunting his building again. He walked past it at least once a week, and it made him angry and sad. It did him no good, brought him no relief, but he kept on doing it.

He was walking by the building right now. David's blinds were still in the windows. Half-drawn, the way he liked them. Tonight there were Christmas lights in the window too. David would have lit a candle. A single candle.

When they first met, David had taken Marty to his studio and lit the candle. They had kissed each other standing in front of the fridge, which had made Marty feel poetic about fridges ever since. Sometimes he patted one as he went past it, as though every fridge everywhere was a benevolent player in their romance.

But Marty was shy, and it took him a week, after that first night, to get back in touch with David.

David, coming in from a run, saw the message, threw his phone in the air and ran out again. He ran all the way to the Columbia Road flower market near Marty's house.

Marty opened the door in his dressing gown that early Sunday morning to find David in shorts and running shoes, leaning on the bell with an armful of flowers and lighting up the narrow hall with globes of pink peonies.

'I didn't think I liked cut flowers,' said Marty.

'It's a sign,' said David.

Soon David was turning Marty's long, thin back yard into a Promised Land of climbing beans and wisteria and old English roses and lavender, and the windows were open onto the street and life came in like music and played in every room.

'Thank you for making me happy.'

Marty said this out loud to the candle. David had loved little twinkly lights. When he made the garden for Marty, that first summer, he had taken Marty out to a bar to eat the night of the summer solstice, and insisted they didn't go home till dusk – nearly eleven o'clock that night, and Marty had to go to work the next day. But David was excited about something. When they got home he ran ahead, leaving the front door open, shouting, 'Don't put the lights on!'

Down the long, narrow hall into the long, narrow yard there was a wavering light. Marty followed it. He stood in the yard. The place was lit up with something like Chinese lanterns – but long, not round – everywhere – on the top of the wall, in between the roses, among the lettuces that shone weirdly green like veg from Mars.

'Glow-worms,' said David. 'Because the sun stands still today – that's what solstice means. From the Latin *sol*: the sun, and the verb *sistere*: to stand still. I want our sun to stand still, just here, just now. Let this be world enough and time.'

They made love on the pull-out bed in the shed.

Marty looked up at the candle that was no longer in the window. Then he turned away to cut through Clerkenwell, carrying the heavy bag that had become his heart.

David had squeezed his hand that final time and whispered, 'I'll send you a sign.'

But there had been no sign. There never is, is there?

Marty didn't believe in life after death. David did. 'It's not interesting as an idea,' argued Marty. 'Why are we even talking about it?'

David said, 'It's fifty-fifty. One of us is right and one of us is wrong. When we're dead, in that split-second when there's still consciousness, one of us will be saying, "Oh, shit."'

Life after death, thought Marty, then out loud, to no one, because no one was on the streets, Marty said, 'So I said to him, and do you believe in Santa Claus too?'

The whiteness was brightness. Deep and crisp and even, reflecting the street lights. But then Marty, looking round in the emptiness for an answer to his question, registered an alteration of light, and a vast shadow darkening the white. He looked up.

In the white snowbound sky, right above his head and big as an airship, floated a giant, peaceful Santa trailing a stream of HO HO HOs behind him. Marty could clearly see his black boots and red hat and the sack slung over the shoulder. Had he come unmoored from some expensive offices? Was he a Christmas publicity stunt? What was he doing flying silently over the silent city?

Marty stood looking up as the Santa hovered in the frozen airstream of midnight. He appeared to be waving at Marty. There was no reason for Marty to wave back but he did. And as he did the Santa seemed to change direction; he wasn't moving west any more.

He was moving east, with Marty.

Marty shoved his hands deeper into his coat pockets and quickened his pace. He liked Christmas, truly he did, but should that warrant being followed home by an inflatable Santa Claus?

'Hey,' David had said, 'don't you love it that you get camels and robins on the same Christmas card?'

'When were Christmas cards invented?' said Marty. 'Victorian, right? Must be.'

'Postal service and cheap printing,' said David. 'Yes, you're right. Henry Cole 1843 in England – guy worked in the newly founded Post Office, responsible for the Penny Post. In America the first commercial Christmas card is 1874 – for once we got there first.'

'I like it that you tell me things,' said Marty.

David drew and wrote their Christmas cards. His last Christmas he was too tired but he had sent Marty out to buy fifty of those slim, round watch batteries and he spent the day in bed cutting up paper. A friend of his had come round and David asked Marty to get everyone champagne.

When Marty returned with the bottles, he went upstairs to find David. The bed was empty. He panicked and ran through the house, shouting DAVID! DAVID! The friend had gone – leaving the door to the back yard open. Marty could hear Judy Garland – '*Next year all our troubles will be miles away…*'

Marty went into the yard. Hanging from the trellis and the hooks and scooped across the door in a chain and fixed onto garden canes in every pot and raised bed were lit-up paper hearts, white and red and pale green.

David was sitting wrapped up in his wheelchair in the shining dark. He was smiling, so pleased with himself and his surprise.

'You loved the glow-worms I made for you that summer we met. So I made you these. I call them glow-hearts. And they are mine and they are yours and I love you.'

Marty knelt down by David's chair and put his head in the rug on David's knees and he cried all the tears he had kept back. And David cried too, wetting Marty's hair, and David said, 'There was a princess in a winter that was never summer and she cried so much for what she had lost that her tears froze to pearls and the birds took them away to decorate their nests. A prince riding by, as princes do in fairy tales, saw the pearly nests and asked the birds where they had found such riches, and the birds flew with him to the princess who had cried so much she was surrounded by pearls. And the story ends when he kissed her, of course, and it stopped being winter that day.'

'That is the most sentimental thing I ever heard,' said Marty, through his tears.

'How wonderful!' said David, and they started to laugh, and Marty opened the champagne and they sat together among the glow-hearts that glowed all Christmas. Except for one. Marty secretly took it away with the battery out so that it would always be David for him.

David knew what Marty was thinking. He held him tight. 'This is for now,' said David. This tonight. This now. 'The Promised Land is never in the future or the past – it is only ever now.'

'Don't leave me,' said Marty.

'Look for the signs,' said David.

Marty arrived home. Two drunks lying in a doorway were pointing skywards. Marty gave them money and didn't look up. He knew the helium-filled Santa was overhead. Now it was hovering over his house like the star in the story.

Marty let himself in and went straight to bed. It was around a quarter to two in the morning. He fell asleep, deeply, but some time later he woke to hear David saying, 'I told you to look for the signs.'

Marty started up. He could see the luminous fingers of the clock – still a quarter to two; must have stopped. The street-lamp was faintly lighting up the bedroom. And David was sitting cross-legged on the bed. He was wearing pyjama bottoms and a tweed jacket. His feet and chest were bare.

'I didn't take any clothes with me,' he said. 'You don't when you die. These are yours.'

'I'm dreaming,' said Marty, 'but don't wake me.'

'Did you like the Santa Claus I sent?'

'You sent it?'

'I was getting desperate – this is my last chance.'

'Christmas Eve – isn't that a bit corny?'

'You are so hard to reach! I can't get through to you!'

'I think about you all the time!'

'That's the problem – you're so busy thinking about me, the dead part of me, that I can't get through. I sent so many signs.'

'Like what?'

'Two comets on the beach last summer – remember those?'

Marty did remember but he wasn't playing games. 'Comets are space phenomena, not signs.'

'That first summer, after the solstice, we saw two comets in France – I said to you, "They are for us."'

Marty remembered. He had loved David's way of making the whole universe party to their love. But he had to protest. 'Romantic, but wrong!'

'So I sent them again – to remind you. And what about that day at the British Library – the woman who walked right up to you and said, "Hello David."'

'I never saw her before in my life. She was a madwoman.'

'She was my auntie,' said David. 'She's clairvoyant. She could see me walking right next to you.'

'How was I to know she was your clairvoyant auntie? Why didn't she say so?'

'You had already strode on by into the crowd – she didn't get a chance! I sent her all the way from Milton Keynes by train.'

'Well, why didn't YOU tell me?'

'I did! You weren't going to the British Library that day – I had to force you. I stood behind you yelling GO TO THE FUCKIN' LIBRARY! Of course, I can't yell because I don't have a voicebox – but you get the idea.'

Marty felt remorseful. He had neglected his lover and been rude to his lover's clairvoyant auntie from Milton Keynes.

'Should I send your auntie a Christmas card?'

'That would be nice; her address is on my iPhone under PA – Psychic Auntie. You still have my iPhone?'

Marty nodded. He had once scrolled through the addresses and stopped – too many men he had never met.

'No regrets,' said David, as if he could read Marty's mind.

Marty had a thought. 'How are you speaking to me if you don't have a voicebox?'

'I have your full attention. We are communicating by thought.'

'It's impossible.'

'Only the impossible is worth the effort.'

Marty put out his hand to touch David. But something like a light barrier was between them. His hand was luminous. He drew back his hand and wiped his eyes. He was suddenly frightened and tired.

'I can't live without you, David. It's like living as a shadow. You were the sun.'

'That's why I'm here. Hey, you didn't even get the soup sign last week. You were at Chez Henri with Dan and Dan ordered my favourite soup, and when the waiter came he gave it to you by mistake. I was right there doing the switch.'

'Are you always there?'

'No, but I come and see you.'

'Hold me.'

'I can't – it's the Einstein thing, $E=mc^2$. All mass is energy but not all energy is mass. You are in mass-form. I am in energy-form. I'm not lost, I'm not wasted, but I don't have a way to hold you. I can warm you up, though. Feel – here – put out your hand again.'

Marty put out his hand towards David's chest. There was nothing solid there. He'd had so much muscle until it started to waste away – but perhaps it wasn't wasting away, perhaps it was becoming what it needed to be. Energy not mass.

Marty felt his fingers tingling and his hand warming. He held out his other hand, as though David were a fire lit on the bed. He started to cry.

'Don't cry, princess,' said David. 'That's why I'm here. For both our sakes you have to stop. I need to go and you need to stay. I'll always be around but I want you to start living again. Life is beautiful and brief. Don't waste it.'

'I can't forget you,' said Marty. 'I don't want to.'

'You won't be forgetting me – you'll be honouring what we had, what we did. Love isn't a prison. You can't be imprisoned inside your love for me. Take our love with you – it is with you; you're not getting over me or moving on or any of that junk, you're taking me with you.'

'Take me with you instead,' said Marty. 'I don't want to be here alone.'

David looked at him with infinite love. 'You have to trust me, like you always did – yes?'

There was a long silence. Then Marty said, 'What should I do?'

'Get up in the morning – have coffee in the yard and I'll be there. You'll know I'll be there. Wait and see. Then we'll walk together to lunch at Chine-Ease and I'll say goodbye to you outside; I'm not eating right now – no stomach for it.'

Marty laughed but he didn't want to laugh.

'And then,' said David, 'I want you to start again.'

Marty fell asleep. When he next woke it was just past 8am and the snow had stopped. He looked out of the window. There was no sign of the inflatable Santa Claus. He rubbed his head.

And David? A dream.

He sighed and went into the shower, shaved, wrapped himself in his dressing gown. Coffee. In the back yard. That's what Dream David had told him to do. In the back yard? It was freezing.

Marty made the coffee, hot and black, slipped on his boots, laces undone, and unbolted the door and went into the yard. The air had ice particles in it and there was a trail of cat paws through the snow. He could see the rough outlines of the box pyramids and doll's house shape of the shed.

And then he saw it.

The glow-heart.

Hanging on its chain from the apple tree was the last glow-heart that Marty had saved from their last Christmas together.

David?

The glow-heart shifted a little in the wind but there was no wind.

Marty took the heart from the tree and hung it round his neck. There was a tiny beat of warmth from it against his chest.

And later, lighter than he'd been, or so it seemed, he arrived at the restaurant. Sarah was just going in. She held out her arm.

'I just have to say goodbye to someone,' said Marty. 'I'll be in soon. Save me a seat next to you.'

Sarah looked surprised but she went inside.

'Goodbye, David,' said Marty, out loud. 'Thank you for coming with me.'

Marty opened the door. 'They seem to be playing your song,' said Sarah.

'Have yourself a merry little Christmas now…'

My
Twelfth Night
Fishcakes

welfth Night is a strange one. January 5th or 6th. Time to take down the decorations and end the holiday season.

Twelfth Night marks the day when the Three Kings came to visit the baby Jesus. In Ireland, and in some parts of Italy, models of the Three Kings are added to the Nativity cribs on Twelfth Night.

The Kings kneeling before the baby in the stable follows the pattern of reversals that midwinter festivals celebrated in pre-Christian times.

The Roman Saturnalia and the Celtic festival Samhain both honour a Lord of Misrule. The period of the festival overturns the normal strict hierarchies of class, wealth and gender. The Italians at carnival time call it *il mondo reverso* – the world turned upside down. High becomes low, low becomes high, women tell the men what to do, and there's plenty of cross-dressing too.

The Catholic Church was genius at grafting its own religious occasions onto existing non-Christian festivals and Twelfth Night was part of the retro-fit.

In Shakespeare's time, Twelfth Night was an important feast. Shakespeare's play *Twelfth Night* dramatises the tradition of reversals – a girl dressed as a boy, a servant who fancies his chances with a high-born lady, a shipwreck where the past is swept away. The chaotic pantomime of the Dark House.

Pantomimes themselves – staple Christmas entertainment – always have a cross-dressed dame, and an ordinary lad or lassie who will become the prince or princess, plus a few villains made to eat dust.

There's a beautiful poem by T. S. Eliot called 'The Journey of the Magi'. It's about the Three Kings making their way to the Christ

Child – and questioning what happened – what was it they had witnessed? Was it a birth? Or a death?

The birth of the Christ Child heralds the death of an existing order.

That's the thing with reversals – and you can find this principle in all the fairy tales too, some reversal of fortune, or circumstances, rags to riches, riches to rags, an end that is really a beginning, a brave new world that is only an animated necropolis, the loss of something precious that allows us to find the treasure that is really there.

The reversal of any fixed situation allows a new possibility to present itself.

Twelfth Night is also known as Epiphany. Epiphany means 'manifestation'. Something is revealed. And what is revealed will be a challenge to the old order.

We hear a lot about disruptive start-ups, like Uber, or Airbnb, challenging the existing order. We're told this is creative and necessary. Maybe it is.

My feeling is that we could do with more stability in our outward-facing lives so that we could risk disruption to our inner lives; our thinking, feeling, imaginative lives.

When we're just like the animals, concentrating on food, territory, survival, mating, being the leader of the pack, then what is the point of being human?

The sad truth is that no political system (and capitalism is a political system) has succeeded in providing most of us with the basics we need, so that we have some freedom to explore what might be happening in the 98 per cent of our brains that we don't use.

That looks like failure to me.

Epiphany is an inspired reversal of power structures and hierarchies, of class systems and the status quo, a reminder that the way we live is propositional: we made it this way – we could remake it in a different way.

The Kings kneel before something bigger than authority – they are kneeling before a possible future, one based on love, not fear; one where there is abundance and not lack.

We know that what follows in the Bible story is King Herod's slaughter of every male child under two years old – his blood-soaked effort to hold on to power, to rigidly enforce what is, and wipe out what will be.

But the child he wants is already gone, wrapped in his mother's arms, trotting across the desert to his destiny.

There is always another chance.

And us?

We've got the ersatz version of Follow Your Star – but what happens when the star leads us to a wormy, dungy stable in a crummy town and we're wearing our best clothes and expecting applause and instead we have to kneel down in the straw and give our gifts (the best of us) to something we don't understand?

Quest stories and gaming make it seem so simple – challenges, monsters, setbacks, and then success. The trouble is that the real quest doesn't have an end, or a happy-ever-after, or a series of moves to follow. A commitment to being conscious, to being creative – whatever that means to you – a commitment to love, a desire for change; that is a life's work.

Stars lead us where they will. What we do when we arrive at the unexpected destination is up to us.

Journeys need food. I love fish, and these easy fishcakes can be left to cool and taken as a packed lunch or picnic supper. Or eat them hot and delicious with home-made mayo or your own tomato sauce.

I don't put potato in my fishcakes because I like eating them with chips. If you want a light and nutritious meal, try these with a squeeze of lemon or lime and a big bowl of seasonal salad. Or a plate of hot buttered cabbage.

YOU NEED

Quantity of mixed fish – this depends on how many fishcakes you fancy. I use a mixture of fresh cod and salmon with about 20 per cent smoked haddock. If you don't like smoked haddock, leave it out. I've tried these with cod and small shrimp. Pretty good.
Chopped onion – not too much, enough to give flavour
Eggs. Eggs work as the binder as you're not using potato.
Breadcrumbs made with day-old bread
Flour
Flat-leaf parsley
Salt and pepper

METHOD

The key here is that these fishcakes are small – too big and fat and the fish won't cook through. Bigger fishcakes with potato need you to cook the potato and fish first – we're not doing that. So think small.

Chop up the fish small and the onion smaller.

Mix together in a big bowl and add the egg or eggs so that you have a viscous mixture. Add parsley and seasoning.

Put some flour onto a board. Using both hands, shape little flat fishcakes, then pat each side into the flour to hold together, and then pat each side into the breadcrumbs.

As you make each one put it aside on a big plate. Make sure each little fishcake is firm.

Chill in the fridge for an hour if you can. If not…

Heat sunflower oil in a pan – get it good and hot and slide the fishcakes in one by one, turning after 4 minutes.

If you want to make a tomato sauce you'll need to do that ahead. The recipe below is very simple and just as good for pasta or rice as it is for fishcakes.

Take some biggish tomatoes with a good flavour and skin them by placing in a big pan of hot water for about half an hour.

Heat some olive oil in a heavy pan and add a bit of garlic. I add onion but you don't have to. I add a fresh red chilli too sometimes, depending on how I feel and if I have one.

When the garlic, onion and chilli are softened, add your peeled, coarse-chopped tomatoes and stir it all around. At this stage I sometimes put in a sprig of rosemary from the garden.

Put the lid on the pan and cook on a medium heat for 30 minutes. Don't let it burn.

If everything has slooped together and it tastes good, take out the rosemary stalk (if you put it in), add seasoning and reduce the sauce to the desired consistency.

You can throw in fresh basil at the end if you like. This is so simple and versatile and pretty quick. Enjoy!

*

CHRISTMAS GREETINGS
FROM THE AUTHOR

ime is a boomerang, not an arrow.

I was adopted by Pentecostals and stamped Missionary. Christmas was important in the missionary calendar. From the beginning of November, either we were preparing packages to send to the Foreign Field or we were preparing packages to deliver to those in Hot Places returning to the Home Front.

It might have been because my parents had been in WWII. It might have been because we lived in End Time, waiting for Armageddon. Whatever the reason, there was a drill to Christmas, from making the mincemeat for the mince pies to singing carols to, or rather at, the unsaved of Accrington. Still, Mrs Winterson loved Christmas. It was the one time of the year when she went out into the world looking as though the world was more than a vale of tears.

She was an unhappy woman, and so this happy time in our house was precious. I am sure I love Christmas because she did.

On December 21st every year my mother went out in her hat and coat while my father and I strung up the paper chains, made by me, from the corners of the parlour cornice to the centre light bulb.

Eventually my mother returned, in what seemed to be a hailstorm, though maybe that was her personal weather. She carried a goose, half-in, half-out of her shopping bag, its slack head hung sideways like a dream nobody can remember. She passed it to me – goose and dream – and I plucked the feathers into a bucket. We kept the feathers to restuff whatever needed restuffing, and we saved the thick goose fat drained from the bird for roasting potatoes through the winter. Apart from Mrs W, who had a thyroid problem, everyone we knew was as thin as a ferret. We needed goose fat.

After I had left home, and later gone to university at Oxford, I went back to the old house, that first Christmas-time. My mother had given me the ultimatum to leave home long since, when I fell in love with a girl, and in a religious house like ours I might as well have married a goat. We hadn't spoken since that time. I had lived in a Mini for a bit, lodged with a teacher and eventually left town.

During my first term at Oxford I received a postcard – one of those postcards that says POST CARD in blue letters at the top. Underneath, in her immaculate copperplate handwriting was the message: ARE YOU COMING HOME THIS CHRISTMAS? LOVE MOTHER.

As I reached our little terraced house at the top of the street I could hear the mostly musical sounds of what is best described as a bossa-nova version of 'In the Bleak Midwinter'. My mother had thrown out the old upright piano and got herself an electronic organ with double keyboard, orchestra stops, drum and bass.

She hadn't seen me for two years. Nothing was said. We spent the next hour admiring the effects of snare drum and trumpet solo on 'Hark! The Herald Angels Sing'.

My Oxford friend from St Lucia was due to visit me at home, which was brave of her, but when I had tried to explain about my family she thought I was exaggerating.

At first the visit was a great success. Mrs W considered a black friend as a missionary endeavour all of its own. She went round to the retired missionaries from the church and asked, 'What do they eat?' Pineapples, came the answer.

When Vicky arrived my mother gave her a wool blanket she had knitted so that Vicky would not be cold. 'They feel the cold,' she told me.

Mrs Winterson was an obsessive and she had been knitting for Jesus all year. The Christmas tree had knitted decorations on it, and the dog was imprisoned inside a Christmas coat of red wool with white snowflakes. There was a knitted Nativity scene, and the shepherds were wearing little scarves because this was Bethlehem on the bus route to Accrington.

My dad opened the door dressed in a knitted waistcoat and matching knitted tie. The whole house had been re-knitted.

Mrs W was in a merry mood. 'Would you like some gammon and pineapple, Vicky? Cheese on toast with pineapple? Pineapples and cream? Pineapple upside-down cake? Pineapple fritters?'

Eventually, after a few days of this fare, Vicky said, 'I don't like pineapple.'

Mrs W's mood changed at once. She didn't speak to us for the rest of the day and she crushed up a papier-mâché robin. The next morning, at breakfast, the table was set with a pyramid of unopened tins of pineapple chunks and a Victorian postcard of two cats on their hind legs dressed up like Mr and Mrs. The caption said NOBODY LOVES US.

That night, when Vicky went to bed, she found that her pillow had been taken out of its pillowcase, and the pillowcase stuffed with warning leaflets about the Apocalypse. She wondered whether to go home, but I'd seen worse and I thought things might improve.

On Christmas Eve we had a group of carol singers round from the church. Mrs W did seem happier. She had forced me and Vicky to wrap several half-cabbages in tinfoil and spear them with cocktail sticks of Cheddar cheese, topped with the rejected pineapple chunks.

She called these things sputniks. It was something to do with the Cold War. Tinfoil? Antennae? The scaremongering that the KGB had listening devices hidden in cheese?

Never mind. The offending pineapples had found a purpose and we were all singing carols quite happily when there was a knock at the door. It turned out to be the Salvation Army singing carols too.

This was reasonable. It was Christmas-time. But Mrs Winterson was having none of it. She opened the front door and shouted, 'Jesus is here. Go away.'

Slam.

When I went away after that Christmas I never went back. I never saw Mrs W again – she was soon too furious about my debut novel, *Oranges Are Not The Only Fruit* (1985). Quote: 'It's the first time I've had to order a book in a false name.'

She died in 1990.

As you get older you remember the dead at Christmas. The Celts, during their midwinter festival of Samhain, expected the dead to join the living. Many cultures would understand that; not ours.

That is a pity. And a loss. If time is a boomerang and not an arrow, then the past is always returning and repeating. Memory, as a creative act, allows us to reawaken the dead, or sometimes to lay them to rest, as at last we understand our past.

*

Last Christmas I was alone in my kitchen, the fire lit – I love having a fire in the kitchen. I was pouring myself a drink when Judy Garland came on the radio singing 'Have Yourself a Merry Little Christmas'. I remembered how Mrs W had played that song on the piano. It was one of those moments we all know, of sadness and sweetness mixed together. Regret? Yes, I think so, for everything we got wrong. But recognition too, because she was a remarkable woman. She deserved a miracle to get her out of her trapped life of no hope, no money, no possibility of change.

Fortunately, she got the miracle. Unfortunately, the miracle was me. I was the Golden Ticket. I could have taken her anywhere. She could have been free…

The Christmas story of the Christ Child is complex. Here's what it tell us about miracles.

Miracles are never convenient (the baby's going to be born whether or not there's a hotel room – and there isn't).

Miracles are not what we expect (an obscure man and woman find themselves parenting the Saviour of the World).

Miracles detonate the existing situation – and the blow-up and the back-blast mean some people get hurt.

What is a miracle? A miracle is an intervention – it breaks through the space-time continuum. A miracle is an intervention that cannot be accounted for purely rationally. Chance and fate are in the mix. A miracle is a benign intervention, yes, but miracles are like the genie in the bottle – let them out and there's a riot. You'll get your Three Wishes, but a whole lot else besides.

Mrs W wanted a baby. She couldn't have one. Along comes me – but as she often said, 'The Devil led us to the wrong crib.' Satan as a faulty star.

That's the fairy-tale element of the story.

Sometimes the thing we long for, the thing we need, the miracle we want, is right there in front of us, and we can't see it, or we run the other way, or, saddest of all, we just don't know what to do with it. Think how many people get the success they want, the partner they want, the money they want, et cetera, and turn it into dust and ashes – like the fairy gold no one can spend.

So at Christmas I think about the Christmas story, and all the Christmas stories since. As a writer I know that we get along badly without space in our lives for imagination and reflection. Religious festivals were designed to be time outside of time. Time where ordinary time was subject to significant time. What we remember. What we invent.

So light a candle to the dead.

And light a candle to miracles, however unlikely, and pray that you recognise yours.

And light a candle to the living; the world of friendship and family that means so much.

And light a candle to the future; that it may happen and not be swallowed up by darkness.

And light a candle to love.

Lucky Love.

ACKNOWLEDGEMENTS

Thanks to everyone who worked to pull this book together with me. My editors in London and New York, Rachel Cugnoni and Elisabeth Schmitz. Áine Mulkeen, Ana Fletcher, Matt Broughton and Neil Bradford at Vintage. Laura Evans on copy-edit and proofs. Kamila Shamsie, Sylvia Whitman at Shakespeare and Company. And my glorious agent Caroline Michel, who loves Christmas as much as I do.

And absent friends: Kathy Acker and Ruth Rendell. And of course, Mrs Winterson and Dad.